Dead

On

Demand

Daniel Campbell

Sean Campbell

Chapter 1: Falling Apart

Edwin cursed. The lawyers were at it again.

Virtually every week since he had become the editor at *The Impartial* newspaper, Edwin had been served with ominous-looking legal forms delivered in innocuous manila envelopes. The court logo visible through the plastic window was the giveaway which set his heart racing. This time was no exception. As Edwin fumbled with the envelope his pulse quickened, and his head began to throb.

Although stressful, such lawsuits were the responsibility of the paper's in-house legal team, who bore responsibility for defending the paper, or settling out of court.

It usually came down to money. Sensational stories sold papers, and profit demanded skirting the line between accuracy and attention-grabbing half-truths.

But today was different. The lawsuit wasn't addressed to *The Impartial*, but to Edwin Murphy. This time, it was personal.

Edwin's hands shook as the papers fell to the desk, and his eyes burned as he skimmed the document. Once he realised why he had been served, Edwin didn't hesitate. He hit the intercom buzzer, leant in towards the fuzzy microphone and said: 'Betty, cancel my morning appointments.'

With a sigh, he switched off his laptop and mobile phone, and then reached for a bottle of brandy which he kept hidden in the bottom drawer of his desk.

He should have seen it coming. His marriage had not been a happy one for a long time. It was fine during their first few years together back in Cambridge. Then, on her twenty-fourth birthday, Eleanor had confessed that she wanted to start a family. Edwin didn't feel ready yet. He thought that they were too young to be tied down. He committed the cardinal sin of saying so.

She said she understood his need for time, but in his mind that time was measured in years rather than months. Before long, Eleanor became frustrated and angry.

In true alpha-male fashion, Edwin did what every red-blooded man confronted with an angry woman does: he hid.

He spent his nights at the office, and convinced himself that he was doing it for both of them. 'I've got to earn enough for two now,' he had declared as his days began to start earlier, and finish later.

Edwin shook his head sadly, and looked around the office which had become his refuge. There were no tumblers in the office, so he upended the dregs of a coffee mug onto his ficus, and set the mug back down on his desk before pouring a generous tot.

He drank the amber liquid in one, setting his lips aflame. Brandy wasn't his tipple of choice, but on this occasion it seemed fitting. It had been a brandy his father-in-law offered when Edwin asked for Eleanor's hand in marriage. He poured himself another tot, then raised his glass to the empty office, a mocking toast to the demise of his marriage.

After several drinks, Edwin reached for the envelope again. His eyes struggled to focus as he read the reason that Eleanor had cited for the divorce: irreconcilable differences, which was as vague as only a legal document could be.

But Edwin knew what it meant. Their marriage had been on the rocks ever since they'd tried to start a family. They'd pretended, postured and tried to convince themselves otherwise but they'd never recovered from the death of their son, Drew.

It wasn't as if Edwin hadn't made an effort. Before Drew had been born, Edwin had taken early paternity leave to decorate the nursery. It was late September at the time, and a chill had begun to rattle through their Belgravia townhouse.

The townhouse was a fix-me-up. It was safe, and it was in one of London's priciest residential areas, but the interior was a shambles.

The room Eleanor chose for the nursery was on the top floor, right across the hall from the master bedroom. It was far too cold for a child. Something had to be done before young Drew arrived, and no expense was spared in making it a nursery fit for a king.

With Edwin's determined supervision, it came together in no time. He added a new stud wall and stuffed the gap with insulating foam, and painted it a vibrant mix of green and blue. The colour scheme had been recommended as soothing by Eleanor's best friend, a child psychologist. Edwin couldn't see what was so special about it, but if it kept the peace it was worth the cost of two tins of Dulux.

It was October 30th when Eleanor felt the fateful contractions during a family dinner. The food was abandoned, and Edwin rushed her straight to Barkantine Birth Centre at St Bartholomew's Hospital. On arrival, it became apparent that something was wrong.

Eleanor had abnormally high blood pressure, and was rushed into an emergency caesarean section, but it was too late. The baby was a breech birth, and Drew was born with his umbilical cord wrapped tight around his neck.

Soon after, Eleanor sank into a deep depression which didn't lift until she fell pregnant again four years later. They stayed together – united in grief at first, and later by the arrival of baby Chelsea. But something had changed, and they drifted apart.

Edwin rested his head on one hand, and lazily flicked through the paperwork with the other. There were pages and pages of legalese which he skimmed before reaching the final document: a financial summary detailing the assets they had to divide up. Their entire marriage had been reduced to a series of valuations. Shares, account balances, even his book collection had been appraised. Underneath the assets were a series of red numbers indicating debts to be taken off.

Edwin clucked at the total printed in bold at the bottom of the page. The sum total of their wealth was dismal, all things considered. They had great jobs. They owned their home. To the outside world, they were the picture-perfect professional couple.

But fate hadn't been kind to their finances. They'd invested heavily in shares, mostly banks and Fortune 500 companies. 'It's the right thing to do,' Eleanor's father had said. 'Look after the pennies, and the pounds will look after themselves

But what went up had to come down. In late 2007 the bottom fell out of the market.

At first it seemed to be confined to the French bank *La Société*, but it quickly became apparent that bad debt had been spread throughout the global banking system. Edwin swirled his brandy around absentmindedly as he remember reporting on the bank collapses with glee. He never thought that mortgages in far-off countries would ever affect his little empire. But they did. In a few short months, the Murphys' allegedly prudent investment into banks and big blue chip companies saw almost two thirds wiped off the family books in a little over a year.

While the losses were only on paper until they needed to sell, the shortfall left the Murphy family in precarious circumstances. They had foregone a repayment mortgage in favour of an interest-only mortgage and the crash wiped out their ability to repay the capital.

Eleanor blamed her husband for losing thousands, and a succession of arguments ensued. Plates were thrown, insults slung and Edwin spent many nights on the sofa.

They tried spending time apart. Eleanor began to spend every other weekend with her parents in Sandbanks. When that failed to improve things, a trial separation lead to Edwin moving out of the townhouse and into a one-bedroom flat in Angel. Soon they were seeing other people, or at least Eleanor was.

Edwin threw himself into his work with a vengeance, spending up to fourteen hours a day in the office. Even on a Sunday, Edwin could be found at his desk tapping away at his laptop, proofing, cutting, and expounding his own views in the Sunday editor's column.

In retrospect the divorce was inevitable. Edwin sighed, scribbled a note to his secretary to find the best divorce solicitors she could and resolved to take the rest of the day off.

***

The following Monday was a beautifully clear morning. The previous weekend's mist had settled further north and for once Edwin's small apartment felt bright and happy as the light splayed across the kitchen worktop, making the metallic sink dance.

Edwin woke early that morning. He had an eight o 'clock meeting with the American owner of *The Impartial*, Derek Wood, and Mr Wood did not like to be kept waiting. Edwin wolfed down a small slice of toast with no butter. He could risk nothing more fancy than that, otherwise his queasy stomach might betray him. As he showered, Edwin ran over the numbers in his mind once more. He could massage the stats only so far. Today was the day he would have to finally come clean and let Mr Wood know that the ad revenues were down for the third successive quarter.

Resolving to be blunt but honest, Edwin patted himself dry and then donned his favourite suit. It was a three-piece in dark navy wool, with a wide pin. Eleanor used to call it his power suit. He carefully donned a matching tie, straightened it using the tiny mirror above the bathroom sink, then pronounced himself respectable and left the flat to flag down a taxi.

***

On the North Bank of the River Thames, a wall of tall and imposing buildings crowded the skyline, stretching from the City all the way to Westminster and beyond.

In the City of London, colloquially known as the Square Mile, office blocks clawed skywards. Men in suits, working mostly in big banks and for insurance companies, could be seen scurrying around behind the windows. Many were clutching coffees, trying to revive vacant stares with an injection of caffeine.

To the west, the skyline changed. St Paul's Cathedral interrupted the office buildings, its iconic domed peak towering three hundred and sixty-five feet above the tourists below.

Further west still were some of London's most prestigious addresses, among which lay *The Impartial*'s head office at One-Sixty-Three Fleet Street. Few tourists ventured into the area, but it was as busy as any other.

The Impartial was in the heart of legal London, a stone's throw from the Royal Courts of Justice. Although many newspapers had been priced out of the area, *The Impartial* was still based on the same site which it had always occupied, a minute away from the Thames.

The original building was long gone, destroyed by a bomb in the Second World War. But *The Impartial* has risen from the ashes inside a new building, clad in glass and steel.

Staying in Fleet Street cost the owner of *The Impartial*, Derek Wood, more than a pretty penny, but it was worth every cent of his investment. On a clear day, Wood could see ten, maybe even twelve miles from the roof terrace. More importantly, London could see him. The bankers might have been masters of the universe, but it was Derek who decided who made the news.

In the top-floor conference room, only a French door away from Wood's private terrace, a secretary laid out a breakfast of fresh fruit and bagels. A pot of freshly brewed coffee sat on a warming plate, waiting to be poured.

Wood always began his mornings with a bagel and a coffee: black, no sugar. He did not believe in tea, and as such it was never served at the meetings he arranged, which greatly annoyed *The Impartial*'s editor-in-chief, Edwin Murphy. Wood considered that a bonus.

Wood's personal assistant, a simpering young man fresh from Oxford, laid out a selection of newspapers at the head of the table and hovered awkwardly as Wood scanned through the headlines. Wood always indulged in this ritual. He simply had to know what the other papers were up to. Three short sharp knocks announced Edwin's arrival.

Wood glanced at his watch, nodded appreciatively at Edwin's punctual appearance and then gestured lazily at a leather chair and carried on reading. When he was finished reading the last paper, he lowered the broadsheet and gazed at Edwin over the dark rims of his designer glasses.

Wood watched Edwin sit and then help himself to a glass of water. Edwin took a quick sip to moisten his lips, and said: 'Good morning, sir. I trust you are well.'

Wood nodded for Edwin to get on with the month's presentation, tapping his watch impatiently.

'Our total readership remained steady this month. We shipped 3.06 million copies per day on the weekdays, and almost 4.7 million for the Sunday edition. This is a 0.12% increase on last month.'

'Good. Revenue is up then. By how much?'

'Well... we forecast retail income at the rate of £2.2 million net per quarter, but our quarterly revenue generated was £2.1 million. This was under-forecast due to some write-downs on bad debt.'

'How does advertising revenue stack up against the same quarter last year?'

Edwin avoided meeting his boss's gaze, and braced himself for the inevitable tongue-lashing that would follow the rest of his report.

'Despite that, sir, our advertising revenues have fallen due to...'

'How much?' Wood interrupted him.

'Well, sir, due to harsh market conditions...'

Wood's eyes narrowed suspiciously. 'The numbers, Murphy, *now*.'

'62%, year on year.'

Mr Wood was an experienced businessman and knew that he had to roll with the punches but no executive could keep their cool when being told that their investment, previously showing a healthy profit, was suddenly a money pit. He exploded in a fit of rage.

'*What?*' Wood roared, spit flying towards Edwin, who ducked instinctively. 'Why the hell am I only hearing about this now? It should have been brought to my attention months ago!'

Edwin cowered, his eyes downcast, afraid to even look at his boss.

'Answer me!'

'Well... sir... it's been a very... ahem, difficult trading environment. It was not my fault that...'

'Not your fault?' Wood mocked; his tone was suddenly cold, his eyes blazing with a fire Edwin had never seen before.

'No, sir. It was Palmer in advertising. He was the one who...'

'Who does Palmer work for?'

'That would be me, sir.'

'Then it's on your shoulders. You're finished here, Murphy.' Wood pressed a discreet button underneath the desk, summoning security. Two burly gentlemen appeared as if by magic in the doorway.

'See Mr Murphy out please, gentlemen. Then get me Palmer.'

As Wood turned his chair away, Edwin found himself flanked by the security team. He tried to shrug them off.

'I'll show myself out,' he declared, trying to keep some dignity.

'We have our orders, Mr Murphy.' Each guard placed a hand underneath one of Edwin's arms, practically hauling him out of the conference room, and then they led him towards his office.

***

Edwin obstinately took his time packing the meagre belongings that he had amassed in the office, neatly stacking a few photo frames inside a cardboard box. He chucked one of the firm's industrial staplers into the box for good measure.

Security turned a blind eye to the stationery theft, and allowed Edwin to shuffle into the lift without further indignity. He was soon standing outside the building he had called home for the last five years, while morning traffic zigzagged by without a care in the world.

As he stood outside the building, a vagrant tugged at his elbow.

'Spare some change, mister?'

Edwin bit back a rude reply, but his mistake was looking down at the elderly man sitting on the pavement. He had a tuft of matted grey hair, and was sitting on a stack of old copies of *The Impartial*, with a skeletal greyhound resting next to him.

Against his better judgement, Edwin thrust a hand into his jacket pocket, and pulled out his wallet. The beggar could barely believe his luck when Edwin shoved a fistful of notes into his hand.

Before the vagrant could say thank you, Edwin flagged down a taxi and asked for the nearest bar that would be serving alcohol at quarter to nine in the morning.

It was nearing eleven o'clock when the barman in Finnigan's Wake finally decided Edwin had probably had enough.

'Hey, pal, how about you order some food?'

'Two more shots. Now.' Edwin upended his wallet, and thrust a fistful of notes at the barman. Food was the last thing Edwin wanted.

'No more booze unless you order some food first.'

'Alright. What have you got?' Edwin slurred. He tried to squint at the menu chalked up on the wall but the text refused to stay in focus.

'How about a burger and fries?'

'All right, and a beer.' As Edwin spoke, another patron cracked a grin and rolled his eyes at the bartender.

The bartender looked at Edwin disapprovingly but reluctantly moved to pour him a pint of London Pride. At least he had moved on from the whiskey.

'Say, pal, what's so bad that you're drinking alone on a Monday morning?'

Edwin, drunk and in no mood to talk, gave a dismissive shrug and finished the beer in one before demanding another.

The bartender grew weary; it was his licence on the line.

'One more, if you let me call someone for you, or call you a taxi.'

'Deal.'

***

In the Murphy residence in Belgravia, a
gorgeous mid-terrace townhouse opposite the
Portuguese embassy, Chelsea Murphy was off
school sick. She had a mild flu, but Eleanor was not
one to take chances. She wrapped up her baby girl
in blankets, put her on the sofa and spent the
morning hovering around checking that she had
enough to drink, and zealously monitoring her
temperature. Eleanor knew she would never cope if
there were ever a real illness in the family.

'Mummy, why do you keep asking me if I like
New York?' Chelsea asked in between brow-
moppings.

'Well, how would you like to see what it's like to
live somewhere new? Didn't you like our weekend
shopping there?'

'Yes, Mummy, but all my friends are here!'
Chelsea protested.

'You'll make new friends, darling. Mummy has
been offered a job over there and without Daddy
around, Mummy needs to work. It'll just be us girls
in a sparkling city of lights. Won't that be
wonderful, baby?'

***

By half past midday, Finnigan's Wake was
heaving with the lunch crowd. The barman decided
that Edwin might put off the regular diners and
shifted him to a booth in the back when he was
joined by his brother-in-law, Mark.

Mark was always the first to agree to a session in the pub, and ever the Wyvern, he soon filled the booth with beers. The fries from Edwin's lunch lay abandoned as the pair got down to the serious business of drinking.

Sometime during his third beer with Mark, Edwin's phone rang. He normally hated answering withheld numbers but his mood was vitriolic and he wanted nothing more than to verbally unload on some unsuspecting telesales person.

'Edwin J Murphy speaking.' Edwin held the phone at arm's length, and giggled as he put on a plummy accent.

'Good afternoon, Mr Murphy, this is Caroline Flack from Huntingdon Fox and Associates. Last week, your secretary retained me on your behalf. I contacted your wife's solicitors. She has given us notice that she intends to leave the country. Are you available to discuss your legal position?'

'My position? I'm glad she's leaving. Good riddance,' Edwin spat, not realising the repercussions of his wife's leaving.

'She intends to take Chelsea to New York with her,' the solicitor said hesitantly.

'Stop her. I don't care how, just do it.'

'Mr Murphy, it may be... difficult to find proper grounds to challenge her.'

An anguished moan escaped from the drunken man as he threw his phone against the wall, watching it shatter into dozens of pieces.

'That *bitch*. I wish she was dead!'

Mark arched an eyebrow, and said after a slightly-too-long pause: 'Hey, that's my sister you're talking about. I think it's time to cut you off.'

***

The next morning, Edwin's head felt like a pneumatic drill had been placed at his temple and set to maximum. He tried to sit up but the effort proved to be in vain. As his eyes slid into focus Edwin realised he was on Mark's sofa.

Mark was splayed across the opposite armchair. Both men were wearing the same clothes as the day (and night) before.

'Water,' Edwin hoarsely demanded of his host.

With a thud Mark tossed a bottle towards him. It landed on Edwin's stomach with a thud. Edwin groaned in pain.

'That's not water,' he complained, always grumpy in the mornings anyway, but even more so with the hangover from hell.

'It's all you're getting unless you want to get up,' Mark replied with a grin, safe in the knowledge that Edwin was going nowhere fast.

Edwin, ungrateful, twisted the top off the bottle of Lucozade and drained the whole bottle into his parched mouth, a few drops missing and dribbling down his cheek to rest on his collar.

Mark slowly stretched out, picked up the television remote between his toes, and then kicked the remote up and caught it left-handed.

'Got any preferences?' he asked, flipping on both the television and the surround-sound system that his sister had bought him the previous Christmas.

'Anything but Jeremy Kyle.'

Mark smirked, and changed the channel to ITV.

'I hate you, you know that.' With that declaration Edwin turned over and went back to sleep.

***

Edwin's hangover persisted late into the day, and his head was still throbbing as he entered the premises of Huntingdon Fox for his four o'clock meeting. Edwin was vaguely aware of the opulence of the law firm's Grosvenor address. He wondered how much of the four hundred pounds per hour fee he was being billed for would be spent maintaining the extravagant decor. The anteroom he was shown to could be described as no less than opulent, and the coffee was clearly not instant. He was soon sat face-to-face with his lawyer. He hadn't chosen her, but his former secretary had assured him she was the best available, and Betty had never led him astray. A pang of loneliness struck Edwin as he realised just how much he had taken Betty's comforting presence for granted.

'Hello,' Edwin croaked. His head pounded as he read the golden nameplate on the lawyer's desk, *Mrs Caroline Flack MA (Hons) (Cantab) LLM (Londis)*.

'Mr Murphy, I asked you here today to discuss your estranged wife. Have you been in contact with her?'

Edwin shook his head, and his lawyer continued her spiel.

'Eleanor has notified us she intends to move to New York to pursue work with a law firm there. She obviously intends to take Chelsea with her. She can do this without your permission, although we can file for what is known as a "First Steps Order" to prevent her. We would need to show the court good reason to prevent her doing so.'

'OK. Do it.'

'This would involve our demonstrating the move is out of malice, or that the move would prevent you from the contact you are entitled to. However, Eleanor's solicitor has confirmed in writing that she would cover the costs of flying Chelsea back to the UK each year over the holidays to see you. It is unlikely that any court will issue such an order on the evidence we have available to us. The court's primary concern is for Chelsea, and Eleanor's proposal may well be sufficient to demonstrate that the best place for her is in New York.'

'So there's no point contesting it?'

'We can contest it, but you would probably not gain anything.' Mrs Flack paused for a moment to sip some water before continuing.

'The other reason I wanted to talk to you is to discuss disposition of your assets in the divorce. Eleanor has cited both irreconcilable differences and unreasonable behaviour as grounds.'

'She thinks I work too much.'

'We could file a cross petition, but again this would require substantial grounds such as her unreasonable behaviour or adultery.'

'So I'm screwed.' It was a statement, not a question. The lawyer didn't deny it.

'Fine!' Edwin snarled. He almost added 'I'll deal with her myself' but thought better of it. The lawyer carried on for a few more minutes, but Edwin tuned her out. By the time he emerged back into Grosvenor, sunlight was fading fast.

***

Edwin thumped a fist on his makeshift desk in anger, causing his mug to leap into the air. It landed on the kitchen floor, cracked and spilt the last drops of coffee onto the laminate. Edwin ignored the mess, rested his hands on the edge of the laptop and typed furiously.

Access Denied flashed across his screen in a blinking bold type. The website he was trying to use was hidden from the public. It wasn't like visiting any old website. It wasn't listed on Google.

This was a darknet site, part of the no-man's-land that few ever ventured onto. Edwin had first found it when he was an undergraduate doing his journalism degree, and writing up the story of a lifetime: a hidden marketplace for accessing illegal goods and services. Drugs, pornography and much more could be bought anonymously, for a price.

The technology wasn't illegal. The United States government had created it for espionage, valuing the ability to send and receive anonymous messages. It had only been a matter of time before the technology had been co-opted by criminals.

Edwin was never allowed to publish the article. The editor of the university paper had glanced at it, and immediately vetoed publication as not being in the public interest. With hindsight, it was probably the right decision. The ability to access a web of criminal activity could prove deadly in the wrong hands.

Edwin entered the right logon credentials, and the laptop beeped three times to indicate a successful connection. Edwin had taken every precaution possible. He had not connected directly to the darknet, but used a series of proxy computers. The effect was like a daisy chain – it was impossible to see where the link began and ended.

Edwin clicked to create a message, enabling a virtual drop box for replies.

Even with his many precautions he was still cautious about what to type.

'Problem solver needed. One problem to fix. Final solution required. Pay negotiable.'

Edwin reread his message. He wasn't sure it would get his intentions across but hopefully it would pique some interest somewhere.

Chapter 2: Red Spot

When his son was born, Yosef Gershwin had paced back and forth frantically.

'Cigarette to calm your nerves, bud?' another of the expectant fathers had asked.

'Thanks, but I'm on the patch.' Yosef slid his sleeve up to reveal a nicotine patch attached.

'Wise. How about a cup of coffee then?'

Yosef smiled He was about to ask if the man had anything stronger when a nurse called out his name to take him through to the recovery room. It was the proudest day of Yosef's life, seeing his son for the first time. He was tiny, and hairless, but he was beautiful.

A year later, Yosef was back in a similar waiting room, but for a much less joyous occasion. Little baby Zachariah was nestled in his broad arms, swaddled in a blanket. The boy yawned, a tremendous effort in his condition.

Just as he was debating calling his wife yet again to let her know they were still waiting, a nurse appeared and led him through to the consultant.

He sat, this time in a much comfier chair, and surveyed the consultant's office. It was leaps and bounds ahead of the waiting room, but still in keeping with the hospital's apparent minimalism.

'I'll be straight to the point. The blood test we conducted shows Zachariah has a deficiency of beta-hexosaminidase. This is an enzyme that breaks down fatty acids in the brain known as gangliocides. The condition is more commonly known as Tay-Sachs disease.'

'What does it mean? More importantly, how do we fix it?'

'Zachariah's nerves will become progressively distended. He will lose the ability to see and hear. He may be unable to move any muscles, which will necessitate the use of a feeding tube. His seizures will become more violent, and Zachariah will be prone to recurring infections. I'm sorry, Yosef, but there is no cure.'

'Why him? What did he do to deserve this?' Yosef was no longer talking to his consultant, but pleading with God for his son.

'I'm afraid it's quite common in the Jewish population. Is your wife also Jewish?'

'What? No, she's not. She's from Slovakia.'

'No Jewish blood at all on her side of the family?'

'Not as far as I know. Are you sure the diagnosis is even right?'

'I'm afraid so. The blood test is straightforward. I only ask as, while the Jewish population have an incidence of around 1 in 3000, it's closer to 1 in 40000 in the general population.'

'Would it happen again if we had another child?'

'It's possible. The gene that causes the problem is recessive. Both parents have to be carriers, and this gives any child of their union a 1 in 4 chance of having Tay-Sachs. Even if they don't have Tay-Sachs it's likely that they would be a carrier.'

'So what happens now?' Yosef asked.

'Well, we will medicate for the convulsions, and monitor Zachariah twice a month to see how his condition progresses. If he needs a tube to keep his airways open then we will address it when the problem arises. If you have any concerns call me, or bring him in straight away. We'll also put you in touch with a support group for other Tay-Sachs parents here in London.'

'Thank you, Doctor.'

***

Edwin checked his darknet account. Nothing: his subtlety had gone unappreciated. He shrugged and pulled his keyboard closer. He ran the same routine precautions as before, concealing his whereabouts using proxies. Again, he took the time to spoof his MAC address, concealing the physical identity of the laptop. This time, he was sure, the messages simply could not be traced back to him. He typed out a new message, deleting the old one as he did so. The time for being coy was over, and Edwin chose to be completely forthright in his new message. 'Contractor needed to eliminate nuisance. Target is mid-thirties. London based job. Contact for further details.' Satisfied, Edwin hit enter and the message floated into cyberspace for all to see.

This time a response came back quickly. In stilted English, the reply informed Edwin that a clean hit could be performed for the fee of £50,000. Payment would be in cash via a drop-box location, and Edwin would never see the killer.

Edwin began to mull it over before he realised how absurd his plan was. While he might be able to scrounge together the cash, it would be child's play for the police to put two and two together. The husband is always the police's first suspect, and with Edwin as the sole beneficiary of Eleanor's rather generous life insurance policy, the police would go over his finances with a fine tooth comb. A £50,000 deficit would stick out like a sore thumb, and Edwin would end up in prison before he could say "It wasn't me."

Then the insurance company would never pay out, and Edwin would lose Chelsea to the foster system. It simply wasn't viable. Edwin would have to find another way.

***

Yosef felt the tension of being a carer flood from his shoulder as he listened to Natan talk. Nat was the leader of the only Tay-Sachs support group in London. Nat had lost a daughter to the disease, but still ran the close-knit group. He had welcomed Yosef warmly the first time he'd walked in, embracing him and baby Zachariah as members of their community.

Nat spoke in a slow, sombre voice that contrasted sharply with his jovial features. He glanced around the room as he spoke, making eye contact with each group member in turn. Nat's grief was still raw, but somehow Yosef found his voice comforting and familiar. Yosef let his mind, and his eyes, wander. He looked around the hall, which had been donated by the Islington Synagogue for their use every other Thursday. It was a small gesture but without it the support group would not exist.

A small cry escaped from Zach's pram as he woke, bringing Yosef's attention back into the moment. He apologised for the disturbance, and picked the boy up gingerly to try and calm him down.

Zach's decline had been swift. He had seemed to grow normally for several months, and Yosef almost believed that the diagnosis had been wrong. Sadly, the set of tests confirmed his worst fears: Zach was suffering from the usual signs of Tay-Sachs. Not long after that, partial paralysis began to set in, and Zachariah became disabled before he had learned to walk.

The cherry-red bright spots in his eyes had been the red flag. Yosef knew his boy would be unlikely to make it past four years of age. The others in the group were further along that awful road. Even now, one woman, Maya, was making her first appearance in the group in months. Maya's daughter had suffered infection after infection, and had been in hospital for over a year.

Yosef squirmed in his seat, imagining Zachariah suffering that same agony, unable to speak or swallow, and barely able to breathe unassisted. Yosef's sense of calm dissipated as he realised once again just how hopeless it was being the carer for a terminal child.

Guilt clutched at Yosef's heart. He had brought this little boy into the world, and it was because of his Jewish ancestry that the boy suffered. He bowed his head in prayer, and made a silent vow that he would not prolong the boy's agony.

Chapter 3: The Plan

Life had been quiet for Edwin since leaving *The Impartial*. With no job to go to, no work to do, and no child to look after he had found himself at a bit of a loose end. For the first few days Edwin had drifted. He had allowed himself to sleep in, to watch daytime TV and to avoid physical exertion generally. He had begun to fall into a stupor. The wakeup call came in an unusual form for Edwin. It was when he realised that he could hum the theme tunes to the major morning television shows that he started to appreciate that, job or no job, he needed some sort of daily routine.

He set his alarm for six o'clock sharp, the time he used to get up for work at *The Impartial*. He forced himself to get dressed, as if he was going to work, but instead spent his mornings at the gym. Edwin didn't consider himself unfit, but he certainly had a slight paunch that had not been there when he was at university. He resolved to get back into trim during his time out from work, which he described to friends as a "career hiatus".

Once he had finished in the gym Edwin's daily routine was to take his laptop and abuse the free Wi-Fi in the British Library to hunt for jobs. It was an auspicious setting that helped Edwin to focus, and he was soon fielding phone calls from recruitment consultants, agents and human resources departments. The loss of work at *The Impartial* was a blot on his résumé but he was still an exceptionally strong candidate. With a first-class undergraduate degree as well as his MBA, many doors were still open to him.

It was scant surprise therefore that within a week Edwin had secured a telephone interview with a business periodical in Vancouver. It was a slightly different role to editing *The Impartial* but Edwin was up for a new challenge and he soon wowed the director for human resources in the telephone interview. She was so impressed with his work ethic that he received an invitation to an in-person interview to take place in one week's time.

***

Edwin liked to do his thinking when it was particularly quiet. He had always found that late in the evening was a particularly productive time for him. As the witching hour approached, the number of distractions decreased exponentially. His phone remained mute, and his social media accounts were of little interest while everyone else was asleep.

Edwin pondered on his problems. A new job might ease the cash flow, but his wife was claiming virtually all their liquid assets and an on-going payment to maintain the lifestyle to which she had become accustomed. After adding in sale fees for the house, child support and the chance of being out of work for a while, Edwin realised that claiming on Eleanor's life insurance policy might be the only way out. He laughed as he realised that the insurance had effectively become a bounty payment for her murder.

The cold mirth echoed around the room, and Edwin clapped his hand over his mouth. He couldn't risk waking the neighbours.

The best thing about the quiet of the night was that it allowed Edwin to make connections in his mind that never seemed to occur to him during daylight hours. It was almost as if his neurons kept working hours that were the direct antithesis of Edwin's waking hours.

Whether it was the silence, or a by-product of his raw desire to carve out a plan, Edwin's brain began to map out a plan to eliminate his wife. He had been on the right track with using the darknet. It was sufficiently anonymous to fox the Metropolitan Police, and it seemed to work. It had, after all, already led him to a contact who appeared to be an assassin.

'What if...?' Edwin whispered. He grabbed a pen and began to scribble on his notepad, a mouse mat between the layers to prevent any indentations left on the paper underneath.

The darknet was an ideal form of communication for finding anonymous contacts, but paying someone to kill Eleanor would require Edwin to renounce his anonymity in making the payment. Spending money would also leave a trail that even the Met could follow successfully right to him.

In order for it to work Edwin would need to exchange not goods or money, but services. One hit in exchange for another, a murder swap.

It was ideal, as neither person would need to identify themselves, only their victims. They would also have absolutely no connection to each other's victims, and thus no motive. Why would the police ever find them?

Edwin stretched out languorously as a yawn escaped him. It was getting late, but Edwin still had a new advert to post on the darknet before he would allow himself to sleep.

Chapter 4: Working Girl

North London's downmarket Caledonian Road area had always been known for being a place in which certain desires could be satiated, at a price. It wasn't completely rundown, but the London housing boom had forced those on the fringe to live in the most affordable places they could find, and Caledonian Road was still relatively affordable, which attracted the undesirable elements of society.

A central London location was essential for Vanhi. Her tiny flat was rented through a shell company, one of a myriad of properties used by her pimp to sell sex.

While prostitution has never been criminalised, solicitation is and always has been illegal. It didn't stop some working girls, who could often be found near roundabouts touting for business from passing cars.

But Vanhi was smatter than that. She advertised online, finding punters in places the law couldn't reach. Business was brisk.

For a city of over seven and a half million people, it was remarkable how lonely many men were. Sex always sold well and it always would. In a city where it was bad form to smile at another commuter on the subway the market thrived.

Vanhi lay splayed out on the four-posted bed, a reluctant participant pretending to be enthralled by the rolls of fat oozing off of the middle-aged man on top of her. Sweat poured off his body, and Vanhi wrinkled her nose as the smell overcame her.

She didn't know the man's name, and she didn't care to. Every time he touched her, she recoiled. But there was no other way.

Her customer didn't notice her pained wince as he mounted her. She closed her eyes as the man came to rest on top of her, and then forced her legs apart.

She tried to let her mind drift, to pretend she was somewhere else, anywhere else. Reality bit back as the man thrust himself inside her, violating every inch of her as his carnal urges took over.

Less than two minutes later, the man grunted as he finished. Vanhi fought the urge to run straight to the shower. A small moan escaped her, one of desperation, but the client smiled as if he had won the lottery.

The big man tossed a few notes on the bed-stand, then slowly got dressed before heading for the door. She closed her eyes as he dressed, willing him to leave quickly.

'Thanks, babe. Same time next week.'

She rolled over and clutched at her illicit haul. It wouldn't go far. She dashed to the shower and ran the hot tap. It was only when searing hot water scalded her that she came back down to reality.

When she was finally satisfied that she had finished her post-punter ritual, she dashed out of the shower to clear away the day's mess. It would only be a couple of hours before Jaison made it back from his cleaning job.

She hastily painted her face to hide her day's activities from her beau, and then pulled out a credit card and a small bag of cocaine. One more hit wouldn't hurt. She just needed to forget.

***

Edwin shifted in his airplane seat, trying not to elbow the woman next to him. His legs were always a problem when flying. They were simply too long. On a previous flight he had fallen asleep with his legs in the aisle and tripped up an air hostess who tried to shuffle by without waking him, and that was only a short-haul flight.

This time, he'd coughed up for premium economy, and asked to be put in the front row, next to the emergency exit. The airlines didn't mind. They needed someone able to open the door in the event of an emergency, and Edwin gained a few extra inches of legroom in return. The airline still refused to confirm that seat until he'd checked in.

He had grudgingly forked out for a travel cushion at Heathrow. He hated wasting money but it was a nine-hour flight, and another £10 made little difference when the bill for the flight had been £1183.

Edwin needn't have worried. He was soon snoozing in his seat, his Kindle tucked under his arm as the 747 soared majestically across the Atlantic.

An automated voice rudely woke him as the plane began the approach to Vancouver International.

'Please remain in your seats with your seatbelts fastened while the pilot begins our final descent. Please keep your seatbelt fastened until the plane has come to a complete stop, and the seatbelt signs have been turned off. Thank you for flying British Airways.'

***

Vanhi yelled out in pain, or she would have if she had not been gagged and bound. She struggled against her bonds, nylon rope cutting into her wrists and drawing blood.

She screamed again as he approached her. His pockmarked face leered down at her with blue eyes, shot through with crimson. He tugged at her hair, pulling her face to within inches of his, parading his power over her. She screamed again, feeling more helpless than ever before. As she screamed he became visibly aroused, advancing on her with a knife in one hand. He held the knife to her throat and slid his hands between her legs.

Vanhi screamed and woke with a start. She was sweating profusely. The dream *again*. She glanced bleary-eyed at the clock. It read 2:32 a.m. She cursed under her breath, careful not to disturb Jaison, and then swung her legs out of bed, before tiptoeing to the kitchen in search of cocaine.

There was none to be found. She searched her purse and found it empty. There wasn't even enough money to buy more, not that it would be easy to score a hit at half two in the morning anyway.

This had to end somehow. It was either her or him.

She pulled a serrated knife from the rack by the sink and placed it above her left wrist. One clean, simple swipe lengthways along the arm and her nightmare would be over.

Just as she was about to use the blade, Vanhi noticed her laptop had a small green LED flashing to indicate a new message had been posted on the darknet site she frequented.

At first, she thought it might be a new punter. She often found clients online, and using an anonymous service avoided being arrested for solicitation. She could find a dealer on there too, one willing to post her drugs to an anonymous PO box. Meeting up meant losing that anonymity, but with careful screening, it was possible to avoid problems.

The message didn't seem to be from a punter or a dealer. It was curiously titled 'You solve my problem, and I'll solve yours.'

The grammar was too perfect for it to be just another druggie looking to score, so Vanhi opened the thread. No author's name was listed, only the message and a time stamp, 1:08 a.m. GMT. Vanhi flicked the scroll wheel to show the body of the message.

'Help me eliminate my problem, and I'll eliminate yours.'

A small text box invited anonymous replies. Vanhi smiled. This was the opportunity she had been waiting for. If she was reading this right she could make sure *that* man never hurt anyone else as he had hurt her, and do it without ever even having to look at his pockmarked face ever again. First she had to make sure the message was what she thought it was. She typed cautiously, praying that the other person wasn't a prankster, or worse, the police.

'Seems like a fair swap. What is your problem?'

Chapter 5: Oh, Canada!

If Edwin hadn't been a Londoner for most of his adult life he would have found Vancouver to be both imposing and impressive in equal measure. The skyline resembled many of the other major cities Edwin had visited. Vast office blocks rose dozens of storeys above the waterline, with beautiful bridges such as the Granville Street Bridge in the north and the remarkably well-lit Lions Gate Bridge breaking up the seaways. It was a most beautiful city, with a vibrant metropolitan community, and a strong economy. It would be an ideal place to live and work for a newly single bachelor looking for a fresh start.

The interview was to take place in downtown Vancouver at 5433 West Georgia Street. It was a swanky address, but having lived and worked in the most exorbitantly expensive parts of London Edwin was not one to be intimidated by a postcode.

He was, however, impressed with the building. His office on Fleet Street had been opulent with incredible views, but the home of the Canadian Business Press Co eclipsed even that office. With over thirty floors, including a central atrium complete with indoor waterfall and a glass elevator, the building was a powerhouse.

Upon arrival Edwin was quickly escorted into the elevator by a businesslike secretary who had plainly been chosen on merit rather than her looks. The ride gave Edwin the opportunity to watch the laid-back attitude the Canadians took to their work. While the foyer at *The Impartial* was a veritable circus, CBC Co had a relaxed atmosphere. Colleagues could be seen chatting over the water cooler and strolling casually among the indoor fauna. It was a culture shock, but a pleasant one.

Equally shocking was the proliferation of proper etiquette. Everywhere Edwin went he was greeted warmly and with a politeness that to an Englishman would seem unnatural, perhaps even false. False it was not, however. There genuinely was a strong culture of being respectful and observing social boundaries.

There was no waiting room for Edwin to sit in and muster his thoughts before the interview. He was led straight into a series of psychometric tests. His brain strained as he fought to recall rules of grammar, and how to solve equations by integration. He was nearing a migraine when the secretary reappeared.

'Time is up, Mr Murphy. If you'd care to follow me, please.' Her tone was pleasant but firm.

Edwin was then led into his first-ever panel interview. A dozen individuals were arrayed down the length of a large, expensive, oak conference table. The secretary gestured for him to sit in the sole chair on the opposing side and left the room without further ado.

Edwin had noticed a coat rack by the door on the way in. He took his time removing his jacket and hanging it neatly before tucking his briefcase under the table and sitting before the waiting CBC executives.

'Good afternoon, Mr Murphy,' the central member of the panel said. He was a youngish man, and judging by the ill-fitting suit he was not truly an executive. Edwin replied with the usual courtesy as his eyes scanned the faces of those watching him. On the far left sat an older gentleman. His attire was nondescript: a simple white cotton shirt and black trousers. This would have been completely unmemorable had there not been a distinct pattern on his wrist, a void where his tan should have continued. Edwin deduced that the man customarily wore a large watch, probably a diver's watch. From the watch's absence it was clear that the man was concealing his wealth. He was probably someone important, but was trying to conceal who he was.

Edwin began to study the rest of the panel when the young man spoke again.

'Mr Murphy,' he began.

'Please, call me Edwin,' Edwin interrupted him.

The younger man frowned at the interruption and began the interview in earnest.

'If you were a dinosaur, what kind of a dinosaur would you be?'

Edwin almost burst out laughing. It was an absurd question, the sort used only by headhunters and human resources personnel.

It was the sort of question that is asked not to find out the answer, but to test how the candidate responds to the unexpected, to test how fast they think on their feet.

Edwin knew this and chose to ignore it entirely.

'I'm sure you have a number of quips ready no matter which of the common answers I give. I expect you're hoping I'll say tyrannosaurus rex. The truth of it is I am not a dinosaur. They are, after all, extinct.' Edwin turned to face the man on the left who was missing his watch.

'Forgive me for being blunt, sir, but I would prefer to deal with those in charge of hiring rather than some spotty-nosed kid.' Edwin flicked his hand at the human resources representative.

The man looked taken aback for a moment, then grinned a wide toothy smile.

'How'd you figure out who I am, son?' he asked

'Putting the important people on the end of the panel is a classic. The lackey chairs from the centre and distracts from the real panel. He asks frankly absurd questions, and you watch how I respond. That, and your tan line is a dead giveaway.'

The CEO guffawed.

'That'll be all, thanks, Tony.'

The younger man rose and left in silence, with three of his colleagues following him. Once they had closed the door the CEO introduced himself properly.

'I'm Barry Robbins, CEO here at CBC. To my left is our in-house counsel, our CFO and our deputy editor, Andy Hodgson. We've seen your work, and you spoke to Andy on the phone. We invited y'all here today to see if we liked the cut of your jib, and whether we think you'd fit in here in Vancouver. We're delighted to say you do fit in.'

***

Back at the Downtown Vancouver Hilton, Edwin practically fell into bed.

It had been a long day. They had most certainly liked him, but he had realised the interview was virtually a formality when they agreed to fly him halfway around the world for a face-to-face interview. It was nearly 7 p.m. Pacific time when he finally got to check his darknet messages. Vancouver lags eight hours behind London so it was no surprise to see the new message indicator flash as soon as he logged on.

'Seems like a fair swap. What is your problem?' he read.

Did she understand what he was proposing? Was she an undercover cop? Did it make a difference even if she was? He was, after all, anonymous.

Edwin pecked out a reply, typing with just two fingers. He 'd become too reliant on Betty's touchtyping.

'A woman. I need her gone.' He hit send, and his message zoomed around the globe in cyberspace, bouncing off relays in Singapore, California, Newfoundland and even Kenya before it reached Vanhi back in London.

***

Vanhi studied the reply. She had not figured that a woman would be the other person's target. Perhaps she had been too rash in responding to the message. But then Vanhi wondered if it even really mattered if her victim was a man or a woman. As long as she didn't have to see *him* ever again it would be worth it.

'Get me a picture.' She typed. *'How and when?'*

A few minutes later, Vanhi had a mini biography on Eleanor. She knew that Eleanor took a run at quarter to eight each morning for a circuit around Belgravia, and she had a clear image of Eleanor's bobbed auburn hair. She knew she had a week to pull off the kill, she just didn't know how to do it yet.

Edwin was a cautious man. He was not one to take risks that could be mitigated. Rather than providing a mere alibi, Edwin wanted to make his visit to Vancouver look genuine. He was a bona fide prospective citizen, so it was only natural to take some time to explore Vancouver. He'd booked a week in Canada, and he was in no rush to get back to London and his drab new apartment. There was no work to return to, and it looked like his choice to take a few days' break would provide the perfect alibi.

While Edwin was not much of a sports fan, a friend had recommended checking out the BC Sports Hall of Fame and its attached museum. Hockey is a national pastime in Canada, and if Edwin were to become a Canadian he would certainly need to know some background on the sport, even if he didn't fancy actually playing it. It was too violent for Edwin really; he had experienced his share of violence as a tight head prop on the school rugby team back at Harrow.

Edwin gladly paid the cover charge, and even picked up a gaudy souvenir t-shirt. He was every bit the tourist, studiously reading every plaque and memorising the names on various medals and trophies on display. He wasn't really interested but his years at *The Impartial* had imparted in him a thirst for knowledge, and the sports records allowed him to quench that thirst. Satiated, he moved on to the exhibits he was really fascinated by. One chronicled the life of Terry Fox, a cancer sufferer who ran cross-country across Canada, traversing 3,339 miles in just 143 days. The exhibit was aptly named the Marathon of Hope. If Edwin had still been an editor he would have loved to see such a great human-interest piece cross his desk.

Still, Terry Fox's story was not the most inspirational. That honour fell to a Paralympian who trekked 40,000 km through thirty-four countries on four continents in a wheelchair to raise awareness of spinal cord injuries. It was at BC Place Stadium that Rick Hansen made his triumphant return to Vancouver, cheered by the crowds in the packed stadium.

Feeling newly invigorated, Edwin left the Sports museum in search of lunch.

***

The syringe was ready. Vanhi had primed it with cocaine mixed with ethanol and put in a new hypodermic needle. Once injected, the coke would take around fifteen seconds to begin to take effect.

Eleanor's running route took her through Battersea Park on a circuitous route around the boating lake and then back across the Thames to Belgravia. The park was perfect. It was large, with plenty of places to hide. Getting away unseen would be easy.

Vanhi could simply stab Eleanor, then go. She didn't even need to wait for her to die. The cocaine would induce respiratory and cardiac arrest. As long as no medical treatment was administered within a few minutes, Eleanor would die and it would be almost impossible to trace. Vanhi knew that all she had to do was remove Eleanor's keys, the only personal possessions she took with her when she went for her daily run, and the police would find it difficult to identify the body.

Vanhi had to avoid the CCTV in the area. In the west the superintendent's office would provide some coverage, while at the east end of the park the Pump House and the park toilets were both monitored. Fortunately Eleanor was not prone to sticking to the busy pedestrian paths, preferring the freedom of a cross-country run. Her return loop would take her past Fountain Lake in the north-west of the park. Vanhi would pretend to sit and enjoy the view while doing her make-up. In reality she would be using the mirror in her make-up case to watch what was going on behind her as well as monitoring everything in front of her. Vanhi had a week to carry out the hit, so she would sit on the same bench each morning waiting for Eleanor to jog past, and only carry out the hit if the coast was clear. If anyone was nearby and likely to render medical assistance, or worse, see what happened, she would abort and wait for the next day to try again.

***

It had been a fantastic break. Edwin had imbibed the culture of Vancouver, playing tourist as well as enjoying the hotel's pool facilities. He could see himself living in Vancouver permanently. It was a beautiful city with plenty of amenities, and the people were as friendly and polite as the stereotypes suggested. Edwin found himself reluctant to leave, and it was with a heavy heart that he left his hotel suite to head back to London's squalor. Edwin wondered if the hit had occurred yet. He had deliberately left his mobile back in London, and had not left his hotel contact details with anyone. There was no one for him to leave them to. His work friends were no more, as was his marriage, and he had long since neglected his university compatriots.

Getting through airport security was painless, though Edwin made sure to keep his belt on as he went through the metal detectors. He wanted to be remembered, just in case.

The flight was equally uneventful. He made a pass at one of the air hostesses, but was shot down in a delightfully polite manner.

Edwin spent most of the nine hours fifteen minutes working out how to minimise the chances of the police catching him. He would have to go to her funeral of course. It would be noticed if he didn't. He might even have to give a eulogy. At the least he'd have to look after Chelsea through the service and the wake.

He'd also have to be careful with the insurance. Fortunately it was an older policy taken out just after he and Eleanor married, so it wouldn't flag any suspicion for being recent. He would have to leave it in a drawer for a while; he mustn't been seen as too eager to claim, otherwise the police would never stop pursuing him. Edwin would simply have to play the aggrieved husband. They were having some troubles, but who wasn't? He and Eleanor had argued before, and they'd always worked it out. He was hopeful that this time would have been no different. He would move back into the townhouse of course; it simply wouldn't do to uproot Chelsea after all she had been through.

Edwin dropped off to sleep over Greenland as these thoughts gambolled through his brain. A slight smile was painted on his aristocratic features.

Chapter 6: Jogging is Murder

Vanhi knew London was a hotbed for closed circuit television. Years of prostitution and drugs had taught her to avoid the bright lights of touristville, and to hide in a crowd when she could.

She was still reluctant to be caught on CCTV on the tube network. Her apartment was above a chip shop in Caledonian Road. She could walk to Battersea Park, but it was almost six miles going straight there, and Vanhi wanted to take a more circumspect route.

Vanhi's route took her on foot to Camden Town tube station. It was on the Northern line, the busiest commuter line on the underground. Vanhi knew she could easily be lost among the foot traffic. She took a train south to Stockwell before doubling back to Oval. To any observer it would look like she had simply missed her stop and gone one station too far.

In reality it let Vanhi know she was not being followed. She didn't expect to be, but few paranoid criminals ever wound up in prison.

From there it was less than half an hour on foot to Battersea Park. As she made her way there Vanhi observed a discernible lack of CCTV near the disused Battersea power station, as well as noticing that New Convent Garden Market was bustling with business, even at this early hour.

By half-past seven she was seated on a bench overlooking Fountain Lake. She sat with a paperback for a while, occasionally glancing at her mobile phone.

The mobile, like the paperback, had been bought just for the occasion. It was an old phone, and wouldn't attract any attention. The SIM card was a pay-as-you-go edition bought in a corner shop. She could have got one for free online, but this way she remained anonymous. She didn't need the phone to communicate, but by pretending to be sending text messages she could while away time without anyone becoming suspicious. Who would look at just another Londoner attached to their mobile?

Vanhi had taken this route several times before, and she now knew Eleanor's jogging route well. It had taken a varied wardrobe not to be noticed on the first three attempts, but each time, Eleanor was absorbed in her run. She probably noticed little beyond the music on her iPod.

For the first few attempts there had been bystanders around when Eleanor jogged by. On the first day an elderly lady sat next to Vanhi on the bench and nattered on about her grandchildren. Vanhi learnt to put her handbag by her side to occupy the whole bench.

The second day another jogger had been with Eleanor. Whether it was planned or not, Vanhi didn't know. The scant information she had been provided with didn't cover jogging partners. On the third day a homeless man had been harassing Eleanor for money, and he wasn't going to give up without a fight. He had clearly missed the fact that Eleanor was running with no bag, no pockets and only her door key around her neck.

On the fourth try, Eleanor appeared like clockwork. She came jogging up from the south of the park, towards the north-western exit. Vanhi's pulse began to race as Eleanor neared her, faster than even on the previous days. Her hands trembled. This time no one was about, she was sure of it.

Now that it came down to the wire Vanhi realised that she couldn't get Eleanor while she was running, and it was unlikely that she would just stop in front of her.

As Eleanor was about to jog on by, Vanhi called out to her in a loud voice, as she knew from experience that Eleanor's iPod would be set to quite a high volume.

'Excuse me, darling, but your shoelace is undone,' she purred in an affected southern drawl.

Eleanor smiled and glanced downwards at her trainers. As she frowned at the obvious lie Vanhi struck, thrusting the needle into her jugular and plunging the syringe down in one movement.

Eleanor moved to strike out at her attacker but she stumbled. A huge dose of cocaine, hundreds of pounds' worth, coursed through her veins. Her heart began to hammer in her ribcage. She was already breathing hard from the continuous jog, and it did not take long for the arrhythmia to set in as her heart rate soared. She tried to scream, but her lungs were burning from a lack of oxygen. Spots appeared before her eyes as she realised her attacker was dumping her on the bench. Where was someone, anyone, when she needed a passerby? She heard a crack as her consciousness failed her. Her key had been torn from her neck.

Vanhi used her sleeve to pull the key off the chain. It was a cheap chain, the kind that could be bought in a hardware store rather than something more decorative. Vanhi flung the key into the lake, watching for a split second to make sure it sank before power-walking towards the south-east of the park. A run would garner attention, and a swift walk would not. She tucked the chain in her pocket to dispose of later, and escaped onto Queenstown Road.

Minutes later she was lost among the crowd at New Covent Garden Market. Vanhi was in no rush to hurry back lest she draw attention to herself. She grabbed a burger at the market, and as she put the wrapper in the bin she slipped the chain and the spent needle in too. She resolved to walk home even though it was quite a trek. As she did so she practically whistled, thinking of the favour she was due to receive in return.

The body was discovered about ten minutes later. An ambulance was quickly called and Eleanor rushed to the Royal London Hospital. The paramedics tried in vain to resuscitate her, but she was too far gone. They suspected drugs, but nothing they tried worked. Eleanor was pronounced dead on arrival, the latest Jane Bloggs in the city of London as she was carrying no ID.

The hospital could not issue a death certificate. Suspected drugs deaths had to be referred to the City of London Coroner's Office as 'violent or unnatural'. Instead the attending doctor completed what is known as a Formal Notice. This would normally be given to the next of kin, but as the deceased was a Jane Bloggs this was not possible, and the doctor was not entirely sure of the procedure. He settled for keeping the notice on file until it was needed.

Eleanor was soon ferried out of the hospital morgue and onto the coroner's slab. The registrar could not register her death, both because of her anonymity and because the coroner had not yet decided how to classify the death.

A post-mortem was then conducted by the coroner. This wasn't always done, but the coroner deemed it prudent to investigate in the circumstances. It was, in fact, a young coroner's assistant who performed the autopsy.

Before the autopsy the body was photographed by a pathology tech. Detailed notes were taken on the body's position ('splayed, no sign of bleeding'), the clothes worn ('expensive, designer, sportswear') and then various samples were taken including fibres from Eleanor's clothes, scrapings from under Eleanor's nails, as well as hair and skin cell samples.

After the clothes were removed an ultraviolet light was used to highlight anything not noticeable to the naked eye. It was here that the assistant coroner noticed the puncture wound to the neck. He scraped around the wound in case any residue remained, then took a number of close-up photographs to measure the extent of the puncture. It was clearly caused by a sharp-pointed object such as a needle.

Satisfied that all the recoverable evidence to be had was recorded in his log the coroner moved on to the internal examination. A rubber body block was placed in the small of Jane Bloggs' back, pushing her chest up higher to expose it to the coroner's waiting knife. Her lifeless arms fell limply by her side as the coroner cut a Y incision from her shoulders, meeting at the sternum. Heavy-duty shears were then used to force the incisions apart, exposing the chest cavity and the organs within.

He was then passed a wicked-looking scalpel by his tech. This was used to slice open the pericardial sack, a fibrous layer that surrounds the heart. A blood sample was then taken from the exposed pulmonary veins, which would be used for toxicological analysis. Satisfied there were no visible blood clots the coroner then removed the heart. Next to be removed were the lungs, and finally the rest of the organs. These would then be weighed.

It was pretty clear from a cursory examination what had happened however, and that was that Jane Bloggs has suffered a heart attack. This was borne out by the paramedic's suspicion that drugs were involved. Toxicology would confirm this in 3-5 days, but the coroner didn't care. It was now a police case.

***

Heathrow posed no problems on Edwin's return. He had half-expected to be met at the gate by the police. Maybe the hit hadn't been carried out yet. He decided to test it by texting his ex-wife when he got home. 'Eleanor, I'm back from my job interview. Can I take Chelsea to the movies next weekend? She can stay over here after.' Edwin figured that if he had no response he could assume the hit had probably taken place. It also seemed to him to be a perfectly legitimate text for a father to send.

His flat looked just as messy as when he had left it. The sink still had plates piled high. At this rate it might be simpler just to chuck the plates and buy new ones. His washing still lay on the floor in a heap in the corner. His appearance mattered less and less each passing day; who was there to try and impress now?

One thing had changed however. His laptop was flashing the indicator message when he turned it on. This meant Edwin had received a darknet message. It was from Vanhi, detailing the target he was supposed to hit. *'White male, six foot two, lives in Brixton, name of Emanuel Richard.* Edwin read aloud. A grainy picture was attached. The picture showed a hand holding up a photo of a man, presumably Emanuel. The person holding the photo couldn't be seen, but in the background, Edwin could see a neon sign. Edwin concentrated on his target.

Emanuel was distinctive-looking, with grey hair beginning to appear around the temples giving him an air of salt-and-pepper sophistication. Both frown and smile lines were evident on his face despite the low resolution, and his lips were curled in a thin smile. He had pockmarked skin, and watery brown eyes, which stopped him from being handsome.

Edwin felt a sinking feeling in the pit of his stomach. Taking this guy out wouldn't be as easy as the whole plan had seemed on paper. He didn't know if he could really do it. Edwin felt his world close in. If he did kill Emanuel, he might leave behind some evidence; even the tiniest part of himself could get him convicted using DNA.

He could just walk away, couldn't he? He mused on this for one happy moment before realising that if he didn't deliver, the other person could easily put two and two together to work out who he was. If they went to the police with what they knew – that he was abroad to provide an alibi – then the police would work it out. Even if the cops couldn't prove it, he would still wind up in the dock.

He still had breathing room for now – he had no confirmation the hit had gone ahead. Perhaps he could even call it all off before it was too late.

Chapter 7: Morton

A trickle of light punctured the blinds in David Morton's office as he entered. His desk was exactly as he had left it on Friday evening, a handful of case files neatly aligned with the top edge of the desk, face up and labelled in the upper right corner. As a Detective Chief Inspector in charge of London's busiest Murder Investigation Team, Morton took great care to examine cold cases every Monday morning. The oldest among them was yellowed with age, an unsolved murder from Morton's first year with the Metropolitan Police.

Nothing had changed in the case since the murder in 1985, the year after Morton had joined the force. Somehow this daily reminder that a victim's family still waited for closure reinforced Morton's determination to one day bring the killer to justice. Morton's work meant dealing with the worst in society, but no matter how hard his workload became, the relief expressed by victims' families when a case was finally closed vindicated Morton's career choice. The cases had long since been passed over to officers specialising in cold cases, but Morton felt, as the first detective to investigate, that he was responsible for getting justice.

Morton tore his gaze away from the case, reaching for the insipid coffee he had grabbed from the force canteen on the way in. He replaced the cold case file, squaring the spine with the neighbouring file so that they were all aligned perfectly, and reached for the paperwork that would be his duty for the morning. He hated dealing with the bureaucracy but without it the whole force would come to a standstill. Finishing his bagel, he reminded himself that he was lucky to still be in the field most of the time. Many of his colleagues had been retired to desk duty by the time they reached his age, but the great Inspector Morton had dodged that particular bullet on the strength of his last annual fitness test, just.

He had some of the dreaded paperwork to fill out, and then his presence was required at the coroner's office. A Jane Bloggs had been found dead under suspicious circumstances, and it had been assigned to the Murder Investigation Team that Morton led.

Peter K. Sugden-Jones tugged at his collar to straighten it as he disembarked. He had travelled first class from his home in Epsom to London. On arrival he had waited for all the other travellers to disembark before he deigned to leave his compartment. No point risking rubbing shoulders with *that* kind of riffraff. He quickly exited Waterloo to find his driver waiting on the double yellows near Station Approach Road. The driver handed him a newspaper and a Thermos cup full of Earl Grey. With one fluid movement Peter tucked the *Financial Times* under his left arm and slid into the back seat.

The driver then turned on the ignition, flooding the car with Vivaldi from every one of the seven Bose speakers mounted in the rear. A small screen flickered to life, showing Bloomberg. As Peter's eyes traversed the morning's market data he sighed contentedly. It was better this way.

The paperwork hadn't taken too long, but several colleagues had asked about his weekend away, and he was only too happy to divulge. Chichester had been a welcome break from the noise of city life. David Morton adored the quaint feel of the town. It had once been a walled town guarded by four gates, and much of the old stonework still stood the test of time. An antiques market had been in town during his visit, and David had managed to snag a lovely Lalique vase for his wife Sarah. She adored the artsy stuff, and while David pretended to protest at its sprawling all over the house, he didn't really mind. As long as she left his television and his Sky Sports subscription well alone, he'd tolerate whatever decorative style was in vogue this season.

He'd also had time to sneak away into Chichester harbour for a spot of fishing while Sarah enjoyed the hotel spa. He had never had much time to fish while the kids were growing up, but now that they were adults forging their own lives he suddenly had a lot more time on his hands. Not coincidentally he also had a lot more in the way of funds with which to fund his hobbies, although his youngest son was still on the scrounge at the ripe old age of twenty-four, and had only last week texted his mother asking her to help out with his rent. He knew which side his bread was buttered, as Sarah had agreed before David had even had the chance to moan about it.

Still, it was good to be back. Morton hit the call button by the lift, and headed for the morgue.

***

Vanhi was beginning to worry. Her contact had not responded to her latest messages. Had he been caught by the police? If he had, would the police be after her now too? A dull thumping began in the back of her skull. Stress always affected her this way. When life got to be too much, migraines were always the warning sign that she needed to cut back.

'Deep breath. In and out. In and out.' Speaking aloud helped regularise her breathing. She had hyperventilated in the past, although not recently. Vanhi began to calm down and quickly typed yet another message. Again, it was a request to fix a date for the reciprocal kill. She needed to know when it would happen so that she could be sure she was out of the way. If he didn't contact her soon, she didn't know what she would do.

Chapter 8: Where's Mummy?

It was not like Eleanor Murphy to forget. School had finished promptly at 3.25 p.m. as usual, the large bronze bell in the schoolyard ringing out to end another week's incarceration for the pupils at the Grosvenor Young Ladies Academy. Chelsea, like all of her friends, was eagerly looking forward to the weekend. Hopefully she'd be able to see her daddy this weekend. She knew he was flying back from Canada tomorrow, and she wondered what he would bring her home. A few months ago he had gone to Amsterdam, and Chelsea treasured the beautiful wooden clogs that Daddy had brought back for her. She was so excited.

Her childlike glee faded to confusion when she couldn't see Mummy waiting in the playground. She always stood under the chestnut tree with Andrea's and Lulu's mothers. Their mums were there, but she couldn't see her own.

'Hello, have you seen my mummy?' she asked Andrea's mum.

'No, sweetie, but we'll wait with you until she gets here, okay?'

'Okay.' Chelsea was sullen at first, but was soon talking animatedly with the other girls.

Fifteen minutes passed before Andrea's mum tried to ring Eleanor on her mobile. It went to voicemail after a dozen rings. 'Hi, Eleanor, Sarah here, Andrea's mum. Chelsea is still waiting for you. Do you want us to take her home with us, and you can pick her up later? Let us know. Talk to you later, doll.'

Half an hour later, and still no sign of Eleanor. Sarah rang her friend's number again and left a message on the answerphone. 'Eleanor, she'll be at our place. We'll drop her back after tea if we don't see you before.'

***

The putrid smell hit Morton as he entered the morgue. The morgue had four rooms available for autopsy, but only one was fitted with proper extraction systems to remove the smell of decay. It was a sweet pervasive smell that Morton could never seem to get out of his nostrils for hours afterwards. The other rooms had venting of course, but none of the carbon-activated filtration that the aptly nicknamed 'bloater' room possessed. The bloater room was used for the worst bodies, those which had putrefied or were in the late stages of decomposition that made it impossible to work in an unventilated room.

Thankfully his corpse was much more intact. She was a Jane Bloggs, brought in over the weekend after dying under suspicious circumstances. The police file so far was remarkably thin. She had been found in Battersea Park unconscious early in the morning, and taken to the Royal London for treatment. She was dead on arrival, and an autopsy was mandated by the coroner.

This had revealed a puncture wound to the neck, and a blood sample had been sent off for toxicological testing, which revealed elevated levels of cocaine and industrial ethanol. Oddly neither substance had any impurities, which meant it wasn't the sort of coke peddled on street corners. It had to have come from one of the criminal gangs operating in London.

Morton eyeballed the body. She was tall – around five foot six – and size ten at most, with neatly cut hair. Her nails were expertly manicured, and she had no train tracks or other indicators of prior drug use. Her lungs were clean; the coroner reported she didn't even smoke. She was also dressed in jogging sweats. It was clear she was a health fanatic. It struck Morton as odd that she would die from drugs. She was clearly from another world entirely. Her haughty features and designer clothes screamed trophy wife, not coke addict. So, who was she? Surely someone with the money to wear Gucci while out running would be missed by somebody.

Edwin's mobile rang, vibrating against his makeshift desk noisily. He snatched it up almost immediately, then let it ring for a few seconds to avoid appearing too keen.

'Hello?' he said warily. Hardly anyone called him on his mobile; it was probably a sales call.

'Hi, Edwin. This is Sarah, Andrea's mum.' Her tone was terse.

'What can I do for you, Sarah?'

'I have your daughter at my house. She came home with us when you didn't pick her up this afternoon. The poor thing was just waiting in the rain alone.'

'She's supposed to be with her mum this afternoon. Eleanor and I aren't together, so I only have Chelsea at weekends.'

'Oh, right.' Sarah's tone began to soften.

'Sorry, I thought everyone would know by now.'

'I'm starting to worry about Eleanor. We've tried calling her, and driven by the house. No one was home. Come to think of it, I haven't heard from her for a few days. Do you know where she is?'

'Sorry, I haven't spoken to her. I only just got back to the UK. Do you want me to come pick Chelsea up?' A smile was plastered across Edwin's face. Eleanor was gone.

It had been a long day. A run on a bank in some third world country had sparked panic early in the morning, and trading had been highly volatile since. Panic really was contagious on the trading floor. Thankfully Peter traded via a broker from his own private office. No one disturbed him there, not even clients. His secretary was allowed to enter, but she was required to knock first and she knew not to disturb him without good reason. She was a vestige of a bygone age. Prim, pressed and proper, Martha was nearing seventy years of age and would retire soon. Peter dreaded the moment she finally packed it in. Interviewing replacements was not a thought he relished, and it was unlikely he could delegate. Even if he did, God knows what kind of riffraff human resources might drag in.

Peter whistled as his private elevator brought him back to earth. His private car was waiting as usual. This time his driver offered him *The Evening Standard*, and he was left to pour his own scotch for the ride home. It was a Friday tradition to enjoy a good single malt, and it certainly made the journey more palatable.

Edwin's message indicator light was flashing again. He tiptoed into the lounge to make certain that Chelsea was still asleep. He needed to be sure that she wouldn't take up and see him messaging. After shutting his bedroom door, Edwin secured the latch, which clicked into place.

Edwin was half afraid to check his messages, but he knew that sooner or later he had to respond.

He had the inevitable chaser message as expected, but he also had a number of other messages. It appeared his first post was still getting interest. He disregarded the new messages. He had enough problems as it was, and Eleanor was already dead even if the police hadn't identified her yet.

He went back to the chaser message and drafted his reply.

'When suits you? It will take a while to plan. How about next month on the second Sunday?'

That would buy him two and a half weeks to work out what he was going to do.

Satisfied, he closed the laptop lid and went to get ready for bed.

Chapter 9: Not Here, Thank You!

The driveway was manicured to perfection. Mrs Sugden didn't do it herself, of course. She wasn't too busy, and she was certainly perfectly able-bodied, but it just wouldn't do to be seen doing her own manual labour.

Identically pruned bay trees lined the driveway to the west of the house. It was extra-long to accommodate Mr Sugden's town car, and was finished with a fine oak carport that protected the vehicle from the weather without making it difficult to get the car out in the morning.

Mr Sugden was as prompt as ever that Friday. His car pulled in at half past eight precisely, and his wife had dinner on the table. This she had made herself. Dinner was the one concession Mrs Sugden made to what she called 'her womanly duties'. She never deigned to clean, but like clockwork fine French food was always served for Mr Sugden. It had been that way for nearly thirty years, and was not likely to change any time soon.

Once Mr Sugden was eating, she waited for him to tackle a particularly rare piece of steak before broaching the subject that had been flitting around inside her skull all day.

'Dear, the new neighbours have moved in. I saw their moving vans this afternoon, all three of them!'

'So what? Can't you see I'm eating, woman?' Peter practically snarled, or at least that's what she thought she heard him say. The steak muffled the noise.

'Well, dear, don't get too angry but they are *those* kind of people.'

'Faggots?'

'No, dear.'

'Lefties?'

'I don't think so, dear.'

'Foreign?'

'Yes, dear.'

'Please tell me they speak English at least.'

'They seem to, dear, but it's not their first language.'

'What is then? Spit it out.'

'I think it's called Urdu, dear,' she practically whispered. She knew her husband would hit the roof. She wasn't disappointed.

Mr Sugden roared in anger. He leapt to his feet, taking the tablecloth with him. Their dinner plates were ripped from the table and thrown to the floor with a loud crash.

'Pakis! Here? In Little Walton?' Mr Sugden steamrollered out of the room in a fit of rage. He had never been a tolerant man.

***

Morton's deputies had been dispatched to collect any CCTV in or around Battersea Park that they could find. The resultant footage had been less than encouraging.

While there was some CCTV in the park, it was primarily centred around the buildings, and the canoe lake. Those areas had been tagged with graffiti a number of times, and Battersea Council had chosen to focus their funds on preventing desecration rather than providing blanket coverage.

This meant that there were a huge number of CCTV dead spots throughout the park. The major entrances were covered, but there were numerous points of egress around the park that were not. The killer could easily have slipped in, and then out again, at any one of those points. Even if the killer had been caught on CCTV, the tapes showed hundreds of individuals in the vicinity at any time. That might mean witnesses could be found, but Londoners were prone to look the other way. It was instinctive in a big city; people were loathe to get involved.

Signs had been put up anyway asking for witnesses, but Morton doubted the free phone number would get anything other than the usual conspiracy-nut time-wasters calling in.

He was more interested in finding the victim on the CCTV. After all, she would have no reason at all for evading the cameras. With a snap of Morton's fingers an audio-visual technician appeared in the doorway.

'I've got an image of our Jane Bloggs here' – Morton indicated the morgue photos on the desk – 'and I've got CCTV in which she will probably have appeared. Can you use facial tracking to find out where she appears on the tape?',

'Yes, sir, but it will take a little time.'

'Do it.' With that, Morton went to find a cup of tea and a custard cream.

***

The tech had worked quickly. Morton was only gone for twenty minutes and by the time he got back the tech was leaning back in a leather office chair playing Angry Birds. He jumped to his feet as Morton entered the room.

'Inspector, I've isolated the instances of the victim appearing on CCTV. She came in here;' he pointed at the first screen, which showed the north-east entrance to the park. 'It looks like her route brought her over the Chelsea Bridge, down round the east of the toilet block closest to the entrance, and then south towards the duck pond, where she disappears from CCTV. She seems to have avoided the main jogging paths, preferring to run freeform. We get another glimpse of her as she passes the boating lake, and then again here.' This time he indicated an intersection of pathways in the centre of the park near an ice cream van. 'After that, nothing.'

'So she jogged in a "U" shape around the park, which means she was probably going to exit in the north-west entrance or return via the north-east entrance.'

'It's north-west, sir. I checked footage from earlier in the week.'

'Good lad. So she probably lives on the north bank, in or around Chelsea, Pimlico or Kensington. Fits with her clothing, I suppose. Odd no one has reported a middle-aged white woman from the rich burbs missing though.'

'Someone did, sir. This morning one Eleanor Murphy was reported missing.'

'Where's she from?'

'Belgravia, sir.'

'That fits too.'

'Yes sir, and one more thing...'

'Yes?'

'When she entered the park, she was carrying a key. The morgue didn't find any possessions on her.'

'Good work. It might have been removed at the Royal London, but I'll look into it.'

***

Edwin made the tactical decision to report Eleanor missing.

If he didn't, the police would want to know why. Even if they weren't together Eleanor was his wife, and the mother of his beautiful little girl. It would look guilty if he didn't.

Edwin had expected it to be a difficult task, but was pleasantly surprised to find that he could do it by phone. It had been straightforward enough, almost as if the policewoman who took down the details was simply reading a script and recording his responses.

'Any relatives in the area?' she asked

'Her parents are about two hundred miles away, and her brother is currently staying with them.'

'Is there anywhere she typically frequents?'

'Her gym. It's the Fitness First round the corner from our townhouse.'

'Anywhere else?' the WPC ventured, moving beyond the standard script.

'She likes to run twice a day. I'm not entirely sure of her route. It changes so often.'

'Does she suffer from any health problems?'

'Stress, maybe. She is a lawyer after all.'

'Finances?'

'What about them?'

'Who does she bank with?'

'HSBC. It's a joint account.' Edwin had not got around to changing this yet.

'Any activity on her cards?'

'None, but she doesn't really trust cards. She tends to stick to cash when she can.' Edwin had pulled up their online banking statement before the call.

'So I'm guessing she isn't on benefits?' The woman carried on down the checklist.

'No. Well, not unless you include child benefit.'

'We don't. Do you have a recent photograph?'

'Yes.'

'Do you have email access?'

'Of course.'

'Email one to us. Missingpersons@met.police.uk.'

'OK. I'll do that at the end of this call.' Edwin scribbled down the email address.

'We'll also need your consent to search your home.' Edwin paled. Did they know something? Of course they meant the townhouse, not his flat.

The policewoman continued. 'It's standard procedure, sir. We will also need a DNA sample; a toothbrush or hairbrush should suffice. We'll collect that when we conduct the search. I assume you are happy to consent to publicity too. The media can be helpful.'

This question shook Edwin. A search was one thing; they wouldn't find much at the townhouse, but if he started going on television to plead for her to come home... Well, that was another thing entirely. It might get him caught in a lie.

'I'll think about it. It's only been a day, and she might have just vanished for personal reasons, right?' Edwin hoped this sounded plausible.

***

The laptop message indicator was still lit. Some were nonsense. Even Edwin couldn't decode *'I wn2 hlp u bt nd drg muni irtn. wl dnefin.'* And one of his undergraduate modules had been on cryptography.

Others were far more straightforward.

'Will eliminate your problem if you sort mine.'

The time limit for the hit he had agreed to was fast approaching. What if he let another one of these crackpots carry it out for him? Then he'd have no link to either kill. He could even be sure to have a firm alibi just in case.

He picked the most promising message, and typed out a brief reply: *'Happy to oblige. Let me know details.'*

Maybe he wouldn't have to kill anyone after all. If he just stiffed the second guy he could get away with it all.

Chapter 10: A Broken Man

Barry Chalmers stared at his lap. His waiter came by every few minutes asking if he was ready to order yet. Each time, he said no in a small voice.

But after three hours, the waiting staff were beginning to talk. His date wasn't turning up. He wished he knew what he was doing wrong. His mother always told him to be the perfect gentleman: to buy dinner, to open doors. It never did him any good.

When he'd met Jessica at a music bar in Basildon, she'd seemed cute. She was a bit coy, and it took him most of the night to work up the courage to say hello.

She wasn't even conventionally beautiful. Barry could understand when the supermodel types turned him down.

When he'd finally got to the end of the night, Barry jumped the gun and went for the kiss a bit too fast, clumsily bumping into her neck.

Somehow, she agreed to go out again. To Barry's amazement, they spent most of the summer together. He didn't even mind that he somehow ended up paying for everything.

Half of the restaurant bill or the whole thing made little difference, and he had asked her out so he gladly paid. Only then she came to expect it, as if he owed her.

Still, he spent the money. Tonight was the night he intended to ask her a question. His friend, for he only had one, had told him it was too soon, but Jessica felt like his last chance at finding love.

Barry absent-mindedly turned the ring box over in his pocket as the clock struck ten. Three hours.

Where was she?

***

Barry learnt the ugly truth the following weekend. He was out of London to visit his mother in hospital when Jessica called and said they needed to talk, urgently, face-to-face. He figured it was serious, and rushed back to Basildon.

He took her out to a nice restaurant, expecting there to be news. He half wondered if she might be pregnant. He pulled out her chair so she could sit down, gave her a bunch of flowers that he'd picked up at the station kiosk, and proceeded to order a bottle of Bordeaux.

'What's up, babe?' he had asked.

'I don't think this is going to work.'

'We can always go to another restaurant.'

'No, Barry, I mean us. It's over.'

'Why?'

'No reason. We just drifted apart. It's not you, it's me.'

Barry's cheeks flushed red. He'd heard that line before. The next line was a classic too.

'We can still be friends, right?'

Chapter 11: Confirmation

The search of the Murphy residence performed by Missing Persons was cursory at best. They picked up a recent photo, supplied by the husband, and obtained a DNA sample from a hairbrush in Eleanor's en-suite.

Nothing was missing from the house, suggesting robbery was not the motive despite Eleanor's door key going missing. It would have been a plum target for a daytime robbery; the Murphys lived a comfortable lifestyle.

The order had come from above not to waste too much time. The legendary DCI David Morton was almost certain that the missing person in question was his Jane Bloggs. The Missing Persons team got in and out, and sent the sample straight to Forensics for analysis.

***

Morton's BlackBerry beeped loudly. He hated carrying two phones, but the force insisted. Everywhere he went he was at the Met's beck and call.

'Detective Chief Inspector Morton, this is Stuart from Forensics. I compared Jane Bloggs with a photo of Eleanor Murphy obtained from the husband by Missing Persons so I went ahead and performed DNA analysis. DNA confirms our Jane Bloggs is Mrs Eleanor Murphy. All sixteen alleles match.'

'Good work. Call the husband in to ID the body – and video his reaction for Dr Jensen to analyse.'

Reaction filtering was a new technique. Potential suspects in violent crimes such as the husband, ex or other persons of interest would be targeted with visual stimuli such as the body or photos of the crime scene. This would be caught on camera, and the resident psychologist would then review the footage to determine if the reaction was normal, and if not, why not.

It was a technique Dr Jensen had pioneered during his PhD in Forensic Psychology. It certainly wasn't mainstream yet, but Morton was willing to try anything that would give him an edge.

***

The police had called about an hour earlier. They thought that Eleanor's body may have been found, and needed next of kin to identify the body. What Edwin didn't know was they were recording the phone call. It was expected he would be under stress but Dr Jensen wanted to use the pitch, tone and timbre of his voice to record which parts of the call he found most stressful.

'Hello?' Edwin's voice was rich, melodious, with a slight hint of that singsong lilt many of Irish descent possess.

'Good morning, Mr Murphy. This is Missing Persons.'

'What can I do for you?' His voice was slightly faster now, a little higher. It wasn't much, but Dr Jensen set this as his baseline, the stress level against which the rest of the conversation would be measured.

'We may have found your wife's body, Mr Murphy. I'm sorry.'

There was a telling delay before the sobbing began. It was only microseconds, and a normal person would never have picked up on it, but the software was exacting. It was the same software used by insurance companies to weed out fraudulent claims.

'Oh, oh God. What happened?' Murphy was pretty convincing, but Dr Jensen's gut reaction was that Edwin Murphy knew his wife was dead, but he didn't know the circumstances of her death. That didn't quite make logical sense yet, but it was his instinctive take on the situation. Dr Jensen was the first to admit his potential fallibility, but he was right more often than not.

'We're not entirely sure yet I'm afraid, Mr Murphy. DNA isn't back yet,' Jensen lied. 'Are you available to come down to the station to ID the body?'

'Yes, yes, of course. Let me drop my daughter at a friend's house, and I'll come straight down.' The concern for his daughter was touching, but the good doctor wondered if this might simply be a ruse to distract the police.

An hour later Edwin Murphy walked into New Scotland Yard, and took the lift down to the morgue. It was recessed in the basement, and the only foot traffic in the area was the coroner, his assistants and technologists as well as the occasional cop.

He was led to a viewing window by the WPC who had phoned earlier, and could see a body underneath a cotton sheet on a gurney. Once he had assured the WPC he was emotionally prepared, the coroner's assistant pulled back the cover. He was careful to show only the face, and not the neck wound.

'That's her. That's my Eleanor.' Edwin's eyes began to water, and he sank to his knees in a fit of sobbing.

***

Most people cannot distinguish fact from fiction, as long as the deception is plausible. Dr Jensen was not most people. As well as being trained in forensic psychology, he had appeared on television as 'the human lie detector'. He was one of the rare individuals who could recognise micro expressions, visual clues that appear on the face for a fraction of a second.

With the subject filmed, and the video played back in slow motion, this could become deadly accurate. He had been thrown out of court for trying to testify as an expert witness, it was true, but that didn't diminish the accuracy of his work. The police knew how valuable his opinion was, and so he spent his days locked up at Met HQ reviewing videos, audio recordings and even photographs to see if he could discern the truth contained within.

'So what are we dealing with, Doc?' called a deep voice from behind.

'I hate it when you sneak up on me, David,' Jensen said, but his tone was more welcoming than his words.

Morton smiled. 'I know, Doc, but old habits die hard.' Prior to joining the Metropolitan Police the inspector had done a stint in the military police.

'Well, the subject isn't being entirely honest with us. He either knew or expected she was dead. That isn't necessarily incriminating. It could just have been deep-seated fear, but I think the slight pauses were the giveaway. Watch him closely.'

'We will, Doc. I'm on my way to question him right now.' Morton tipped an invisible hat to Dr Jensen, and left whispering a barely audible 'thank you' as he strode towards the door.

***

The gold-embossed envelope fluttered onto the doormat while the Sugden family were still asleep. The maid brought it up with the paper, resisting the temptation to open it. Mr Sugden set it aside at first. Even in front of his staff he maintained an air of indifference. It had to look like gold-embossed envelopes were an everyday occurrence, rather than something to get excited about. After he had supped his coffee, Mrs Sugden passed him his letter opener. It too was embossed, a beautiful handmade antique. It was a relic of the Afro-Crimean war, and had been in his family for generations.

He flipped the envelope over gingerly between his fingertips. It was addressed simply to Mr and Mrs Peter Sugden. That puzzled him at first. Usually when one goes to the trouble of using such an elaborate overture as gold-embossed silk envelopes, one takes the time to address the recipient in a more formal manner.

The reverse had not been written on, though a wax seal had been applied to the seams. The crest imprinted in the wax was not a design that Peter was familiar with, and he was knowledgeable of such matters. His family was in Debrett's after all. The figure depicted was a famous imam, but Peter had subconsciously discounted the invitation possibly being from *those* sort of people and he didn't notice it.

The envelope eviscerated neatly along the top edge; Peter tugged the invitation from the cotton and held it between his thumb and forefinger.

'Dear Mr and Mrs Sugden,

His Excellency Qadi Qumas and his exalted wife request the pleasure of your company on Saturday for the occasion of a Garden Party to be held in celebration of their purchase of Lyddington Manor. '

The note was on foil-backed card, and was signed by both Mr and Mrs Qumas.

'First they move in next door, now they outdo us on social occasions!' Mrs Sugden's voice was as shrill as it had ever been in recent memory. Mr Sugden's baritone was far more serious.

'This just won't do. Those sort of people can't live here, and I'll be damned if I'm going to their glorified barbecue.' Mr Sugden defiantly tore up the envelope.

'I'll take care of them, dear. You mark my words; they'll be gone before Christmas.'

Chapter 12: Interrogation

The day after identifying his wife's body, Edwin was summoned back to the station as he had expected. On arrival, he was given half an hour to compose himself and make a few phone calls before being shown into an interview suite where DCI Morton waited.

'Mr Murphy, we've asked you to answer our questions today regarding your wife's death. You are here of your own free will, and you may leave at any time. Do you understand that?'

'Yes.'

'We will be tape recording this interview today.' Morton gestured at the tape recorder on the table between them, then proceeded to open a brand new tape and insert it into the machine. 'From this point on everything said will be recorded. For the benefit of the tape, Mr Murphy has attended the station today on a voluntary basis.'

Edwin leant forward and picked up his coffee in his left hand, absently stirring in a sweetener with his right.

'You do not have to say anything but it may harm your defence if you do not mention, when questioned, something which you later rely on in Court. Anything you do say may be given in evidence.'

'Am I under arrest, officer?' Edwin frowned as if confused.

'No, Mr Murphy, not at the present time.' Morton said simply. It was clear the policeman would not give away information freely.

'Did your wife have any enemies?' Morton asked, watching Edwin closely.

'No, not that I know of. A few irked ex-clients, I suppose.'

'What sort of clients?'

'She's a lawyer. She dabbles, but it's mostly corporate work.'

'Do you have a copy of her client list?' Morton humoured Edwin. It was unlikely a simple company dispute would have led to her death.

'Her firm would. Is that all you need from me, officer?' Edwin began to rise.

'We have a few more questions yet, Mr Murphy.' Morton gestured for him to sit back down.

'What is your relationship with your wife?'

'We're married.' Edwin smirked inwardly. If he was going to have to discuss his marital problems, he wasn't going to make it easy.

'Was it a happy marriage?' Morton asked.

'For the most part. We'd recently had an argument. It happened from time to time.'

'What were you arguing about?'

'Work mostly. She felt I spent too much time in the office. Bit of a moot point now I suppose.' Edwin thought that a candid approach would garner the least suspicion.

'Why is that?'

'I'm working a lot less than I was before.' It was true, of a fashion.

'I see. We found the divorce papers among your wife's possessions,' Morton confronted him.

'I didn't kill her if that's what you think!' The denial slipped out before Edwin could work out if it would help or hinder his position.

'Would you be willing to submit to a DNA test to prove that?' There was no DNA evidence to compare it to, but Edwin didn't know that.

'Yes, of course. I can also provide an alibi.' It was too quick to offer an alibi, and Edwin knew it.

'We haven't told you when she died yet.' Morton's eyebrow arched suspiciously.

'Well, when did she die?'

'Friday.' Morton didn't give a time.

'I was on a plane over the Atlantic for most of the day. Ask anyone,' Edwin protested.

'We will. Interview terminated, 11.29 a.m.'

With that, Edwin was free to go. He grabbed his briefcase, which was now more of a fashion accessory than a genuine business accoutrement, and scurried out of the interview suite.

***

Peter K Sugden smiled. He had just made over a million pounds short selling in less than four hours. The financial papers had dubbed him a guru, able to foresee market movements with pinpoint precision. In reality, it was less to do with luck or skill than it was to do with networking. Over the years he had built a huge circle of acquaintances who would scratch his back in return for a favour. Some served on company boards as directors, others were at financial institutions such as banks and hedge funds. The commonality between them was that they all had their pulse on the heartbeat of the London Stock Exchange.

Some of it was perfectly legitimate. Brokers and fund managers often trade rumours. The price of a stock is based as much on perceived value as it is the intrinsic value of the company's assets.

That perception could be manipulated, to pump and dump certain shares, or to crash their value when short selling them. These were unethical, but the law rarely caught up with those involved. Instead it concentrated on those involved in insider trading. Having knowledge of a company that the public doesn't possess allows for a huge potential profit. Good news means buying up all the stock you can, and flogging it for a hideous profit. Bad news was even easier. Traders borrowed stock from institutions such as pension funds, paying them for the privilege. They then sold them, and rebought the same number and type of share within the loan period. If the stock fell, then the trader made a profit.

This was what Peter and his coterie did. By trading tips on the innermost workings of public companies he and his cronies were able to manipulate prices to their own advantage every day. The industry average growth was around 8%, and Peter promised investors 15%. He kept every penny above this, and it had made him rich.

The genius in the system was how they communicated. In the past the system would have been open to wiretaps, police surveillance and counterintelligence measures. Now, they simply used the darknet to communicate, a private network hidden deep in the Internet.

The set-up had been suggested by the son of one of the parties to the project, and it allowed them to exchange information without anyone else ever seeing it. It was private, anonymous and heavily encrypted. Codenamed the Aesop Network, it allowed the group to openly share confidential information for profit, and they did. It took a while for Peter to become proficient with the technology, but once he did, the sky was the limit.

***

Edwin's way out was confirmed. The previous message seemed serious. The guy was asking for two kills, his ex-girlfriend and her new boyfriend. A two for one deal was insane really, but Edwin had no intention of following through so it didn't hurt him to agree. Of course he needed the other guy to come through first.

'Multiples no problem, as long as you go first,' he typed.

As long as the guy agreed to that, Edwin was free and clear. The contact had no possible way to find out who he was, so it was highly unlikely the police would ever trace it back to him.

Detective Chief Inspector Morton struck Edwin as thorough, and his record was impeccable, but no one could link Edwin to a man whom he had never met, nor had any reason to meet. He'd also make sure he had a solid alibi for the night of the kill, one even Morton wouldn't question.

***

The plan had seemed clean even if it was amoral, but Edwin had not expected it to be so hard to break the news of Eleanor's death to Chelsea. He wondered how he could do it and more importantly how he could continue to lie to his little girl, every day, for the rest of his life.

It was too late now. What was done was done, he rationalised, but the guilt stayed with him. He tried to justify it as self-defence, that he was defending his relationship with his little girl, and that financially it was just self-preservation. Deep down he knew that he would never convince himself, but he could at least explain to Chelsea why Mummy wasn't around anymore.

Chelsea had never experienced bereavement before. Not real grief. There had been a great-aunt that had died, and Eleanor had made a big fuss over explaining that she was in a better place, but Chelsea had barely known her, so it wasn't much of a loss really.

***

'Right, thanks. The plane landed on time at four o'clock. OK, thanks. You've been very helpful.' Morton hung up the phone, then swore loudly. Edwin Murphy's alibi checked out.

But Morton couldn't shake the niggling doubt that screamed that Murphy was shifty. You can't fake being mid-Atlantic though. The stewardess even remembered the slimy git hitting on her.

Murphy's finances didn't turn up much either. The accounts were frozen pending probate as joint accounts, and there were no withdrawals out of the ordinary. It was the usual hodgepodge of car payments, mortgage interest and shopping. If he had hired a professional then either he had got one hell of a deal and paid with pocket change, or he had thousands stashed away from some unknown source that had never touched the family finances.

Morton didn't think either was likely, and he reluctantly scrubbed Edwin Murphy as a suspect.

If he didn't kill her, or pay someone else to, then he couldn't be prosecuted.

***

Edwin was feeling smug. He was in jail, but that was the best place for him that night. He had pondered on the best alibi money could buy, and thought about buying a whole bar a drink or something else that would get him remembered, but it was out of character and would look desperate.

He'd settled on letting the police provide him with the alibi. He went to a pub in Red Lion Street in Camden. He started off gentle, and then ramped up the booze after dinner. Edwin was obnoxious, but all the time he was buying doubles every five minutes, the landlady didn't mind.

Edwin challenged every man in sight to a drinking contest. Eventually one took him up on his offer. A row of Jameson's Irish whiskey shots was laid out along the bar, a road map to liver failure. The row was two thick, and each man started at opposing ends of the bar. The pretty landlady was roped in to judge, and on her word the men charged. Edwin pandered to the crowd, roaring his delight as the fiery alcohol slid down his throat.

The other man was much more businesslike, staying low to the bar and quickly knocking back each of his shots in quick succession. He finished first, but Edwin was having none of it.

'Ah don't fink so, pal. You were way slowa than I were,' Edwin slurred. He had become progressively more Irish with every tot.

'A bet's a bet, pal; £50 please, now.' The bigger man flexed his muscles, a tattoo stretching taut over his left bicep.

'Nar, dun tink so, buddy. Get lost.'

Seconds later fists were flying and the landlady was on the phone to the cops. Holborn Police Station was only a few hundred feet away and so within minutes both men found themselves in the drunk tank, its first occupants that evening.

Chapter 13: Too Far

Vanhi was more subtle with her alibi. She visited an old friend in the Scottish Highlands; far enough away that even flying wouldn't get her back in time to commit the crime. She made sure she took public transport. It would be impossible for a lone woman on foot to get back to London in time to commit a murder and not be seen. Fort Augustus was so far removed from the city not only geographically but in time too. Everything seemed to be done at a slower pace, and it was small enough that any stranger was the subject of much interest.

Vanhi took her friend out for dinner at a lovely restaurant on the pier. It was one of only three restaurants in Fort Augustus, and was by far the nicest. There were a few other parties there, but Vanhi's was the only one to stay for the entire evening enjoying themselves. By the time Vanhi collapsed into bed in the guest room at her friend's cottage she had all but forgotten that the trip was only a cover for an alibi.

Chapter 14: Unknown Territory

Barry had never killed someone before. He'd been in a few fights, but that was about it. He wondered how he should do it. He discounted poison straight away. He didn't have the know-how, and even if he did it just seemed too cowardly.

Barry knew his target lived in Brixton. It wasn't as rough as it had once been, but it was still pretty bad. Barry agreed to carry out the hit on the Sunday evening so the other guy could get an alibi in place. It hadn't taken long to find the target's house the previous week, and he'd sat watching the building for a while.

Quite a few people were coming and going. They were mostly in their late teens to early twenties, and although there were two flats in the maisonette he doubted they were all visiting the elderly lady on the ground floor.

It was probably drugs. The guys coming and going looked like addicts. Barry wondered if he was getting mixed up in something gang-related. The guy might just be dealing on someone else's patch. Barry wasn't the judge and jury though, he was just the hired gun. He was doing as he was told, not choosing his victim himself. He mentally passed the buck, and thought about which weapon to use. Guns were too loud, even with a silencer. The cops would come running in no time.

Barry settled on a knife. It was sharp, cheap and disposable. The one he was going to use had been a present when he'd moved into his current flat, and it hadn't yet made it out of the box.

Barry put a disposable glove on his right hand and used the newly gloved hand to put the knife inside his jacket. He'd put a wedge of paper inside to line the pocket so the knife wouldn't slip straight through.

When it came time to head out to do the deed, Barry felt self-conscious. It wasn't just the knife either, he felt conspicuous being one of the few white faces in Brixton, walking alone through the rough end of town. His bald spot shone under the streetlamps, practically a beacon for potential muggers.

He made it to the target's property without incident, and rapped smartly on the door with his knuckles. There was no doorbell.

Heavy feet could be heard stomping inside the house, growing progressively louder until the door swung open with a loud creak.

Barry didn't want any prying eyes seeing him carry out the hit, so he had to get inside.

'Hi, my mate said you might help a fella out?' Barry spoke quickly, trying to throw a hint of desperation into his tone, as if he needed a hit.

The man nodded, looked him up and down, before beckoning him in and bounding up the stairs just inside the door.

Barry followed him.

'What can I do ya for?' the man asked.

Barry could have rushed him straight away, but he was a coward and wanted to minimise the chance of the victim defending himself.

'An eighth of Moroccan black.' He didn't know what kind of drug he was asking for but he had heard it in a movie.

'Last of the big spenders, eh?' the big man chuckled and turned around to fish in a drawer. It was now or never, and Barry leapt forward, pulling the gloved hand from his pocket and thrusting the knife towards his victim. The knife cut into his back as if it was butter, sticking there. Barry yanked the knife from its resting place and rammed it back in, again and again in quick succession. On the last thrust he ploughed the blade into the back of the man's neck. Blood was everywhere, and it was clear the man would bleed out.

Barry removed his outer clothing, stripping down to his shorts and vest. He tucked his bloodstained clothes into his rucksack and left Emanuel to die.

***

The night before the funeral, Eleanor's parents arrived in London. Edwin had rashly offered them use of the guestroom, which they had gladly accepted. When they rang the doorbell, Edwin wondered how he would ever look them in the eye, but his guilt disappeared as he took a perverse pleasured in playing nice.

He was finally free. He had his little girl, and she wouldn't be dragged halfway round the world at the whim of her mother. He also owned the house now. It had been in joint names, and the right of survivorship applied. This meant that at the moment of Eleanor's death, he became the sole owner of 51 Belgrave Square. It would be his free and clear soon enough, as the life insurance policy would pay off the remainder of the mortgage.

Edwin wouldn't get the money Eleanor had in her own bank account. Her will meant that money would go into a trust for Chelsea. It was of little consequence to Edwin.

The funeral arrangements had been left to Edwin, as her parents felt it was a husband's duty. He had half considered getting his brother-in-law to assist, but figured it would be easier to do it without Mark turning it into another excuse to hit the booze.

Eleanor hadn't left funeral instructions. Of course she hadn't, she hadn't expected to die anytime soon. He chose an ornate oak casket, not a cheap one. He played every bit the part of the mourning husband. Flowers, bagpipes and the church at which they had got married were soon booked in a flurry of open wallets, the kind Edwin hadn't been able to indulge in for a while.

Before he knew it the funeral was upon them; Eleanor's extended family were soon sitting in contemplative silence in the back of a procession of black town cars.

The funeral had a large number of attendees. It seems murder brings all sorts of acquaintances out of the woodwork. School friends, teachers, even a hairdresser or two. They all turned out to pay their respects to the late Eleanor Murphy.

Edwin thought few remembered her accurately. The eulogies from Eleanor's parents and her best friends were heartwarming, but it was little Chelsea standing up to speak that had every eye in the room damp.

'My Daddy says Mummy has gone to a better place. I know she didn't want to go, because she loves me so much. I don't want her to go either, but I guess God thinks he waited long enough. I know Mummy will be watching over us, and I'll miss her every day, but Daddy says she's gone somewhere no one can hurt her anymore. I love you, Mummy.'

Edwin was the last to deliver his eulogy, and he was frank about the difficulties that there had been in their marriage, and closed with his regrets that he never got the chance to put things right.

***

Cause of death took no time at all to establish. Emanuel Richard bled out after being stabbed multiple times. That much could be established on-site.

The old lady downstairs had rung environmental health when she first smelt the decomposition, and they had in turn called in the police.

As the whole flat was a crime scene it was quickly sealed off, and an officer was posted at the door. Morton was forced to wear a plastic coverall before he could enter the scene. It covered Morton from head to toes, and prevented him contaminating the crime scene.

'No matter how many times I wear one of these I never get used to it,' he moaned half-heartedly.

The coroner grinned. 'It's like wearing a giant condom.'

Morton flipped a V at the doctor, and gestured at the body.

'What do you think, Doc? Our vic stiff someone on a drug deal?' Crime scene techs had found cocaine, methamphetamine and marijuana stashed inside the downstairs toilet. Robbery didn't appear to be the motive: the man still had his wallet. Morton read aloud from the man's driver's licence.

'Emanuel Richard. Sounds familiar.' Morton had heard the name before, but he couldn't quite place it. He made a mental note to ask narcotics when he got back to New Scotland Yard.

'Get trace from around the wound. It's not uncommon to get nicked when using a knife to stab someone. Any sign of the knife itself?'

'Nope, nothing. The killer must have taken it with him. Chances are he'd be covered in blood too – there's plenty on the floor, but the contact spray would have at least spattered the attacker as well. Local CCTV might be able to pick something up there.'

Chapter 15: Patsy

Anthony Duvall had been a university student when the bust went down, and he took the rap for another's crime.

He was new in Portsmouth, having transferred to the city's university for the final year of his BA in International Relations. His finances weren't in great shape, and the opportunity had seemed like a godsend. It had never crossed his mind that anything dodgy was involved. The man who hired him, Jake, was a doctoral candidate within the School of Social Historical and Literary Studies. He'd seemed like an upstanding guy, and when he said he needed a parcel picked up for a birthday present, nothing had struck Ant as being out of the ordinary. As Ant understood it, Jake was only a few days away from a submissions deadline before his viva voce, and he didn't have time to travel up to Liverpool to pick up the parcel.

Ant wasn't all that busy; his dissertation was mostly done, as he had spent the summer working on it, and it was worth a third of his final year's mark. It seemed odd that the final year only had eight hours a week timetabled, but Ant wasn't complaining.

He'd rearranged his Thursday and Friday seminars to earlier in the week, and Jake gave him first class train tickets up to Liverpool.

Ant's instructions were straightforward enough: meet Diane, the girl who had Jake's present, in the city centre a couple of minutes away from Liverpool Lime Street. Give her the money, get the parcel, bring it back.

As he had Friday off he'd chosen to book into a hotel and come back the next day. There was no point rushing back; he didn't know many people in Portsmouth so he wouldn't be missing out on a social life.

The handover had taken place in his hotel bar. A gorgeous leggy brunette had walked in and introduced herself as Diane.

'Hey, hun, you the guy Jake sent up?' It wasn't a Liverpudlian accent.

Ant nodded.

'You got my money, babe?' she whispered.

Anthony slid over the banker's draft that Jake had given him. He had said it was an antique for his mother's birthday, a rare piece of pottery for her collection. Sure enough the parcel he was given did appear to be pottery, but it didn't look like anything special to him. Then again, who was he to give an opinion on what was and wasn't tasteful? Pottery wasn't his thing.

Anthony didn't bother inspecting the goods. He had already been paid, and he wouldn't know what to look for even if he tried. He therefore missed the false bottom covered with a fresh layer of new clay.

Diane didn't stay long, and Ant was left to wander before returning to his room at the hotel. In the morning he wished he hadn't bothered. A bachelorette party had occurred in the main bar, and stayed on in the hotel late bar. It had been impossible to get a good night's sleep, and the half-cold cooked breakfast hadn't been worth the price of admission either.

At least the return journey gave him time to read through his seminar material for the following week, even if the swinging Pendolino trains did make him feel vaguely nauseous.

It was on his return home that the difficulty began. He tried to find Jake to deliver the goods, but he was nowhere to be found. He had skipped teaching his Global Political Economy class that afternoon, and the blinds were drawn on his Victorian home in Southsea when Ant tried to deliver the goods there.

Reluctantly Ant gave up and took the goods home, intending to bring them to the university on the following Monday. They never made it. At 5 a.m. the next morning the police burst through the front door, smashing it to splinters to get in. The pottery was seized, and Anthony frogmarched to the station. He was barely given time to throw on jeans and a t-shirt before he found himself up before a judge. He tried to protest his innocence, but the jury was having none of it. There was almost £100,000 pounds of heroin sealed inside the base of the pottery.

Anthony was sentenced to four years inside, and served nearly three before being granted parole. The young man sent down that fateful day was not the man who emerged three years later from HM Prison Dorchester. Gone was the youthful exuberance, replaced by a tattooed punk who had spent three hellish years enduring prison food, regular fights with other inmates and worse. The honest and helpful undergraduate soon became a world-weary convict aged beyond his years. He went in young and healthy, but came out psychologically scarred and HIV positive. His life would never be the same again.

***

Morton had to wait to get his CCTV footage. Lambeth Co-Operative Council had to be subpoenaed before they released the footage they had of the area, and Lambeth only had control of part of Brixton's CCTV coverage.

London is plastered with CCTV cameras but they're not linked to one big system, so for every camera, Morton had to ask someone new for the footage.

There was some suggestion from the Mayor's office that the CCTV would eventually be put onto a central system, which would save money and make Morton's job easier, but it hadn't happened yet.

Raeburn Street, the victim's road, wasn't covered by CCTV, but the roads it bisected did, so all those passing through were caught by the council's surveillance at one end or the other. It was a necessary evil in Brixton as crime was rife, especially among the gangs in the area.

Only a few dozen individuals were seen leaving the area after the estimated time of death. That gave a window of around six hours to look through, and that job fell to an unlucky uniformed officer. He found only one suspicious individual, and immediately paged Detective Chief Inspector Morton.

'Sir, we've got one individual who appears to change clothes between entering and exiting the road. He could be a resident but he wasn't among the neighbours we canvassed going door-to-door.'

Morton thought it over for a moment. The killer could be a resident, in which case he should show up on footage from the previous week.

'Run a scan for him on the previous couple of days. If he's a resident it's almost certain he would be coming and going regularly.'

'Already done, sir. Nothing flagged up. It isn't a great angle though, sir. He kept his head down as he passed the CCTV. Looks like he knew there were cameras about.'

'He's white. Not a huge number of white guys that wander alone in Brixton in the evening. Can we trace where he went after he left Raeburn Street?' Morton figured the suspect would slip up and show his face at some point.

'I've got him, sir. We can see him heading south to the A2217. He disappears off CCTV there, in a blind spot between Concanon Road and Trinity Gardens. Traffic might have something though, if anyone got flashed for speeding as he went past?'

'It's a long shot. Worth checking, though. Hang on, freeze on the Concanon/A2217 camera.'

It was angled down above a row of shops, but caught the corner on film neatly.

'Aha! The bag disappeared somewhere between Raebarn Court and the A road. We might just have found the dump spot for our murder weapon. Good work, lads.'

Chapter 16: Weak Links

Although her victim was now dead, Vanhi was still a weak link. If she got caught, Edwin knew she would turn on him in no time if it would save her from a life sentence in jail. While plea bargaining wasn't officially encouraged or sanctioned, it did happen in practice.

The prosecutor in charge would simply reduce the charge to manslaughter; Vanhi would turn Queen's Evidence.

If Edwin could eliminate Vanhi, he could massively reduce his exposure. Her death would end any investigation into Eleanor's death as well as removing the only darknet contact that had enough information to work out who he was.

He couldn't kill her himself, of course. That would be counterproductive. Instead he settled on a new course of action. He would demand two kills from the man who called himself Barry. He wanted his ex-girlfriend and her new lover dead. It was only fair. If Barry wanted two kills, then Edwin wanted two kills. He'd still never follow through, but Barry didn't know that.

'If you want two. I want two. Will advise on who second is if this is acceptable.'

He knew the other man would be fuming when he read it, but he could hardly complain to the police. Without Edwin's identity he couldn't exact his revenge personally either. Worst case scenario, Edwin was no worse off than he was before he sent the message.

***

The bag turned up, but not before the lab techs from Forensics had to climb into a rubbish bin. It seemed the suspect had been smart enough to head south past the A2217 towards the council flats before he dumped the bag in a huge communal bin. There were CCTV cameras on the apartment building, but they were all just for show. The council maintained that the perception of CCTV was just as effective as real CCTV but at five percent of the cost. Unsurprisingly Morton didn't agree.

'Paper-pushing morons. I'd like to see them catch a criminal.' The bin was ripe with food, a testament to the failure of the then-Labour government's biweekly bin collection program. It certainly wouldn't help the lab when it came to particulate analysis, and it could create reasonable defence in the hands of a vaguely competent criminal defence barrister.

The contents were untouched though, and the clothes inside were soaked in blood. It would almost certainly be just the victim's blood, but there was an off chance that the aggressor nicked himself with the blade and left a little piece of himself behind. Even a partial fingerprint would do; Morton just needed something to go on. He gestured at a constable. 'Get this bagged, tagged and back to the lab. Now.' He was in no mood for pleasantries.

***

The bag didn't reveal any major surprises. There were no fingerprints anywhere on or inside the bag, which suggested the killer may have worn gloves. The only blood to be found was the victim's, and the clothes were distinctly disposable. They were the generic mass-produced clothes that can be bought in any supermarket.

There was one ray of hope, a small hair trapped underneath the strap on the backpack. It didn't have a follicular tag attached, so DNA was a no-go on this occasion. The hair could be compared manually though, should a sample from a suspect be obtained. It also suggested that the killer had light brown hair. This was compiled with other data from the CCTV to produce an e-fit image of what the man could look like. It was guesswork at best, as there were no direct profiles of his face on CCTV, but by combining the angles it was possible for an educated guess to be made.

He was Caucasian so the ratios on distance between the eyes, the size and breadth of the nose, as well as the jaw line shape, could be predicted with some accuracy. His height and build were visually discernible, and combined with the knowledge of his real hair colour a profile was beginning to take shape.

The e-fit would be flashed around the area, and hopefully someone would have seen him.

***

'Not happy. You should have asked upfront.'

Despite his protests Barry knew that two for two was a fair deal. It wasn't too fair to find it out halfway through the deal, but he had little choice. He wouldn't get what he wanted from the deal if he didn't hold up his end and carry out two hits. The first had been much easier than he thought it would be. He was already in it up to his neck. Two life sentences is still life. Barry had nothing to lose, but a hell of a lot to gain.

He soon capitulated.

***

Once Edwin had convinced Barry to do a second hit, he had to work out who the target was. He had nothing from her except a brief message telling him not to carry out the kill they'd asked for in the vicinity of the Caledonian Road.

Edwin also had the photo of Emanuel, the victim. He clicked on his downloads folder, and brought up the image which showed a photograph being held by hands with painted fingernails. *A woman! And in the background – what does that neon sign say?*

Edwin brought up an image enhancement program, and clicked 'interpolate', which caused the computer to try and guess at the detail by adding new pixels between the blurry image regions based on the colour change. It wasn't a great picture, but it did reveal two things. The neon sign was for a fish and chip shop across the street. The sign read *"'Oh My Cod!'"*

Edwin laughed, then brought up Google. Oh My Cod! was halfway along the Caledonian Road. Edwin clicked to bring up a street-view map of the road, and looked at the apartment opposite.

The flat from the webcam picture had to be one floor up, based on the angle of the sign. There were only two flats in that building that were on the first floor, and faced the road. That narrowed it down a bit.

Another trip to the world's most famous search engine brought up Electoral Roll records for the two flats. Only one had a woman living there, Vanhi Deepak, age twenty-seven. Edwin smirked again. It was almost too easy.

He typed out a message to Barry with the details, and then added *'Change your modus operandi. Don't use the knife again. Get it done.'*

Chapter 17: Data Trail

If he couldn't use a knife again, then a gun was Barry's second choice. But getting a gun in the UK isn't easy. He could legally apply for, and probably get, a Firearm Certificate. They weren't too hard to come by, but the police would want to fingerprint him as well as inspect his gun cabinet to make sure it was up to par. He'd also have to wait a while, and even then if he used it the police would trace it straight back to him.

That left him two options as he saw it, if he wanted to shoot Vanhi. Number one was to buy a lawful gun such as an air rifle and then modify it to fire lethal pellets. It wasn't a bad plan, but it would still leave a wide paper trial for the police to follow.

Behind door number two was the idea of acquiring an illegal gun. Barry thought this was essentially two sub-options, namely getting an otherwise legal gun illegally or getting a completely illegal gun.

The former could be as simple as buying a licensed firearm from someone else, or stealing it. Farmers, ex-military personnel and the police are allowed some weapons. The problem was they would almost certainly ask questions, as well as remember whom they sold the gun to.

The latter option meant finding someone willing to sell a gun, no questions asked, and to conveniently forget where it went should they ever be found. Barry decided this approach was much safer, and started his search by simply asking for one on the same darknet he had made his murder swap deal on.

***

Morton was at a loss on the Brixton stabbing. The victim lived alone, and had no friends or family. He was on narcotics' radar, but his dealing was low-level. He was one of thousands of petty criminals in London, and didn't have anything in his record to suggest anyone would want to kill him. He'd lived in Brixton for five years. Morton knew that much from council records, as the man claimed single person reduction for his council tax. Before that, there was nothing at all to suggest who he was.

It wasn't even the only unsolved murder on Morton's desk. He had overseen dozens of investigations during his career, and this was one of only three times he'd been truly stumped. It was almost as if members of the public were randomly killing each other in elaborate ways without leaving any evidence, and without there being any apparent motive.

The other detectives were starting to talk. Morton knew they couldn't do any better given the evidence on the table, but it didn't quell the rumours he was getting old and would soon be heading for retirement. If he didn't crack at least one of these cases soon then it might be the final bell tolling on his career. It would be an unglamorous way to go out, but he'd have his pension intact, and he'd be secure in the knowledge he did his best for several decades of service. That wouldn't make it any easier to look his colleagues in the eye at the retirement party however, and Morton would sooner forgo his pension than his reputation.

***

It hadn't taken long to get a nibble on the darknet. Barry's instinct had been right. The darknet was a world where anything goes. His seller wasn't strictly in London, but they met in Guilford. The weapon was concealed inside a guitar case, and cost Barry five hundred pounds in cash. Barry had to empty the slush fund under his bed, but that money bought him a double-barrelled sawn-off shotgun. It was old, and could do with a spot of polish, but Barry was sure it would work. It was bound to be loud, but there was no escaping that.

Barry also bought one box of ammo – twenty-four shells – with the gun, for an extra twenty pounds. He probably wouldn't need a whole box, but it wouldn't hurt. He'd ditch both the gun and the ammo in the Thames after the hit. It was twelve-bore ammo, the most common kind, so it wouldn't attract too much attention should it be found, and the ammo wasn't illegal anyway, just the gun.

Barry's second task was to home in on his victim. He knew she lived across from a chip shop, and he found her place easily enough. He loitered in a nearby coffee shop, and tried to keep an eye on her comings and goings, to work out when and where the hit would go down.

***

Morton was beginning to make progress investigating the Brixton stabbing. The victim, Emanuel Richard, was in the system, having been arrested a number of times for rape and sexual assault. None of the charges had stuck, but if the accusations were true, it could explain motive.

The conviction rate in rape cases was notoriously low, often hinging on a he said, she said case with the defendant claiming that the sex was consensual.

Sometimes witnesses were reluctant to testify for fear of being victimised again on the stand. That was often more than enough to give rise to reasonable doubt, and so Mr Richard walked free each time.

Morton wondered if his death was the result of vigilante justice. It could give him a lead, but could just as easily be a red herring. There were a huge number of victims that might want to see him dead, and Morton suspected that more might exist that never found the strength of conviction to come forward.

The slight hole in the theory was the statistic that over eighty-five percent of violent stabbings were committed by men, and as far as Morton knew, Emanuel Richard did not swing that way. It was possible of course, but considering the number of victims it was unlikely.

'Men often hide it out of shame. They don't want to be seen as the victim of rape.' Morton's colleague, Linda had read his mind. She was often the voice of reason in the squad room despite her relative youth. She was, at forty, an experienced detective but Morton considered her a relative newcomer nonetheless. He was demanding that way.

'I agree, but it's more likely that a brother or father of a victim would carry out a vigilante hit. We've got an e-fit, so let's see if it matches up with anyone connected to the known victims.'

The south end of the Caledonian Road was attracted a reasonable amount of foot traffic. Barry couldn't simply loiter, or he would be noticed. There wasn't a convenient cafe to sit in and watch the property, so Barry was forced to improvise. Across the street, above and to the right of the chip shop, was the Regal Fitness Centre and Gym. On the fourth floor a number of treadmills gave a clean view across the street towards his target's apartment building. The front door was off to the side, with an alleyway leading towards the bins at the rear of the property, and Caledonian Road at the front. Barry decided to take out membership at the gym and use it as an opportunity to spy on the property and its occupant.

When he entered the gym he realised that there was a remote chance that a paper trail could come back to bite him. Barry bought a gift certificate for one month's membership, waited until the girl who sold him it went off shift, and redeemed it himself under an alias. That way he neatly avoided needing to sign up to a minimum twelve-month contract, and without his real name it would be difficult to track him via the gym.

***

The relatives hadn't turned up anything. No one admitted to knowing the suspect from the e-fit, and none of the relatives the uniforms saw when interviewing the rape victims met the description. It could be the work of a phenomenal poker face in play, but it seemed that the vigilante angle was a dead end.

A broad canvass of the streets had turned up a witness, but he might be unreliable. When the canvassing officer, Bertram Ayala, met him, the witness reeked of marijuana.

Normally Ayala would have him straight in for possession, but if he could be a lead in the stabbing case then the greater good demanded that Ayala stay his handcuffs – this time.

Ayala paged Morton, who drove straight down to Brixton to interview the potential witness in person. He had with him six e-fits, of which only one was the e-fit of the killer. Morton needed to know whether or not the witness was reliable. He might be called upon to testify, and as a traditional line-up was not possible without the suspect in custody, Morton chose to proceed with an e-fit line-up.

He needn't have worried. The young man identified the correct e-fit at once.

'That's him, blud. Skinny li'l white dude. Big blue eyes. He legged it, like he was in a hurry.'

'Which way did he go?'

'He stopped at the bus stop, didn't he? Heading north towards Liverpool Street.'

All London buses had CCTV installed, so if this was true the man could be tracked further, which might help to ID him.

'You remember anything else?'

'Naw. You gonna spare me an Adam Smith?'

It was a reference to the twenty note printed with the likeness of the famous Scottish economist. Morton was impressed the young man knew who he was. He decided that it was a small price to pay to catch a killer.

'Here. I'll throw in a tip for free. Ditch the weed.'

Chapter 18: **Déjà** Death

The second kill wasn't as easy as the first, and Barry was becoming desperate. The target didn't have any discernible pattern to her movements, and each time he tried to follow her by leaving the gym he had to get his bag from the locker before he could pursue her. By then she was long gone. Clearly the gym-based surveillance wasn't the smartest idea Barry had ever had.

He debated simply knocking on the door and shooting her, but the sound would resonate in the alleyway, and it would be impossible to get away unseen. It was also far too similar to his first hit, and that would get him caught.

He eventually decided to follow her, no gun, and make small talk in the laundrette she used down the street. He needed to get her somewhere quiet before he could take her out, so his aim was to set up a meeting at another time when it would be easier to conceal the gun.

The target seemed pleasant enough, and Barry wondered again what she had done to deserve death. She was shy and retiring, and was slow to come out of her shell. Barry needed an opening to get her talking, and then he could find out where she went when she left the house.

Eventually, he feigned a lack of soap and asked to borrow a cup. She nodded, and gestured at the powder sitting on top of the machine that would be hers for the next hour.

It wasn't much of an opener, and Barry resorted to asking her about the film magazine she was reading half an hour later.

'I don't know why everyone likes that movie,' he ventured when he saw a slight frown on her face while reading.

'I know! It's so predictable. The killer is obvious in the first five minutes.'

'The book was way better anyway. I hate being told what characters look like after I've built them up in my imagination.'

'Me too.' She became animated, and Barry knew he was in.

'I'm Larry,' Barry said, extending his hand. Lying under pressure was not one of his strong points.

'Vanhi.'

'I just moved into the area. Care to show me around?' Barry winked in what he hoped was a salacious manner.

'Err. Sorry, I'm busy.' Vanhi turned away, picking the magazine back up to shield herself from the awkwardness of the conversation.

Strikeout. Barry had overdone it, and he would have to try again another time.

***

Barry tried the laundrette again the following week. Same time of day, same day of the week, and there she was sitting doing her laundry like clockwork.

He needed to play it cool. She hadn't responded to his sexual advances, and he knew he'd need to try a more platonic approach to get her to open up.

'Remembered my soap powder this time.' Barry indicated his box as he took a seat nearby and flicked open a magazine.

When she didn't respond Barry decided to give her a few moments. If he pushed too hard, she would clam up and he'd never get anything out of her.

'You got change for a five? Seems the machine doesn't like my pound coin.' It was plausible. He had seen a television show on Channel Four once that said almost a quarter of all pound coins in London were counterfeit.

'Sure. Here you go.' There was the hint of a smile as she passed him the coins. He hoped it was amusement at his misfortune – he could work with that.

He feigned trying another coin.

'Damn it! This one doesn't work either.'

Vanhi began to giggle. The poor man was having no luck that evening.

'Not your night, is it?'

'Naw, nothing's gone right for me since I moved to London.'

'Where you from then?'

'Kent.'

'Nice part of the country.'

'Yeah, and much easier to find my way around. With mostly fields around, the houses stick out more,' Barry joked.

'Well, if you're still having trouble finding your feet, I can show you the sights, such as they are.'

'Really? That would be awesome, though knowing my luck, I'd probably get mugged.' Barry decided to play up the hapless loser; that persona would lower her defences and get her talking.

'Ha-ha, I promise not to mug you. You ever been to the One Eyed Dog?'

'Nope. Pub?'

'Yup. I work there.'

With that, Barry knew where she would die. He would get to know her shift pattern, and shoot her at closing. The only witnesses would be too drunk to remember a thing.

***

Morton's witness was right. The suspect who ditched the bag did board the 133 bus. CCTV showed that he boarded the bus at the Brixton Road stop, then rode all the way to Liverpool Street Station before heading for the underground. From there, he took a train north. Morton had ordered Ayala to follow the suspect on the CCTV footage at subsequent stations. Once Ayala had the suspect's home location down, Morton would take the e-fit out and show it around. Hopefully it would get a hit.

***

Vanhi worked most nights, but only Tuesday was really quiet enough for Barry to take his shot. He would be seen, that much was guaranteed. Barry had slowly become a regular late-night drinker in the area, and he would keep up that pretence after the kill to avoid arousing suspicion.

The gun was secured inside his overcoat. It was the thick padded kind, as only that could conceal the lumps and bumps of the shotgun. At least the weather was cold, so it didn't look out of place. The cold was also a great excuse for wearing gloves. It made the gun cumbersome, and Barry would have to ditch them after pulling the trigger as they would be covered in gunshot residue, a dead giveaway if the police pulled him for being in the area; but it avoided Barry's risking exposure by fingerprint.

At closing time on Tuesday night, two 'clock in the morning, Barry leant against the wall in the alley adjacent to the pub.

He held a lit cigarette in one hand and a bottle of cola in the other. He didn't normally smoke, but it was good camouflage. He avoided talking to other customers by pretending to be outrageously drunk.

The truth was that no alcohol had passed his lips that evening. Each of the shots he had bought was carefully tipped down his shirt to make him smell of alcohol. He'd even gargled a double vodka so that his breath matched the rest of his persona.

The Coca-Cola was multi-purpose. Barry did enjoy drinking it, but it was primarily a plastic silencer to reduce the number of people who would hear the shot. It wouldn't do much – Barry planned to fire a shotgun in an enclosed alleyway – but, with a bit of luck, any witnesses would mistake the sound for a car backfiring.

At around ten past two Vanhi emerged, and saw Barry. She smiled, and asked to borrow a cigarette. Vanhi smoked prolifically, and Barry knew this from his weeks watching her. She lit up and leant against the fence.

She was about to engage him in conversation when her phone rang. She turned away from Barry to answer it. No one had actually called her. It was Barry hitting redial on the phone in his pocket.

As she lifted the handset to her ear, Barry lifted his shotgun, spread his legs in anticipation of the recoil, then slipped the empty Coke bottle over the barrel and ended the call. She began to turn as Barry raised the gun but didn't have time to react. With one fluid motion, Barry flicked the gun to a horizontal position and unloaded one shot into the side of Vanhi's head. The sound felt deafening to Barry, and he nearly legged it down the street to get away.

There was no time to conceal the weapon and dump it in the Thames as he had originally planned. Adrenaline flooded through him, and he ripped the gloves off, tossing them, the gun and the bottle against the fence. He nudged Vanhi's body on top of the gun to cover it up, and threw the bin bags over her body loosely, before striding off into the night. It was done.

Chapter 19: Worry

Vanhi hadn't come home, and Jaison was worried. He'd been her boyfriend for four years, and they'd lived together for two. Not once had she ever been late home from work. He wanted to call the police, but something was stopping him.

Jaison was an illegal. He'd arrived in the UK properly, but that had been on a student visa and Jaison had now outstayed his welcome by over two years. His heart was torn in two. On the one hand he was sure something had happened to Vanhi. On the other hand he would almost certainly find himself on the first plane back to India if he went to the authorities.

Jaison knew that they would never disregard the overstay. Many of his friends had been caught, and every time they had been deported. Unless he married a British citizen he would never gain leave to remain in the United Kingdom.

Jaison dithered, phone in hand as he tried to decide what to do. If he got deported he'd never see her again, and he had no one to go back to in Mumbai, but if something happened to her because he didn't call he'd never forgive himself.

He decided to wait twenty-four hours, and then make his decision.

***

'Damn it, those bloody kids have done it again,' Lucas Johnson, landlord at the One Eyed Dog, spoke aloud to no one in particular. He was alone in the alleyway, save for his trusty German shepherd, Scruffy. The kids loved to play games with Lucas. They knew he couldn't see, and found it highly amusing when he tripped over his own rubbish bags. Sometimes they emptied the bags, or moved the recycling bins around the corner.

Once they had even broken into his wife's car only to put it in neutral and leave it one block north. They hadn't even hotwired it, so it must have taken quite a while to manually push that far.

This time, it was the bins again. Rubbish bags had been flung all over, a row of them scattered up against the fence dividing the One Eyed Dog from the flat block next door.

Out of the blue, Scruffy began to bark.

'What is it, boy?' Lucas moved closer to the mutt, nudging the bag with his toe. He leant down to feel what the dog was barking at, then realised that he was touching flesh.

Lucas almost screamed. It was human, and it wasn't moving. He quickly grabbed the dog's collar and dragged him inside. 'Vera!' he shouted, calling for his wife. 'Call the police.'

Fifteen minutes later, Detective Chief Inspector David Morton stepped out of his car. He was in a suit, as he had been set to appear on television that morning to publicise the Metropolitan Police's ten most wanted list.

His polished shoes gleamed, reflecting the early morning sunshine as he strode towards the body. A uniform had already taped off the scene. He slipped plastic covers over his designer shoes, and ducked under the tape.

She was a young woman, in her late twenties or early thirties, and of Asian descent. Rigor had set in but had not begun to wear off, putting time of death at six to eight hours ago.

As Morton inspected the scene, the coroner rolled over the body to inspect the exit wound.

'Well, I was going to suggest shotgun as possible cause of death, but this confirms it.' The coroner gestured at a sawn-off shotgun tucked underneath the body, nestled among the rubbish.

'Well, that's not legal.' Morton's sense of humour often missed the mark.

Morton donned a glove, and picked up the weapon gingerly. There were no visible prints, and the serial number had been ground down. An acid wash might bring out the original etching.

As Morton inspected the body, crime scene techs began taking samples for particulate analysis, as well as dusting for fingerprints.

A camera flashed as the in situ photographs of the scene were taken. The Met still used film SLRs to capture crime scenes, as digital photographs were more open to digital manipulation.

Morton was unconcerned with the physical evidence for the moment. His job was not to collect or process that evidence, but to analyse it later on. He went inside the One Eyed Dog to find the landlord.

'You told my officer that you know the deceased.' It was a statement, not a question. Morton was old school in his interviewing technique, and liked to establish that he was in control of the conversation early on.

'Yes. The lassie had been working for me. Good barmaid, popular with the punters. Name of Vanhi Deepak.' Lucas spoke with a trace of a Scottish accent. His voice was slow and even. Morton imagined he was a tremendous barman; his mannerisms gave rise to trust and confidence.

'How long had she been working here?'

'A few years. I don't recall the exact date. I can check if you want.' Lucas was sipping a warm cup of sweet tea, no doubt prepared by his doting wife to help him deal with the shock.

'Did she have any problems with punters last night?'

'Nae, it was mostly a quiet night. Not a fight all evening.' Caledonian Road was known for being home to many disorderly establishments. The One Eyed Dog was surprisingly genteel for the area.

'You got an address?' Morton hoped her home might give clues as to who would want her dead, unless it was a random killing – which wasn't unheard of, not in Caledonian Road.

***

Morton decided to carry out the search of Vanhi Deepak's flat himself. He could have sent Ayala to conduct the search, but years of experience meant he spotted things that more junior officers missed. It wasn't a big flat, but waitressing had never paid well and central London was excessively expensive.

He didn't know if the flat was shared, so he knocked before using the key he had obtained from her landlady. A young Indian man answered wearing old-fashioned flannel pyjamas. He looked tired, as if he hadn't slept well. Morton wondered if the rings under his eyes were the product of a guilty conscience.

'Detective Chief Inspector David Morton, Metropolitan Police. May I come in?'

Without waiting for an answer David moved towards the door, forcing the young man to retreat through the nearest doorway to the safety of the sitting room.

'I'm here regarding Ms Vanhi Deepak,' Morton announced once they were both sitting down.

The younger man simply looked at him without saying anything, and Morton took the opportunity to visually sweep the room. On the mantelpiece were a number of photographs of the victim. Several of them featured her with the young man sitting opposite him; they were clearly a couple.

'What's your name?' Morton asked.

'Jaison.'

'Do you live here?'

'Yes.'

With that formality out of the way, Morton handed him a copy of the search warrant authorising him to look around the apartment of the deceased.

He watched Jaison read it. His eyes appeared to gloss over as he read. It appeared his English was not up to dealing with legal jargon.

'How long have you been in England, Jaison?' He watched the younger man closely as he asked. Facial expressions often gave away far more than the verbal answer.

'Not long.' Jaison tried to be vague and obscure the truth, but no police officer was going to buy it.

'I'm not from immigration, Jaison.'

'Four years. I've lived here with Vanhi for two.' The shy witness was beginning to relax. He may have had something to hide, but it was his immigration status rather than having killed someone.

'You're a couple.'

'Yes. I love her.'

'I'm sorry to inform you that Miss Deepak's body was found this morning outside the One Eyed Dog.' Informing the families of the dead was every policeman's worst duty, one any of them would avoid if they could so choose. Morton had been duty-bound to break the news to families dozens of times over the years, and it never got any easier.

As most relatives did, Jaison broke down immediately. Tears began to stream from his hazel eyes, his head sank, and he would not meet Morton's gaze. Now was not the time for mourning however.

'We didn't find a purse or a key on her. Was she in the habit of carrying one?' The absence of any valuables on her person could indicate robbery was a motive.

'No, sir, she didn't need it at work, and when she come home, I always let her in.' His English began to break down under stress, becoming fractured and disjointed.

'Who would want to kill her?' Morton preferred to be direct. Beating around the bush simply wasn't his style.

'Nobody, sir.' It soon became clear that Jaison knew nothing of value. Morton could have tipped off immigration – the man was in the UK illegally – but his conscience would not allow him to be party to the deportation of a man who had just lost the love of his life.

Instead he ventured into the cramped living areas of the apartment to execute the search warrant. It yielded little, but he took her mobile and her laptop for the IT department to investigate. Data storage devices often proved valuable data mines in criminal investigations – Morton hoped that this occasion would be one of those times.

***

There had been no DNA at the One Eyed Dog other than that of the victim. The crime scene techs had been hopeful that the gloves found in the bin might yield epithelial cells. The skin was a rich source of DNA, and would have made it easy to put the gun in the hand of its owner.

There were a number of fingerprints at the scene, which was no surprise for a public thoroughfare that was used by the residents of an adjoining flat block.

A few fingerprints were found on the fencing, as if people had taken to leaning on the wall in the alleyway. The landlord had explained that since the smoking ban indoors had taken effect, the smokers had taken to loitering in the alleyway to get their nicotine hit.

The sheer number of prints would make heavy work of processing the scene. In all, over two hundred prints were lifted, but not all of those would be unique.

It took a while to process fingerprints. The lifting had to be done carefully, and then every fingerprint had to be individually scanned into the system. Once that was done it was all down to the computer. The first stage of processing the computer would undertake would be to compare the fingerprints to each other to determine how many unique individuals were at the scene. One finger from each of these people would then be compared with the Police Fingerprint Database.

The database was extensive, as every suspect, whether or not they were then charged, was printed and their data added into the system. With many crimes being repeat offences the database proved immensely valuable.

It wasn't exhaustive, however, as there was no general requirement for the public to be fingerprinted. This gap meant that first-time offenders, as well as those coming from outside the UK, would not be on the system, and the prints would be flagged as unknown.

There were thirty-two unique individuals, and virtually all of them were unknown. Of the few individuals who were on the system, none had a record for violence so there was no prime suspect.

Chapter 20: Hope

'Dear Mr. Murphy, I am delighted to inform you that we wish to offer you the position of editor-in-chief.'

Edwin blinked, and reread that line again to make sure he hadn't imagined it. The letter arrived that morning by snail mail, postmarked two weeks earlier. He had been offered the Vancouver job. It had seemed an ideal move when he was a single man escaping a loveless marriage and a lonely London existence. Now that he was a homeowner again, with full custody of his little girl, the rose-tinted view had begun to wear off.

Edwin didn't know anyone in Canada. It was a lovely place to visit, but visiting a place and living there were two entirely different propositions. He would talk it over with Chelsea of course, even if she didn't really understand. He'd probably have to discuss it with Eleanor's parents too, though how they could object when Eleanor had been planning to take Chelsea to New York for work herself Edwin didn't know.

At least Edwin didn't have to rush his reply. The Canadians had given him a thirty-day grace period to make his decision, and he wouldn't inform them until it was necessary to do so. He had other irons in the fire, and if they didn't come off he might just take the role to avoid a protracted period of unemployment.

***

There were fingerprints all over the big bags in the alley. Not only did the One Eyed Dog use the alley, but local residents did too, so the fingerprints could belong to virtually any of them.

Morton zoned in on a pair of gloves found near the shotgun. After flipping them inside out, the forensics team had been able to find several smudged partial prints inside, but there were no epithelial cells so DNA was out.

Gunshot residue was present on the outside of the gloves, but it had been commingled with rubbish so it was impossible to exclude the possibility that it was transfer.

The partial fingerprints from the glove were a match to a record , but the file wasn't readily available. It was marked as having been sealed by judicial order, which probably meant that the fingerprint belonged to a juvenile defendant. Juvenile prints were routinely expunged from the database, but sometimes the file managed to evade the recycle bin. Morton was, for once, thankful for the IT department's hideous inefficiency.

It took Morton's pet prosecutor, Kiaran O'Connor, considerable effort to persuade a family law judge to unseal the file. If defence counsel had been present, the judge probably would have sided with them, but it was an unopposed application with only the prosecutor and the judge in the courtroom at the time. In the end, it was the connection to an open murder investigation that swung it, and Morton was soon sat at his desk with a Starbucks coffee, reading about the owner of the print.

The print belonged to a Barry Fitzgerald. He was resident in London, but council records confirmed he was not local to the Caledonian Road area. It was therefore unlikely that the presence of his fingerprints on the bag had been put there innocently. Still, without further corroboration it was highly speculative, and David Morton wanted to approach him with kid gloves on. If he was the killer he was obviously armed, and therefore dangerous.

Chapter 21: Suffering

'Hello, handsome. You got a parking permit yet?' Jeanine joked as Yosef walked through the front doors of the hospital. She was Zachariah's nursing assistant, and Yosef had been on first-name terms with her since Zach's first visit.

Yosef shook his head sadly, but did manage a weak smile.

'Routine visit?' Zachariah had regular visits to the hospital, designed to monitor his deterioration. They say that at rock bottom, the only way is up. But Yosef seemed to be bouncing along the bottom.

'No. Not today.'

Zachariah was doing well, compared to most Tay-Sachs sufferers.

He couldn't crawl, sit or turn over unassisted. He was registered blind, had a severe hearing impairment, and was slipping into permanent paralysis. His mental development was slow, but he was alive and in relatively little pain.

Like all victims of infantile Tay-Sachs, Zach suffered from infections often. This one wasn't serious – the antibiotics were working. But that might not be true the next time, or the time after that.

It was that realisation, that Zachariah would be taken from her, that drove Yosef's wife, Zachariah's mother, to take her life shortly before the baby's first birthday.

In her suicide note she decried the helplessness and desperation that had meant that the whole family was victimised by the disease. Yosef's father often said that the measure of a man isn't his success in life, but in how he picks himself up after failure. In that regard Yosef proved himself a worthy son. He had endured so many knock-backs, and never once given up on Zachariah.

When his wife had fallen to pieces as Zachariah's condition worsened, he had continued to provide financially, as well as nursing the boy all hours of the day and night.

Soon it would become his duty to go one step further in relation to the boy. He would not allow him to suffer for years before an infection finally got to him. Yosef would sooner send him to join his forefathers in heaven. This much faith he still had. No god could fail to provide in death for a boy who had suffered so much in life.

***

'Barry Fitzgerald! It's the police. Open up,' Morton called out loudly, then paused to listen for any movement within. In his experience the guilty often fell straight into fight or flight mode. Adrenaline started to pump through their system, and they often ran out of the rear door, or tried to escape through a window or fire escape.

Deputies had been posted outside to watch for any activity, each with a fuzzy e-fit.

Inside, Barry was quietly grabbing a knife from the kitchen. He knew the police would barge in at any moment, and he would only get one chance to get past them. He had stuffed all his spare money into his trouser leg pocket, and was pulling a second layer of clothing on as he heard the crunch that indicated they were breaking the door in.

On the third crunch the door swung inwards, coming off its hinges and hitting the floor with a fierce thud. Barry was crouched underneath the breakfast bar in the kitchenette, and watched the policeman enter in the reflective microwave door above him. When the man turned to go into the bedroom Barry threw the knife towards him and ran out of the door. He heard the man yell, and knew he had hit his target.

The policeman would be radioing for backup at any moment, and Barry had to make good his escape. He knew the police would be on both the front and the back door of the flat block, so he went up one flight before knocking on the door of another flat. As soon as the occupant opened the door he punched her in the jaw, making her fly backwards and land, unconscious, with a thud.

His victim was eighty-two, and hard of hearing. Her television was on maximum volume, and that masked the sound to the adjacent flats. Barry shut the door behind him quietly, and then made himself at home. He knew the police would search the surrounding streets first; it was the logical thing to do. He didn't know where he would go next, but they'd be watching his flat now.

Stripping off the extra layer of clothes he had donned to disguise his appearance should the policeman ID him, he flicked the television over to "Countdown" and mentally played along with the numbers game.

***

Blood was slowly dripping out of Morton's leg where he had been stabbed. He had been smart enough to leave the knife in his leg where it had struck him, but he knew his body was going into shock. That was as dangerous as the blood loss, if not more so.

Out of instinct, Morton had radioed for help immediately, but knew that the men posted on the doors would stay there to prevent the suspect from escaping rather than assist him. He had trained them himself, and it was what he would do.

Morton's man at the front door radioed back. A medical team was en route, estimated time of arrival, ten minutes.

By the time they had arrived, Morton had passed out. He awoke four hours later in the Royal London, with twenty-six stitches in his upper leg. The wound had required a blood transfusion, and he was still woozy when he came to. The first question on his lips was not how bad his injuries were, but 'Did we get him?'

'No, sir, I'm afraid he escaped.'

Morton let the darkness envelope him once again, and hoped that the response had been a figment of his imagination.

***

Barry didn't leave the old woman's flat for several hours. He gagged and bound the original occupant, and left her in the bathroom to prevent her calling the cops anytime soon. He wouldn't leave her there for too long; his plan was to tip off the police anonymously when he was as far away as he could be.

The flat had yielded a few useful items. Breakfast bars were now stuffed inside an overcoat that fitted Barry neatly. Several hundred pounds in cash was also a massive boon, and an unexpected one at that.

The old lady had also been mercifully vain. In her bathroom was a full stock of hair dye. Barry's efforts wouldn't win any design awards, but the peroxide drained the brown pigment from his hair in virtually no time at all. Judicious use of scissors cropped his locks to alter his face shape, and a slow swagger altered his gait.

The flat wasn't large, and with the real owner tied up in the bathroom Barry was left to meander around the lounge and bedroom. Fortunately the lounge had a large window with a clear view of the rear entrance to the building. The police were still out there, and didn't show any signs of moving.

It was six hours before Barry decided to leave. He decided against the rear exit, as leaving via the back door was too obvious. With his changed appearance in place, he decided that his best option was to hide in plain sight. With that in mind he walked straight out of the front door. Sure enough, a number of police were in the area, but they appeared to be the beat cops that periodically strolled around the neighbourhood rather than the Met police who Barry knew would be looking for him.

He wasn't sure where to go. Friends and family were out; he'd be found in no time.

He could flee London entirely, but eventually his face would appear on "Crimewatch", and someone would ID him. If he did leave then he would have to either take his car or risk public transport.

The former option was clearly a poor choice. There was no doubt that the police would have put out an alert on his number plates, and a stolen car would be even easier to find. Besides, Barry didn't know how to hotwire a modern car. It wasn't quite as simple as it had been when he had boosted cars in his youth. His conviction for teen joyriding was long past, and that skill set had atrophied over the years.

Public transport would allow him to hide in a crowd. Adverts on the tube proclaimed boldly that over a million people entered London by public transport every single day. With that large a crowd, it would certainly be possible to disappear.

If he was going to go on the run for good he'd need new papers. Lord Lucan might have managed to disappear for good back in 'Seventy-four, but that was before the advent of DNA. If he was picked up for any reason whatsoever it would be child's play for the police to link the crimes back to him. Leaving the country was always an option, but many countries now had extradition treaties with the UK to haul criminals back home to face justice. If he stayed within Europe then Interpol could come after him with a European Arrest Warrant. To leave he'd need a false passport to travel on, not to mention the language skills to help him survive wherever he wound up.

It simply wasn't practical to run like that, so Barry decided to stay relatively local. He knew London well. He would adopt an accent of some kind, perhaps Welsh like his mother's, and he'd keep changing his appearance to muddy the waters.

The biggest problem for Barry, at least initially, was to find somewhere to stay. He might be able to stomach living rough, but the homeless were often picked up by the police under vague vagrancy laws that criminalised being homeless. If that happened, and they printed him, it would be game over.

Instead he needed somewhere to lie low. A cheap travel lodge would be fantastic. The bigger chains wouldn't bat an eye at someone staying in their room for a week straight. It would give him the chance to hide until the initial enthusiasm of the manhunt began to die down. It wouldn't take long. There would soon be another criminal, more interesting to the media, that would take the limelight. There would still be coverage but it would be far less intense.

The problem with the budget national chains was that they would all require a credit or debit card; cash would raise too many eyebrows. Barry didn't intend to make use of the incidentals, but that wouldn't stop them wanting to ring fence funds on a card just in case. He might be able to kick up a fuss and give a cash deposit instead, but at best they'd think he was a pimp, and at worst they'd call the police for suspicious behaviour.

A smaller hotel or bed and breakfast might be happy with cash, but Barry would have to make a show of being a tourist and leaving each day. It just wasn't normal to hide away in a B&B for a week, especially not alone. Somewhere with free Internet would also be handy. Barry would need to check in with his darknet contact at some point to make sure that he reciprocated.

Barry decided his best bet was to start in south London away from the big hotels in the centre, and look for a medium-sized business which would take cash and not ask too many questions.

Chapter 22: Done and Dusted?

The Deepak murder hit the papers the next morning. A woman had been shot in Caledonian Road, point blank, with a sawn-off shotgun. Her body had been dumped under bin bags in an alley, and the police were in pursuit of a suspect in connection with the murder.

If Edwin had still been the editor of *The Impartial,* he would have found out about the news before it broke, but he was now reduced to finding out about it in his old newspaper. It was an odd feeling to be relegated to reading the news rather than writing it. He felt out of the loop, and oddly exposed.

His initial link to Eleanor's murder was now dead. The police would have a hard time tracking him without a tangible link to the victims. There was the possibility Barry would be caught, or they'd check Vanhi's computer, but at best they could only link the deaths to an anonymous deep web account. Reasonable doubt seemed pretty certain should Edwin ever end up in the dock.

The issue for Edwin was that media interest would now intensify greatly in both Barry's run from the law, and the life of the victim. If he was unlucky an overly enthusiastic journalist would begin to dig too deep. On the other hand if Barry were to disappear permanently with no sightings of him, then the trail would run cold. Perhaps it was time to delve into the darknet messages once more, and add a further stumbling block for the police to trip over before they came anywhere near the root cause of the trouble.

Edwin's biggest risk of exposure would be if Barry was caught and allowed the police to link the previous deaths together. He had made the error of getting his own hit out of the way first, which would always implicate whoever benefited from that death. He had to make sure the police didn't suspect the kills were linked, or at the least had to eliminate witnesses who knew enough to point the police in the right direction. Around 170 murders were committed each year in London, as well as a huge number of deaths that went under the radar. It would take the police extraordinary luck to correctly link the incidents that Edwin was involved in.

There were still a few more darknet contacts left that had expressed interest in his initial post. He had ignored them until now, as so far he had only really needed one of them. Another death would have the police reeling; if Barry were simply to disappear it would be even better. Barry might become famous for having disappeared but then the spotlight would be on him, and not Edwin. Now was not the time for a light touch. If Barry disappeared, Edwin could stiff the next guy, and put the whole sorry saga to bed for good.

Chapter 23: Officer Down

Sarah Morton stayed with David in the hospital for almost a week straight. Her husband's condition had stabilised quickly, but Sarah had always had a morbid fear that her husband would come to harm while on duty. David had laughed off her concerns with his typical machismo, but he hadn't refused when Sarah offered to sleep on a camp bed in his hospital room to keep an eye on him.

A week later and David was beginning to tire of his wife's company. He loved her dearly, but his work was his true calling in life and he had several investigations on the go to sink his teeth into. He had almost discharged himself twice already, but had stayed after Sarah begged him to.

David frowned. There were dozens of live cases within his purview, and all he could do was flick through the few papers that the other officers deigned to allow him in his hospital room. Between the frustration of not being able to do anything and the other ward residents moaning and screaming at odd times, David was having a hard time getting any quality sleep.

He knew the tedium of watching hospital television would eventually get to him though; while he was desperate to be back out investigating he knew he would need to be well rested. Human resources had already tried to suggest he take an extended break by being reassigned to desk duty for a while.

If there was one part of being a policeman that David detested, it was paper pushing. When he had started out in the force the work had been about being on the beat, helping to build the community and arresting criminals. Now he spent more time filling in incident reports, documenting the chain of custody for evidence and analysing performance targets. He would sooner retire than be forced to sit at a desk for a few weeks. No, he'd just need to block out the noise and get some quality rest before he went back to work.

The one saving grace was that his deputies had visited a few times, but the visits had been more social in nature than professional. Although they had brought him up to date on case progression it had been professional courtesy. It seemed the younger detectives were hungry for the opportunity to prove themselves by taking up the slack.

Perhaps some of them even shared Sarah's concerns that he was getting too old to investigate murders. David didn't want to believe it though; his injury could just as easily have happened to a younger man. When someone throws a knife at your back you're pretty lucky to escape with only a flesh wound. The blade had missed the major arteries in the leg, and he had been taken to hospital before the blood loss had approached fatal levels. He was ashamed of passing out, but he had always been terribly squeamish about the sight of his own blood.

At least he would be back at work soon.

***

Edwin had several unanswered darknet messages in response to his original posting. One of them was from a man who wanted a problem neighbour removed. His request was simple, but as always with Edwin it didn't matter what he asked for. Edwin could promise the earth, but with no intention of ever delivering, it wouldn't cost a penny.

The slight problem was that Edwin would have to find out where Barry was in order to send someone after him. He would need to be quicker than the police, and this time element made the job urgent.

'If you can eliminate my problems in next 48 hrs, I can sort yours after that.' Edwin typed, feeling the same surge of energy he had on the previous occasions. There was no getting around it: playing puppet master was *fun.*

The other man might not agree to go first, but if he didn't, Edwin would simply move onto another prospect. There seemed to be no lack of unscrupulous individuals on the Internet.

Chapter 24: One of Ours

The ground-down serial number had not been entirely removed. They rarely were. It took considerable effort to complete smooth out metal, but it was much easier to use an acid bath to reinvigorate the etchings to reveal the serial numbers.

It was odd however. The serial numbers concerned showed the gun had been confiscated by the police during a drugs raid, and subsequently destroyed. The technician made a mental note to investigate personally. He could simply pass the information on up the chain of command, but without knowing how the gun went from the police locker to the black market no one, the inspectors included, could be trusted implicitly.

It took another week before the hospital pronounced David Morton fit to go home. It was about time, for Morton was not one to stand idly by when there was work to be done. Sarah begged him to come home and rest for a while. He had more than enough holiday days banked to take a week off to recuperate, but Morton had decided that he was needed down at the station, and when he made his mind up he was incredibly stubborn about changing it.

He was greeted warmly as he entered his office. His wife had evidently called ahead, as his squad mates had managed to pull together not only a cake but balloons as well. They all congratulated him on his war wounds, masking the tension in the room with laughter.

It was not until the Director of Human Resources said 'David, have you got a moment?' that the room fell silent. While Morton was gone it had become first rumour, and then agreed common knowledge, that the Superintendent wanted him on desk duty. He was too old, went the rumours. He got lucky this time, but his luck would run out. Others argued that his pension age wasn't all that far away, and that he should be allowed to continue doing his duty until he was physically unable.

In the end, the decision came down to the director. Morton would be placed on desk duty for the determinable future.

'Afternoon, David. How's your leg?'

'Better, thanks. I'm fit to get back out in the field.' Morton was in significant pain still, but he was damned if he would let it show.

'Glad to hear it. David, I'm going to place you on desk duty, at least for a little while. We can't risk your leg in the field. I'll be assigning your active cases to Charles Rosenburg.' The director's words all came out in a rush. He was afraid to pause for fear of giving Morton the opportunity to interject.

Morton's face turned ashen. To avoid getting fired he remained silent, nodded, then turned and left.

Minutes later he was in the station gym. Health and safety buffs had insisted on a punch bag being placed on site to help relieve high stress levels. David hated to admit it, but it worked.

He was sweating profusely from attacking the vaguely man-shaped bag when his long-time colleague Alan Sheppard walked in.

'You seem upset. What's up?' Alan asked.

Morton glanced around and saw they were not alone in the gym.

'I'll tell you later,' he said apologetically. 'In private.'

***

It took a while to get a response, but Edwin's contact agreed to carry out the hit. It was on the condition that Edwin carried out his hit simultaneously, which Edwin had no intention of doing.

To gain his trust Edwin had to be particularly cruel. He asked questions about the intended victim, plotting an elaborate kill that he knew would never take place. The plan was to cut the brake cables on the man's car while he was at mosque. The car park at the mosque would be deserted, with no CCTV in place.

The plotting made Edwin feel dirty. While he was more than happy to play puppet master for his own ends, he would never feel comfortable directly bringing about the death of another. Perhaps it was his upbringing. His parents had drummed into him the sanctity of life. Somehow he could disassociate himself from it if someone else did the actual deed. All he was doing was sending some messages on the Internet, after all.

***

'I fucking hate that guy.' The beer had begun to loosen Morton's tongue. The Hog's Head was not a policeman's bar, and Morton felt that he could talk freely sat in a quiet booth towards the rear of the pub.

'Who?' asked his drinking buddy, Alan Sheppard.

'Rosenburg.'

'Why? He's always seemed like a nice guy to me.'

'He's a sycophantic tosser,' Morton said

'How?' Alan had been an usher at Rosenburg's wedding.

'He stole my cases!'

Alan laughed. 'I think you'll find the Superintendent stole your cases. You wouldn't like me if I'd had them passed over.'

'True enough.' It would not be long before Morton began to slip back into his usual morose persona.

While he did hate the fact he'd lost all of his cases, his problems with Rosenburg had started long before the stabbing incident. Rosenburg had once attempted to seduce Sarah, and Morton considered it a point of honour that he owed him a beating.

Chapter 25: Incognito

It took a while for Barry to be able to find an Internet connection. He had managed to snatch a briefcase containing a laptop while its owner was talking on his mobile a few feet away. It was bold, but Barry had been fully prepared to take it by force if he was caught.

Finding somewhere he wouldn't be overlooked, and the Wi-Fi wouldn't be monitored, had been a bit more difficult. People are often careless about their Internet security and leave their connection unencrypted, but finding one within range of a place he could sit without being noticed proved more difficult.

The solution had been a coffee shop at the base of a block of flats. Barry sat with his back to the wall, and booted up the laptop. There wasn't much battery left, but the owner of the coffee shop became amenable to letting him plug it in when it became evident he would be staying for a while.

Barry kept the coffee flowing for two reasons. First, it greatly extended his welcome. The owner was happy to mind his own business and only ventured over to top Barry up every hour or so. Secondly it helped him concentrate. The combination of sugar and caffeine fired up neurons that hadn't been active in a long time.

Barry looked more gaunt than he had previously been. He wasn't eating well, with the only proper meal of each day being the breakfast he had at the bed and breakfast. He was on to his fourth B&B. Changing every few days stopped anyone noticing him. He still needed to get out and about, however, to avoid suspicion, so he spent a lot of time walking about London. He walked as if he had a purpose but it was really more of a wander.

Four cups of coffee later, and Barry broke the security on the laptop. It hadn't taken much in the end. There was no BIOS administrator password set, so a brute force change of password was simple enough. Once he was in, he looked to see what Internet connections were available. He knew the coffee shop offered free Wi-Fi, that much was advertised in the window. What Barry didn't expect was to find a number of flats above had left their Wi-Fi unsecured, and the signal was strong enough to maintain a steady connection.

Barry didn't take an elaborate route to connecting to the darknet. He knew how, but keeping his identity secret was the least of his worries. The police already had CCTV images of him, and that meant they probably had fingerprints and maybe even a DNA sample too.

He fired off a quick message.

'Still alive. Need help. Running out of funds. Can you help?'

Then, he sat and waited. Hopefully his contact would come good. It was his fault that he had gotten into the mess after all.

***

For Edwin, the message was manna from heaven. He had needed to pin down a location at which he could find the errant Barry, and now he had the perfect excuse to arrange a meeting.

Being a devious fellow Edwin knew not to agree too quickly. If he was too eager then Barry might smell a rat and disappear off his radar. The concern that it might also be the police posing as his contact also crossed Edwin's mind. He was a smart man, but it manifested in being overly paranoid sometimes.

'How much? Might be able to come up with some, but will take time.'

Edwin thought that was sufficiently interested to keep the conversation open, but not so eager as to scare anyone off. He hit send, and leant back in his chair. He didn't know how quickly a reply might come, but he had to pick Chelsea up from school in half an hour; so his contact would simply have to wait until she went to bed for a reply.

***

Barry waited all day, but if he was going to walk back to his B&B before dark he would have to leave soon. He didn't want to come back a second day running to see the reply, but it didn't look like he would have much choice. He could try and find somewhere else again, but it had been a stroke of luck to find the first coffee shop. He'd managed to stay there for most of a day without being bothered by anyone other than the owner who kept on topping up his coffee. At least he'd been kind enough to watch his (password-locked) laptop when he needed to go to the bathroom.

***

Edwin got the a reply from Barry next morning after he had taken Chelsea to school.

'Meet me at the Thames Barrier. Nine o'clock tonight. Bring as much as you can.'

It was short notice, and Edwin needed to get his latest darknet victim to be there, preferably armed.

He quickly sent the details over to the car-brakes guy, setting Barry up. With any luck his last loose link would disappear in just a few hours, and Edwin would be free to flit off into the Canadian sunset.

Peter K Sugden didn't like lying to his wife. He wouldn't normally so much as think of deceiving her, but tonight was different. He couldn't exactly waltz into the parlour and announce 'Hello, dear, I'm off – out for the evening to off someone.'

Instead, he used Skype to phone his mobile, and staged a conversation with himself in which he was asked to meet a client urgently regarding their account.

'Sorry, dear, I know I'm deserting you, but one of my clients has got themselves all in a tizz. If I don't go in I might lose the account.' It was believable if only because Peter was notoriously competitive.

The mere thought of losing business to a rival broker brought him out in hives. His wife didn't really mind either. An evening of peace and quiet, with a hot bath and a trashy novel (of which Peter disapproved) proved most alluring, and she readily allowed Peter to excuse himself.

Peter drove his town car to the station. It would attract attention, but his wife would be extremely suspicious if he called a taxi, and it was too far to go on foot. He could have called his driver, but the overtime would be logged in the company files, and Peter was too smart for that.

He took the train as far as Waterloo before changing to the underground. He hated the closeness of it all. People were crammed into the carriages like sardines, and there was no first class.

He waited for a while, hoping to find a carriage that was empty, or at least only full of white people. If Peter had been a more regular traveller on the London Underground he would have realised the impossibility of this. It was when a group of darker youths surrounded him that he decided he had best take the plunge. At the Bank interchange he changed for SLR, which runs both over- and underground heading to the east of London. He disembarked at the Woolwich Arsenal station, and paused on a nearby bench after leaving the station.

It was unfamiliar territory for Peter, and he had to use his BlackBerry to get his bearing.

The barrier itself was a little over a mile away, but the target point wasn't at the visitors' centre, as it would be closed for the evening. Peter began walking towards what he hoped was the river as his phone robotically called out instructions. He realised halfway there that the phone could be used to track him so he promptly switched it off.

By then he was nearly there, although he was breathing heavily. Mr Sugden was a portly man, and his exercise regime consisted mostly of fetching biscuits from the biscuit tin and lifting them to his dribbling jowls. He was a diabetic as result of his weight, and his plan was to use the insulin to induce stupor by hypoglycaemia. At that point he could simply lift the body over the barrier and into the Thames, where it would become yet another drowning victim in the gloomy icy waters.

He had to get there first. If he didn't catch his breath soon he would be late. His contact had told him the man was expecting a meeting, and expecting to be given cash. Peter wasn't carrying any, and he wouldn't give it up if he was. He would simply pretend to open his wallet and then inject the man.

The road began to get shorter, and the water came into view. He was almost there. As he waddled the last few feet he tugged his sleeves down to cover his left hand, in which the needle was situated. He hoped being a leftie would give him an element of surprise, although it was not a fact he normally broadcasted.

Chapter 26: The Barrier

Barry arrived at the Thames Barrier early. He noticed that there was more CCTV in the area than he remembered, but it was only a hand-off of some cash, and this was unlikely to be considered worthy of any attention, particularly as it was unlikely to be a significant amount.

He saw the fat man approaching long before he arrived. The spot he had chosen was near the visitors' centre, with a deserted car park to his left and the Thames path to his right. The path ran for many miles down towards Hampton Court, and was popular in the early morning with joggers.

The terminus was not so popular however. A few tourist boats sailed out far enough to look at the barrier itself, but this was only during the daytime. Even the Thames Clipper service terminated at Greenwich, so it was highly unlikely there would be passers-by. Barry assumed the fat man was his contact, but waited until he strolled straight towards him before speaking.

As the distance closed between them to around ten feet Barry called out.

'You got my money?'

The fat man tried to respond, but his speech was wheezy, as if he was asthmatic.

'Yeth,' he rasped. He doubled over to catch his breath before straightening up and moving towards Barry. It was clear his wallet was in his breast pocket, but he made to move his left hand – which couldn't possibly give him access to the correct pocket without his removing his jacket.

Barry sensed that something was wrong. The man raised a pudgy left arm with surprising speed, something metal glinting in the moonlight. Barry reacted by instinct. He had been in close-quarters physical combat many times while in prison. He elbowed the older man in the stomach, rolled forward onto his knees and lifted the man. As he did so, he toppled over backwards under the weight, the man rolling at first onto the wall behind him, and then with a crack onto the rocks below.

Before Barry could react, the tidal nature of the Thames took over, waves lapping at the man, inching him slowly deeper. Barry fled. There was nothing he could do without compromising himself. His contact was dead.

Chapter 27: Rosenburg

Detective Inspector Rosenburg pulled the floater case the next morning. A body had washed up on an inlet near Creekmouth early in the morning near Breckton dock, and the police had been called by a dog walker on his early morning jaunt. It wasn't an area the police were often called to. Apart from the sewage treatment works there was little in that part of London. It was too far east to attract tourists, and really only contained a few residential properties.

Rosenburg had the misfortune of being the duty officer, and was roused from a satisfying sleep by his wife. She was a light sleeper, and the incessant beeping of his pager could not be ignored. She didn't know how her husband could sleep through it, but he had even slept through a fire alarm on a previous occasion.

Once she had awoken her husband, she filled his thermos with instant coffee as he dressed, and pecked him on the cheek as he made for the door. They had planned to spend the day together, as Rosenburg was in the middle of the off-work period mandated by the Met's four days on, two off policy.

Work had been even more hectic than usual lately. With the senior inspector off active duty due to injury the work had cascaded downwards, and Rosenburg had caught more than his share. He now had a dozen murder cases to investigate.

Rosenburg liked to give each file at least ten minutes every day. That way none slipped his attention entirely. He could have done with an extra day or two a week to really keep up. The Met was understaffed, as much as the taxpayer might moan about the cost. The crime lab was backed up for weeks at a time, and investigations dragged on because of it. It was OK for Morton. He was the big man in the office, and his requests were always fast-tracked. For all Charles knew, Morton didn't even realise there was a shortage of resources.

The morning's floater hadn't been in the water long. Time of death was estimated at thirty to forty hours. It was long enough for the skin to start to pimple and roughen, and the fatty layer underneath showed only minimal adipocere. If the body had been submersed for a protracted period the fat would have begun to turn soapy, and it would have obscured any surface marks. With the body mass this victim had, the ensuing results would have severely stalled the investigation.

The body had been found face down, with the head hanging beneath the water. Severe lacerations were evident on the face and neck, but there did not appear to be any blood, which indicated they were probably post-mortem, caused by the rough tidal waters.

The lungs had been weighed during autopsy and been found to be significantly heavier than expected. This was almost certainly due to water retention, but it was not conclusive evidence of drowning.

Compression fractures suggested that the body had suffered a fall of some kind. Rosenburg was immediately mindful of a body-dump scenario, although if the victim had drowned it would be hard to marry those facts. Who would dump a live body?

It was possible the victim couldn't swim, and that he had been murdered by ineptitude. It was a risky way to off someone though, as the Thames was busy and passers-by would almost certainly render aid.

Rosenburg hoped it was simply an accident. If he could write it off he'd have more time to investigate his other cases. No one in London had reported the man missing, and Rosenburg had enough work to do chasing after those who were missed, without creating work. Maybe the coroner could be persuaded to rule this one an accident.

The investigators were not the only ones suffering from an increased workload. The morgue was backed up ten deep, with most gurneys in use. The coroner didn't have the luxury of working with just the confirmed murder cases, but had to examine anything unexpected or suspicious. He had an assistant and several techs, but his signature was on every report and he took pride in making sure every piece of work done in his lab was up to par. Larry Chiswick had not always been a coroner. He'd originally trained as an accountant because his parents wanted him to. As a postgraduate he'd rebelled and become a lawyer only to find that the calling was not for him. While he was distinctly middle-class he didn't go to Harrow, nor did he play rugby, and he found he had nothing in common with the vast majority of the legal profession.

At the time education was free. He didn't have to pay, and got a small government grant as well as benefits to live on. It wasn't the high life, but Larry wanted to stretch it out for as long as he could. He liked being irresponsible. Medicine was the longest course he could get onto, and it was in med school that he really found his calling. He met his wife over an autopsy table, and soon qualified as a doctor.

Realising the unique skill set he possessed, he became a coroner. There wasn't much competition; few individuals ever take the time to train as both a lawyer and a doctor, and the combination ensured a diligent and faithful servant to London's legion of the dead.

He had been his typically diligent self with the latest floater to be found. Weight and fat percentage as well as bone density were recorded in his charts. It was not information required by law but Larry believed in being thorough. The information could help to determine buoyancy, which would allow the crime scene techs to work out how fast, and therefore how far, he had floated.

Combining that with time of death they would be able to estimate where he entered the water, and hopefully use that to determine how he entered it. The damage to the body perimortem showed a significant fall followed by drowning. It wasn't conclusive, and the death could just as easily be either accident or murder.

Larry had no choice but to rule the death suspicious and so require further investigation by the Met.

Chapter 28: Flow

Rosenburg hated Wednesdays. He always had. They were as far as he could get from the weekend. He still had to work some weekends, but it was mostly by being on call rather than active duty. Even police inspectors need a break sometimes.

The floater still hadn't been identified. His skin had been macerated while in the water, and only the exposed dermis was left. Without fingerprints it became exponentially more difficult to determine who he was. The lab would try to create reverse fingerprints from the exposed dermis, but it was expensive and slow, so Charles would have to start the investigation on the basis of what they already had, which wasn't much.

Water currents in the Thames had been studied for decades, and the Met had an accurate water flow simulator that could use known weather conditions such as temperature and wind speed to compute how fast an object in the river would move.

Toxicology had confirmed there was no alcohol in the man's system, so the chances of its being an accident were becoming more remote. While the nerds in the basement ran simulations to try and discern point of entry into the Thames, Charles studied the man's clothing. He was impeccably attired. The suit was flattering despite his bulk, and that suggested a quality tailor, which wouldn't have been cheap. He should have been missed. There wasn't a wallet on him, but the Thames was known to churn violently, and anything in his pockets was probably on the riverbed within minutes of his entering the water.

***

The boys in the basement came good for Rosenburg in less time than he expected.

The man weighed approximately twenty-two stone, which, combined with a flow rate at that end of the river of almost one point two billion gallons a day, put the point of entry near the Thames Barrier.

The barrier would normally trap anything that passed through, but it was raised on the night the man entered the river, allowing the body to pass onwards to the East out of the built-up part of the city and towards the suburbs. It had only stopped because of a sandbank built up around the sewage works that had caught the body and prevented it carrying on much further. The speed of the Thames carries on increasing as it meanders towards the sea, as more inlets join it. If it hadn't been caught the body could easily have turned up many miles downstream.

***

The entry point was well lit, but relatively sheltered. It was near the popular running routes for the area as well as the tourist centre, but the start of the Thames Path was sheltered behind industrial-use land. It received some foot traffic, but not at the time the body was estimated to enter the water.

Rosenburg was on scene for only a moment before a constable called out.

'Over there! Look.' The constable waved his hand upwards.

Above the point of origin of the path was a CCTV camera. It was aimed at the entrance to the pier below and to the side, but it appeared to be wide-angle, which meant it might have caught something.

'The wires go down to the Barrier Control Building,' another officer chipped in.

The building was the home of the major controls for raising and lowering the barrier. It was used to study changes in the waterway to prevent the flooding that had devastated London several times before the construction of the barrier.

Rosenburg hated formalities. He should go to the Crown Prosecution Service and get a warrant. It was private CCTV and he couldn't compel the owner to hand over any footage. Blustering had worked in the past, so he walked straight into the building and thrust his badge at the poor girl on the desk.

The colour drained from her face. She was clearly feeling guilty about something.

'I didn't mean to. It just sort of slipped in.'

Rosenburg frowned. He had no idea what she was referring to, but he wasn't going to overlook a chance to get her to hand over the CCTV.

'We might be able to overlook that.' He smiled confidently.

'Really?'

'If you can get me the CCTV for that,' he pointed out the window at the camera in question, 'in the next ten minutes, I'll forget all about it.'

She bolted from her desk in a flurry of guilt. Gary, the CCTV guy, worked in the back monitoring the feed, and he was sweet on her.

'Hey, doll, come to ask me out to lunch?' It was a long-standing joke between them. Gary was decades older and a widower.

'Naw. I need a favour.' She smiled coyly.

'Anything for you.'

'I need some CCTV tapes.'

'Except that.'

'Aww, why not?' she fluttered her eyelids.

'Company policy. What do you want them for anyway?' Gary raised an eyebrow.

'There's a copper in reception. He wants 'em, don't he?'

'Well, send him in. If he's got a badge, I'll sort him out.'

***

After the tenth phone call pleading with him to go on television and appeal for information, Edwin agreed. He also offered to stump up a modest reward. He never expected to pay up, but it gave him a veneer of respectability. Once he said yes the Met moved startlingly quickly. Barely a day later Edwin found himself in a drab conference room on the second floor of New Scotland Yard. A solitary window offered a view over Dacre Street, but Edwin couldn't have taken the time to stop and stare if he had wanted to. The room was full of journalists. The BBC, Sky News, *The Times*, as well as international names such as Reuters were all represented. A few independents filled out the rest of the seats, with everyone else left to stand at the back of the room behind them.

Eleanor's murder had been big news. She was white, middle class, a lawyer, and lived in Belgravia. The tabloids had already run features with headlines like "Murder in Paradise". None had printed anything negative about Edwin, but that was only because they didn't want to fall foul of the Press Complaints Commission.

An officer had prepped him before he walked out to the waiting carnivores. A dozen cameras flashed as he made his way to the lectern facing the journalists.

Edwin cleared his throat, took a sip of the provided water and began. He knew these people. They were, until his recent departure, his people. He was brief, but managed to moisten the eye of every journalist present. Some of them had even met Eleanor at various industry functions. Edwin may have been acting, but none of them noticed. He was preaching to the choir.

***

They kept CCTV on site for only 24 hours. After that it was backed up to a central server for a further 28 days by an outside contractor. Gary couldn't supply Rosenburg with what he wanted.

The contractor was wary of liability should they hand over the footage, and wanted a court order.

Rosenburg hated it, but he had to go cap in hand to the prosecutor assigned to the case, a young shyster called Kiaran O'Connor.

'I need CCTV from a private firm for a murder investigation.' It came through gritted death. Rosenburg and lawyers did not generally mix.

'Ya gotta give me more ta go on tan that.' Kiaran typically dropped his accent when dealing with the police, but he knew Rosenburg hated it, and enjoyed making him uncomfortable. It was one of the few perks of being a criminal lawyer.

'A body was dumped in the Thames near the barrier. Private CCTV on a dock there has a wide-angle lens that covers the dump site. The CCTV is processed locally, and the local centre was cooperative, but CCTV is archived off site. We need access to the archives.'

'That's better. Why couldn't you have said that in the first place?' he teased. 'Consider it done.'

***

The CCTV was clear-cut. A man was shown loitering against the barrier when the victim came down the hill. He spoke to the victim, but without audio Rosenburg had no idea what they discussed.

As the distance between them closed the victim raised his left arm, with something metallic visible in his hand, at which point the first man flipped him over his shoulder and past the barrier.

If Morton had still been on the case he would have recognised the man in a heartbeat, but Rosenburg had failed to dedicate much time to any of his adopted cases. He had given each a cursory read, but without having looked at the primary evidence himself he was flying blind.

Rosenburg was therefore highly curious about the identity of both parties, and what was said between them before the incident. It was clearly self-defence, and thus it was not a job for Charles Rosenburg, but the police would still need to identify the victim. As far as homicide was concerned, it was case closed.

Once the case had been deemed self-defence, uniforms were drafted in to trace the victim's identity so that the family could be informed. It was a fairly simple affair in the end. CCTV in the area was used in conjunction with facial recognition to check public transport. The man had clearly arrived on foot, and so the logical point to disembark for the barrier was the local train station, or the tube.

The man was large and distinctive, and was easily spotted on CCTV. He had disembarked at Woolwich Arsenal tube, and the Oyster card he had swiped was registered to a Peter Kevin Sugden-Jones. His home address was listed, as was his email and other contact details.

It would now be down to the local police station to inform the next of kin.

Chapter 29: By Self-Defence

The tension in the small drawing room could have been cut with a knife. Mrs Sugden sat with her sister, desperate to know where her husband was. Though there was no love lost between Mr Sugden and his sister-in-law, she would be the first to admit that he was reliable. For Mrs Sugden he had always been her rock. Steady, dependable and usually honest, it was not like him to lie about a business meeting and disappear for days on end.

The sisters had devoured enough tea to last a lifetime, and the conversation had been rehashed many times. There was nothing more to be said, so the sisters sat in silence.

Mrs Sugden didn't know how long she had been sat there when the doorbell shrieked out in the silence. It was a nasty piercing doorbell, but anything softer could never be heard in the back of the house. She looked up, an ashen expression on her face.

'Don't worry, I'll get it,' her sister said as she rose.

WPC Hayley Lancaster introduced herself at the door, and asked simply to come in. Her hat had been removed, and was dangling limply at her side. Her gait was slow and steady, signposting the bad news she was about to deliver.

'Mrs Sugden.' Hayley took the seat opposing her before continuing. 'I'm sorry to inform you that your husband has died.'

Hayley knew that there was no concern regarding criminal liability, and that made the delivery of the news much easier. She was used to delivering news to persons who might have some connection with the death. With suspicion clouding her judgement, it was often hard to be sufficiently empathetic.

The news clearly came as a shock. Mrs Sugden just sat there, silent. A tear rolled down her cheek.

It was her sister who broke the silence.

'How did Peter die?'

Hayley paused. It was an odd situation. She had dealt with murder victims, accidental deaths and even cot deaths in the past. Death by self-defence was not in her repertoire of expertise.

'He drowned in the River Thames. I'm ever so sorry.' It was the truth. The widow didn't need to know the specifics of how he ended up in the river.

As Mrs Sugden sobbed, her sister brought in a tray of tea.

Hayley nodded appreciatively before asking if there was anyone she could call.

'I'm all she's got left,' her sister interjected. Her diction betrayed her upbringing. While Mr Sugden was as blueblood as they come, his in-laws were, at best, nouveau riche.

Standard procedure was to never leave the widow alone, but she was well cared for by her sister, and didn't seem to need any additional support. She would need to formally ID the body at some point, but that could wait for another day. She clearly wasn't up to it that day.

***

A plate zinged through the air, missing David by millimetres. He ducked through the doorway, and retreated into the den.

He and Sarah rarely argued, but when they did it was as if a volcano had erupted. Months of petty squabbles and disagreements were regurgitated in a fit of unrepentant rage.

She never forgot a thing either. Insults, snide comments and sarcasm that had long vacated his memory came back to haunt him in quick succession.

The evening had begun normally enough. He had come home from work a little after five. Now that he was on desk duty his hours were far more regular, and they had slipped back into the habit of sharing dinner around six o'clock.

It was work that transformed a pleasant dinner into the slanging match from hell. David had been offered early retirement in light of his years of service. It would reduce his pension somewhat, but the house was already paid for so the Mortons were on fairly good financial footing.

Sarah wanted him to take it. The force had always been the third person in their marriage, beckoning him away in the dead of night and consuming his thoughts even when he was home. David had been a career man for a long time, and Sarah wanted her husband back.

It was an impasse, and the yelling soon kicked off.

'I will not stay at home and watch television when there are criminals to catch!' David boldly declared.

'You can't right every wrong, but you can start by spending some time with me.'

'I do spend time with you! I need to get back on active duty. I'm a policeman, it's who I am.'

✳✳✳

The second gold-embossed note fell through the letterbox on the day the neighbourhood found out about Mr Sugden's death.

'Dear Mrs Sugden,

My wife and I were truly sorry to hear of the loss of your husband in such tragic circumstances. Please allow us to extend our deepest sympathies to you and your family at this difficult time. I know you have many friends in the area to find solace in, but if we can support you in any way please do not hesitate to ask. We're here to help make things a little easier for you, if that is at all possible.

Our warmest thoughts and most sincere condolences,

Qadi Qumas'

Mrs Sugden's eyes welled with tears as she read such heartfelt words from a family whom her husband had shown nothing but scorn.

Chapter 30: No Luck

Edwin's plan to eliminate Barry and remove himself one step further from the original kill had backfired spectacularly.

The death of Peter K Sugden had been big news for the last few days, and Edwin was sweating it badly. Rather than closing a loose end he'd opened a whole new can of worms. If the police became suspicious, the whole plan could unravel faster than Edwin could fathom. He wondered if he'd ever be free of the mess that he had created.

As well as being a killer on the run, Edwin now had the curiosity of the press piqued. They wanted to know why Sugden would attack an apparent stranger, and who the stranger was. If either issue was investigated thoroughly then Edwin could be exposed. Finding Barry would give the game away. He'd already panicked once, and if his neck was on the line he'd give up his online contact if he thought it would help. Through Barry's first victim, Vanhi, he could then be tied to Eleanor.

If the press hounded the Sugden widow they might find out he was plotting online, and that would lead just as quickly back to Edwin. It seemed to Edwin that at this point in time all roads led back to him.

He needed Barry taken out, and he needed him gone. Soon.

***

It was half five when WPC Stevenson, arrived to pick Rosenburg up.

'Morning, sir. Nice flat.' Stevenson's comment implied a question as to how a policeman, even a detective inspector, could afford such a nice duplex.

'G' mornin',' Rosenburg replied drowsily. The overtime was killing him. He had been jacked up on coffee for a week straight, and was beginning to crash.

'We've got a witness in the Eleanor Murphy death. Called the toll-free number last night in a fit of guilt. He won't give a name, sir, but dispatch thinks it's genuine.'

'Get him to come in.' Rosenburg knew immediately after saying it that it wouldn't be that easy, or she'd already have done so.

'He said he'll only meet a detective personally. Won't come near the station.'

'I don't do home visits, Stevenson.'

'You might want to make an exception for this one, sir.'

'Why is that?' Rosenburg ducked into the squad car, his broad frame brushing the ceiling as he sat, legs crushed in the foot well.

'He lives in the park, sir.'

'Our star witness is a tramp? Kiaran O'Connor will love that.' Rosenburg wasn't above massaging evidence and coaching a witness, but even he couldn't work with just the word of a tramp to go on.

'Will you at least talk to him, sir?'

'Fine. Drive slowly; I need a nap on the way there.' With that he turned away, leant on the window and closed his eyes.

***

'Shit,' Morton yelped in pain. A few other officers looked over, at first in concern but then to giggle profusely. The great David Morton, thirty-year veteran of the Met and stabbing victim, had stubbed his toe doing desk work.

'Great, the entire department will know it by lunchtime. Bloody Facebook. Can't keep anything quiet anymore,' he muttered to no one in particular.

A secretary was already opening up the dreaded social media site. At least no one had caught it on camera. At the policeman's ball the previous Christmas a number of events had been caught on camera phones, and the embarrassment caused when a few had found their way onto YouTube led to a department-wide edict banning them from the office. Despite its being against policy nearly everyone still had one. Even Morton had an iPhone tucked inside his breast pocket, although it rarely saw much action. In truth he didn't really know how to use it, but he wouldn't let Sarah know that, as she had bought it for him on their last anniversary. It had seemed like an insanely generous gift at the time but he was the one the bill for it went to, so it wasn't quite a freebie.

The one up side was the number of games on it. Now Morton was spending his days deskbound there really wasn't much work to do. He was a slow typist, preferring the one index finger at a time method over the touch typing required of those in the secretarial pool, and he wasn't really earning his wages anymore. He was desperate to get back to active duty, but the Superintendent had flat-out refused to review his case for at least a month after the injury. Thirteen days down, eighteen more to go, he thought as he scanned BBC News for something juicy to read.

***

Chelsea was at a friend's house for a sleepover, and Edwin had the house to himself. He found it a genuine pleasure being able to bask in the silence without having to worry about the school run or any other interruptions.

It gave Edwin a chance to think, to put things in perspective, and to plot his next move.

Clearly Barry was capable. An amateur had died attempting to take him out, and the police hadn't managed to catch him. A professional was needed, but Edwin couldn't simply pay for him to be eliminated. There had to be another way of getting it done properly, without leaving more loose ends to grate on Edwin's frayed nerves.

The obvious solution was to simply pay the man who had responded to his first darknet message. Now that he was back in the house he could liquidise cash assets without being noticed so easily. Some of the furniture was antique, and would certainly sell for a pretty penny. It would leave a paper trail, but feigning being broke was not difficult when one was out of work. There were a few niggles with that plan. Edwin didn't want to pay. It was a pleasant change to be back living in West London luxury, complete with all the trappings. To sell the family jewels off would diminish his victory over Eleanor.

Secondly, some of it was probably technically in probate. He had been married to a lawyer long enough to know that the furniture didn't simply come with the house, but had been her personal possessions. Selling them could even amount to theft from the estate. At best, if it was discovered by the judge dealing with probate, or the executor of her estate (a friend of Eleanor's from law school that Edwin had never been fond of) then he would be ordered to repay the sale proceeds to the estate, which he couldn't do if he had spent them.

Finally, while it closed one loose end it opened another, and Edwin was a perfectionist. He wanted a neat end to the whole sorry saga, and the closure that would go with that. If he could finish off by tying up every loose end he could start to sleep well at night, safe in the knowledge the police would never darken his door again.

***

The solution was staring Edwin in the face. A professional would be an ideal get-out-of-jail-free. They would be sure to finish the job cleanly, unlike another amateur who would leave the web open for the police to investigate. If Barry were to disappear without a trace, Edwin would be safe, and while he couldn't pay for one himself, there was no reason he couldn't extort someone else into paying. He had a number of darknet contacts still to try, and hopefully at least one of them would agree to a transaction involving cold hard cash.

***

The cash Barry had stolen was running out. He'd managed to steal food a few times, but his reserves were fast evaporating. Including the stash from the old woman's apartment, he'd started out with a little over £700. In London, that didn't go far. Barry considered ditching on the last B&B without paying, but they knew what he looked like, and the last thing he needed was another police report.

Bill paid, Barry left with less than £200. He needed to get out of London. He could go virtually anywhere, and the choice was so wide it was almost paralysing. Scotland would give him a huge area in which to hide, but a stranger in a small town would garner attention. Likewise, Wales was discounted. His fake accent would never fool a local.

Barry really needed to leave the country. He spoke fluent French, as his mother had taught him as a small boy and helped him hone his skills with a summer-long sojourn to southern France every year during school. Flying was out of the question. There was no way he could get by without a passport there. The Eurostar might work, but the best bet was to try and take a ferry. Customs and Excise at ports were much more concerned with keeping foreigners out than keeping people in. A foot passenger could board at Dover, Portsmouth or Southampton and be in France in less than five hours. Barry still had family in France, and they wouldn't ever have thought him a criminal. None of them spoke much English, so unless the police involved Interpol he could simply disappear.

Dover was the busiest route, but customs had always been quite heavy there. Southampton would involve going via Portsmouth anyway, so it would be quickest to go direct. The train to get to the port would take around £30 of his remaining funds, and the ferry would be another £27.50.

Barry was amused that the relatively short train journey would cost more than an international ferry, but now was not the time to comment on the extortionate price of rail travel in the UK. All in, Barry would arrive in France with £140. With the euro stronger than the pound, he'd need to be frugal when he got there, but it was certainly doable. He'd travel down to Portsmouth in the morning.

***

Edwin's plan had received some responses. They were a mixed bunch. A couple flat-out said no to paying for a hit. One offered to pay after the hit, which was a possibility if Edwin could borrow the money temporarily, but it wasn't ideal. A final contact had appeared more interested.

'Possible, how much?' the message had asked.

Edwin replied quickly, quoting the £50,000 he had first received.

'LOL' came the reply. Edwin was ready to give up when the contact messaged him again.

'Can't do £50k. How about part cash part swap?'

The man clearly thought Edwin's first post had not been fulfilled. It wouldn't work of course; Edwin couldn't kill someone without exposing himself to too much risk. The money would be helpful, but it would simply complicate the paper trail.

***

They found the witness where he had promised, sleeping under a bench in Battersea Park near the toilets. Rosenburg kicked him none too gently.

'Wake up.'

'Five more minutes,' the homeless man mumbled.

He was used to be abused and moved along. In London it was a crime to be a vagrant. The law saying so was 180 years old, and as vague as Parliament had ever been, but it was still on the statute books, so homeless people like Frank got kicked to the kerb every day. It didn't help that a number of beggars weren't really homeless, and it stopped those genuinely in trouble getting the help they needed.

'Get up you, worthless shit.' Rosenburg pulled his leg back to kick him again.

Slowly, Frank rolled over and sat up. He was shivering badly. WPC Stevenson leant forward towards him.

'Coffee?' she smiled.

Frank returned a toothy grin. It was rare for him to receive a kindness. One Christmas a lady had helped him into a shelter, but it had closed in the New Year, with the rich feeling they had done their bit by housing him for a couple of weeks. He'd even had a job interview lined up when he was last cast out onto the streets. Ever since he'd been living on soup and curry handed to him by charity workers. It rarely tasted good, and his weight was a slim fraction of what it had been before the streets.

'You rang us. Start talking,' Rosenburg demanded.

Frank glared at him. He didn't like this one. He turned back towards the kind one with the coffee.

'I saw someone. Every day that week that lady died. She stole my bench, kept her bag spread across it like, so I couldn't even share it. Never so much as glanced at me proper.'

'Did you see her kill the woman?' WPC Stevenson asked

'Naw, she was looking mighty shifty though.'

'This is getting us nowhere!' Rosenburg was tired, and he had no patience after several double shifts had left him sleep-deprived.

'What did you see?' the WPC continued, ignoring her supervisor's temper tantrum.

'She sit in same place all week, and she was there ever' day. Never saw her before or since, and I've been here for months.' Frank tried to explain, but he was less than eloquent. He hadn't had a conversation this long since the shelter.

'What'd she look like?'

'Pretty lady. Asian. 'Bout your height I guess.' Frank had been drinking to numb the cold, and his recollection wasn't perfect.

'Anything else?'

'She had a mobile, and did her make-up.'

'Thanks.' Stevenson tossed him a pre-packed sandwich.

Frank grabbed at it greedily, tearing the packaging and discarding it to the floor as he stuffed the whole sandwich in his mouth. He hadn't eaten in almost a day.

"Fanks,' he said with a mouthful of BLT.

***

'Single to Portsmouth pl,ease.' It had taken less than ten minutes to get through the queue at Waterloo.

'Got a railcard?'

Barry dithered. He did have a railcard, but it had his name on it, as well as an old photo. Would it give him away? Before he had a chance to reply the man had printed his ticket.

'£31.80 please.' Barry shook his head, and gingerly handed over two twenties.

Ninety seconds later he was stood under the big clock staring glumly up at the big screens with the departure times. The 10.31 to Portsmouth Harbour didn't have a platform number yet, but Barry still had a quarter of an hour to wait. He grabbed a copy of the *Metro*, and leant against a sign to read while he waited.

By the time he'd read a story about himself (thankfully without a picture!) the board had refreshed and platform 14 was glowing luminescent on the board above him.

***

David knew he had to apologise. He didn't really think he was in the wrong, and he wouldn't give up on getting back on active duty, but he was going to apologise to Sarah.

She was out at her mother's for a day, and wouldn't be back until around seven. She hated to leave during rush hour, so David knew he had plenty of time to make good his apology.

He took a day off from his accrued time off in lieu, and began to clean the house. He usually hated doing it, but somehow the action was cathartic. It certainly beat data-entry work all day. Once the house was sparkling he made a trip out to Sainsbury's. Flowers and fine food were the order of the day.

It had to be orchids of course. They had always been his signature flowers at university, though Sarah never knew that. She thought he bought them because they were her favourite colour, purple. He wasn't going to disabuse her of that notion. With the flowers sorted, he picked up a couple of decent wines and sea bass. David couldn't cook much, but those recipes he could cook he had practised to excess. Tonight would be Szechuan sea bass with sautéed potatoes and a starter of edamame.

The edamame was easy enough. Boiled, tossed in sea salt and chilli flakes and served, it looked like hard work but was the essence of simplicity.

The sea bass was a bit harder. It was easy to overcook, and balancing the flavours took real effort. David started with deboning the fish, and removing the guts. Sarah would have cheated and bought fillets, but it was far more manly a task if done properly, and not one for the squeamish. Once that was done he chopped onions, chillies, lemongrass, ginger and garlic for later. He'd deep-fry it while she ate the starter and grabbed a glass of pinot grigio.

A few rose petals scattered about the kitchen leading up to the bedroom finished off his preparation. He was nothing if not an old-fashioned romantic, and wanted to take full advantage of being well rested after desk duty.

Chapter 31: Sunrise

Edwin's brother-in-law turned up at five o'clock the next morning, banging on the doors. Edwin was not amused. He could catch up on the sleep; he had all day to do that. The problem was that the neighbours might hear. It was unseemly to have night-time visitors in Belgrave Square, especially ones who bang doors loudly at such an ungodly hour.

Edwin was tempted to tell him to get lost. He wasn't his brother after all, but he had been there for Edwin when he'd lost his job, and could be relied upon for babysitting services occasionally.

Knowing he might regret it, Edwin unbolted the French doors, and allowed him in. Mark had always been a pest, for as long as Edwin had known Eleanor. He was unreliable, lazy and had an addictive personality, but somehow he was still a loveable rogue. His partying ways made Edwin feel young again, and he always invited Edwin on nights out. Many a bottle had disappeared in an orgy of drink-induced partying, and he had always managed to get Edwin home no matter how drunk he personally was.

This time, it was he who needed help. He was in withdrawal. Mark had been clean, on and off, for a long time. He'd probably been addicted to every substance known to man at some point or another. Drink, drugs, even certain foods. Mark had many demons, but the current one was heroin, and if he didn't get help soon it would kill him.

'I'm ill, man,' he moaned, throwing himself onto the leather divan in the drawing room.

'Couldn't it have waited till sunrise?' Edwin was always grumpy before his morning coffee.

'I'm on the brink, I need help. Now.' It was a plea Edwin had heard a few times before, when he and Eleanor had helped put Mark into rehab.

'What do you want from me?' Edwin felt a pang of conscience. He had killed the man's sister, so it was unreasonable for him to be angry at the early intrusion.

'Help me get back into the Sunrise Centre.'

The Sunrise Centre was a secure lockdown facility. Inmates could leave at any time, but if they did they were not permitted to come back. They were reduced to a regime of exercise and a balanced diet, with group counselling every day. Mark had been there once before, and had walked out after two weeks, straight back into the welcoming arms of his dealer.

It would be difficult to get him back into the program, but Edwin knew a donation to the centre's work would open doors. The Sunrise Centre didn't charge, but it still needed to get funding from somewhere, and the government stipend was notoriously stingy.

'I can try. No guarantees,' Edwin offered, letting guilt get the better of him for the first time in months.

'Make the call, Ed. I need to get off the skag, otherwise it's going to kill me.' He was already shaking, visibly suffering from the withdrawal.

'Fine, but I can't call for a few hours. Want some breakfast?' Edwin knew he couldn't risk going back to bed until he had seen Mark safely into the hands of professionals who could deal with him.

'Bacon and eggs, fried bread, hash browns and beans please.' Withdrawal always gave Mark the munchies.

Edwin rolled his eyes, and headed for the Aga.

***

It was a logical solution, if he could persuade both parties to go along with it.

Edwin decided to communicate again with the earlier assassin – the first to answer his darknet messages – and offer a part-exchange deal. Edwin, or rather Edwin's latest contact, would do one kill for the assassin and pay him a cash surplus.

This would give Edwin two benefits. Firstly, he would be massively distanced from the kill he was paid to do, and secondly he would get the extra money.

Edwin knew his contact would pay up. He had as good as said as much. If he could now persuade the assassin then the whole plan could proceed without Edwin's being involved.

The assassin would then track down and eliminate Barry, closing the largest loophole. His contact would then complete the assassin's kill, and then Edwin would stiff his contact. The contact would then have knowledge only of the assassin, and be nothing to do with Edwin.

He typed out a message to the assassin.

'Interested in a swap? We do your kill, and you do ours.' Edwin figured he would only mention the cash if he had to.

Chapter 32: The Frenchman

The assassin was a Frenchman who went simply by Pierre, although that was not his real name. He was a professional, though you couldn't tell it just by looking at him. He was plain, even bland-looking, the sort of man you look at and then forget in an instant. He was of medium build, around five foot ten, and had no features that really stuck out. It was his job to be a nobody, to be passed on the street but forgotten in a second. His entire being was consumed with pretending. He monitored his clothes, his gait, his mannerisms and his accent religiously to ensure that he stayed in the persona he had assumed. Contrary to popular belief he was not a seasoned criminal, a hard man or any of the other stereotypes his enemies thought of when they imagined him. He was meek, unassuming and dedicated to getting the job done.

With a talent for accents he could pass for any one of a dozen nationalities, and regularly did so. He had a habit of travelling in and out of countries on different passports. It was illegal of course, in most countries at least, but he did it anyway. He had been in the military when he was younger, but had been thought dead in action. It didn't take him long to realise the benefits of no longer officially existing, and his fame and fortune soon began to wax.

The message he had received was intriguing, but he knew he could get extra out of this contact. He'd already enquired about a paid hit once.

'Sounds interesting. What's in it for me?'

The messages went back and forth for a while before a deal was agreed. The assassin would go second, and on completion would be paid £5,000 cash in unmarked bills.

As it wasn't Edwin's money, he agreed.

***

Zach's condition kept on deteriorating. It would be cruel to delay it, and Yosef knew he wouldn't be able to bring himself to do it.

£5,000 seemed like a low price to pay to end his son's suffering. He had spent six of the last eight months in hospital, and that ratio was likely to increase in the future. He spent his days tanked up on a morphine drip, breathing through a respirator. He could only hear the loudest of sounds, and his sight was restricted to seeing whether the room was light or dark. It was no way to live. Yosef couldn't allow his son to suffer any longer.

'Deal, if you go first.'

The next cheap ferry wouldn't be for another few days, so Barry decided to lurk near the port. Portsmouth was much cheaper than London, and his remaining money stretched more easily. A B&B was costing him fifteen pounds a night. It was a bit downmarket, but he only needed somewhere to lay down his head.

The crowds along the seafront allowed him to hide effectively. No one was ever suspicious of a tourist wandering along the seafront, and there was enough seafront that he never needed to walk the same stretch twice.

His diet consisted of chips, chips and more chips. Portsmouth didn't have a huge culinary repertoire. The seafront was scattered with fish and chip shops, and at not much over a pound a bag they were hot, filling and didn't stretch the budget. There were plenty of pubs but Barry couldn't afford to avail himself of their services no matter how nice a crisp cold beer would taste in the sunshine.

He did let himself enjoy an ice cream while sitting on a pier, but it was really only an excuse to loiter without arousing suspicion. Hopefully he'd still have over a hundred pounds by the time his ferry came around.

***

Both contacts wanted the other to go first, and neither was willing to budge.

Edwin was at a loss. If neither compromised then the plan would fall to pieces. The professional would never compromise, and Edwin's other contact was just as adamant. With such a large sum of money involved he was prone to be stubborn. Ideally, one of them would have compromised and agreed to go first; that would have allowed Edwin to close any link to him without any further action.

As it stood, Edwin needed another individual to join the mix. If they did, and were willing to go first, they could perform one of the hits, and then the second hit would fall into place. Barry would then stiff the newcomer by never carrying out his side of the deal. He could even give out the details of one of the other parties to the last of the killers. If that one then sought retribution, the only details he would have would lead him to either an elusive hit man who would be long gone, or one of the earlier dupes who had committed murder at Edwin's behest.

This would leave Edwin free and clear, as Edwin's name would never feature into the deal, and the police couldn't possibly match up the myriad London murders to find the ones that were linked. Even if they did link the last few kills, Edwin was well removed from them, as the only victim he could be concretely linked to was Eleanor, and he had been on a plane at the time of her death.

Edwin would have orchestrated a number of murders, but paid for none of them, and he had a solid alibi for all of them. It was, in Edwin's humble opinion, a stroke of genius on his part. It was no wonder the crime rate was so high when it was so easy to manipulate pawns into carrying out his orders unwittingly. It was a beautiful spider's web of criminality, in which Edwin was at the centre, but no one would ever find out.

The web was soon to be closed for good.

Chapter 33: Paper Trail

Luke Garth, the tech who had used acid etching to reveal the serial number, did not remain idle for long. The gun had been seized in a drug raid conducted by narcotics in the summer of the previous year in accordance with Code B of the Police and Criminal Evidence Act 1984, the major legislation controlling seizure of property in the UK. In total 391 guns had been seized, of a variety of calibres and types. It had been a major raid that year, and the criminal litigation was still ongoing. Pursuant to department policy, once forensic data had been gathered and independently verified the guns were sent for destruction. A C57A form was still on record for the items, but it was redundant as the owners would never be able to reclaim the guns.

David Morton had completed the correct form F103A, dated 11th December, that was required to mandate destruction of the weaponry. The guns were due to be shredded after Christmas, but had clearly gone missing after this point. The guns would have been stored in the evidence locker pending destruction, and should have been signed out to be destroyed. The correct form had been lodged for their removal, citing a civilian contractor as the point of disposal for shredding.

Luke wanted to call the company and see if the shipment had reached them, but doing so would alert them that the disappearance was being investigated. If they hadn't received an expected shipment they surely would have contacted the police, Luke reasoned. It was fair to assume therefore that someone at the recipient company, ARM Disposal UK Ltd, was involved.

Luke swivelled his chair round to face his computer terminal. Bringing up the UK's company-house search service, Webcheck, Luke typed in the details for ARM and requested a list of their directors.

'Name & Registered Office:
ARM DISPOSAL UK LTD
POST RESTANTE
10 WATERLOO PLACE
LONDON
ENGLAND
SW1Y 4AN
Company No. 907304166
Directors:
Arthur Friedrich
Jane Friedrich
Secretary:
Jane Friedrich'

Oddly enough, the address pertained to a post office collection box in the heart of London. A quick search for the directors showed that neither name brought up anyone licensed to dispose of armaments. It was time to turn over the investigation to the professionals.

Luke printed out what he had found, filled in an internal IPCC referral form that would turn over jurisdiction to the Internal Investigations Unit at the IPCC, and filled in the requisite information.

***

Pierre was used to travelling, and loved to people-watch as he travelled. He had found the money in a locker at Victoria Station as promised, wrapped in an old gym bag. There was a mixture of £5, £10 and £20 notes in non-sequential numbers. After a quick check while in the disabled bathroom, Pierre put the bag back into another locker. He didn't handle cash himself, preferring to leave the administrative details to the man who could loosely be called his banker. The banker was a fixer of sorts, catering to a variety of clientele, moving money, exchanging money and occasionally rendering a service of some kind. He was a fixer, and his job was to take the money in London, and pay the same amount minus his fee of ten percent in euros back in France. It was illegal of course, but extremely lucrative. Maintaining clients in multiple countries, he simply swapped their money between them when required, and pocketed a commission from both of them for the pleasure.

He also supplied a small gun. Pierre had asked him to offset the money he was depositing against a Saturday night special, any cheap and untraceable gun that could be found at short notice. This was placed back into yet another locker to be collected by another of Pierre's lackeys.

It cost him £350, but the piece was well worth every penny. He had tracked his prey by CCTV. Unlike the police he didn't bother with warrants, simply hiring individuals who could obtain the information without asking questions. He knew that on Sunday the man would take a ferry from Portsmouth to Le Havre, taking an inside cabin for the five-hour journey.

The plan was simple. He would board the ship, kill the man in his own cabin and dump the weapon in the sea. Then he'd walk away never to be seen again. With a shipboard capacity of almost 6000 it would take the police a long time to work through who was who, and by then he'd be far away and have changed his appearance significantly. With any luck the British and French would spend so much time arguing over jurisdiction that the trail would be arctic by the time any investigation started.

Chapter 34: Hot Pursuit

The suspect still hadn't surfaced. He had been on the run for a while now, and Rosenburg suspected that he had some help. His finances showed no withdrawals, and none of the CCTV systems the police actively monitored had caught him. Rosenburg cursed. If only London had sprung for an integrated CCTV system it would be far quicker to find those the police were investigating.

'Sir, we might have to consider he has fled London,' an officer suggested gingerly.

'Maybe. Where does he have connections to?'

'Mostly the north, sir, he's lived all over Yorkshire but his heritage is mixed. He could have relatives anywhere.'

'Get on with tracking the possibilities. Call all known associates personally, and fish for information. He's got to turn up sooner or later.'

'Yes, sir.'

Rosenburg turned back to the squad room's active investigations board. He still had more work than he could possibly handle. Finding one man among the 62 million or so living on the tiny island that is the United Kingdom was easier said than done. He simply didn't have the manpower, or the computing power to keep searching indefinitely. Once thirty days had passed he could pass it to the cold case squad. At least then it wouldn't count against him in his annual review. Likewise, if he could fob it off on Interpol it would no longer be his problem. All he had to do was evidence a reasonable belief that Barry had fled the country, and he'd be out of Rosenburg's hair.

***

The letter had arrived that morning. It was addressed to David Morton, but Sarah opened it first as her husband was still asleep. It was from the human resources department, and contained an offer for early retirement. The Met was offering to top up his pensions contribution as if he had been pensioned off at his normal retirement age. It was a generous offer, and Sarah knew that the girls in HR must have fought hard to get him it. She also knew her husband would not take it. His stubborn determination had been one of the qualities she had most admired in him when they were courting. He was fiercely loyal, and he never backed down when he thought he was right, and he believed that his future was in the force. He still had potentially a decade before he needed to retire, and if he carried on catching them as he had for the last few decades then his work would keep dozens of violent criminals off the streets. It wasn't something he would willingly give up in return for cash.

She'd have to take him up the letter sooner or later, but it wouldn't hurt to get him in a good mood first. She set the letter on the table, and turned on the Aga to cook him breakfast.

The last swap was arranged without much ado. The final piece of Edwin's puzzle fell into place. The final contact would fulfil the assassin's kill request. The assassin would then kill Barry to close the loop, and the final contact would kill for the final contact. Edwin would then cut his last contact loose, knowing that he had no information on him personally, and even if he did he wouldn't be able to turn to the police to pursue the non-performance. Edwin chuckled as he imagined that conversation. 'Hi, officer, a man stole my money when I paid him to commit murder for me, but I don't know who he is.' With any luck they might even find him a nice tight straitjacket.

Even Edwin was impressed with the deviousness of his plan. It was every inch as clever as he could have hoped, and he knew he was going to quite literally get away with murder. He allowed himself a few moments to bask in his own evil, a smug expression fixed on his features.

Edwin breathed, exhaling deeply and letting the stress of the last few weeks go out of him. It would be over soon, and he could go back to just being a dad, and maybe even take an exciting new job in Vancouver.

***

David didn't suspect a thing when his wife appeared by the bed with a cup of coffee and a large cooked breakfast. He loved to surprise her, and she occasionally reciprocated. It wasn't until he was satiated by the grease that she broached the subject of the letter.

'This came for you, dear,' she said, passing it over nonchalantly.

His eyes narrowed. It was obvious she had read it, and in hindsight the obvious bribery of the fry-up meant it was important, and that he wouldn't like the contents.

***

Pierre had been incredibly specific about his requirements. A businessman was travelling with a lady companion. The man had cheated a client of his, and the client wanted retribution. The man was to die in great pain, and the woman was to watch.

The contact, Ant, had no problem with this as long as the requisite items were supplied along with a concrete plan. He had grown to enjoy violence in prison. It was sick, but after being victimised he felt the need to victimise others to reassert his own status.

The target was having dinner at a small restaurant in Camden Lock. The All-American Diner was a quiet venue, with a number of private booths. The couple were to be seated in the rear booth, near the kitchen door, through which a fire escape could be found. The owner had been bribed to look the other way, and to ensure that the old-fashioned CCTV system was out of tape.

Ant arrived a little after six. He knew the couple wouldn't finish dinner till about seven, and he wanted them to be a little tipsy.

The plan was simple enough. Red wine would be laced with Rohypnol, and the couple would be led out the rear door to a waiting car that Pierre had supplied. They would then be taken to an old warehouse in Dukes Road, Euston. It was isolated, and would be an ideal place for Pierre's demands to be carried out.

Chapter 35: Quis Custodiet Ipsos Custodes?

Theresa West rubbed her eyes, desperately trying to avert a yawn. The document before her was potentially the most explosive issue she had dealt with since joining the Internal Investigations Unit.

She was used to dealing with cops who had accepted bribes, or vice cops looking the other way in return for favours. Her pulse quickened as she read the Garth Report.

It was an alarming internal report that guns may have been trafficked out of the evidence locker and back onto the street. If it was proven to be true the Metropolitan police would suffer a shellacking in the press the likes of which they had never seen before. It would almost certainly result in a judicial inquiry, and would have repercussions for many years to come.

As far as Theresa could tell the guns had been properly confiscated. The raid had been meticulously planned, and the execution was one of the many fables that built up the legend of Detective Chief Inspector David Morton. It had been a stroke of genius to use stun gas to take out their armament store, and had probably saved more than a few police lives. The gang concerned was prepared for a protracted conflict, and even the heavy riot gear would not suppress such high-calibre fire all the time.

The guns had been properly transported in secure vans back to the evidence locker. It was clear from the records that none of the guns had disappeared before the destruction forms were completed by the commanding officer who had seized them.

It was odd that the form had been completed just before Christmas, giving a full three-week period for the guns to go AWOL without anyone being any the wiser, but Morton had never been a fan of paperwork and may well have simply dealt with it at the most expedient time for him. He had always kept a heavy workload, and that year was no exception.

Despite his reputation he would still be the primary focus of the investigation. The guns were his responsibility until they reached the civilian contractors engaged to dispose of the weaponry, and there was no evidence that any impropriety had taken place on this occasion. The uniforms engaged in the transport of the guns would also be interviewed individually and possibly even subjected to a polygraph if the Internal Investigations Unit thought it useful. Luke Garth would be put on record to confirm that the method of recovery of the serial was correct in case it was needed for a criminal prosecution, and the recipient civilian firm would eventually be searched in a dawn raid to check any evidence that the consignment had made it that far.

Ant had checked out the plan meticulously. If there was one thing that he had been taught in prison, it was that more criminals were caught by being careless than by bad luck. One slip-up could leave forensic evidence tying him to the crime, and he knew the police probably had his DNA on file from before.

The warehouse was fairly large, with one main point of entry at the front. It was unbolted, as promised, with a key inside. Ant would lock it after his initial reconnaissance. The interior was sparse, with a few stud walls pushed up against the extremities. They were clearly designed to help divide the internal floor space between shared use, or for different purposes.

Ant wheeled a few of them together to create a box in the centre of the warehouse, giving in effect a second pair of curtains should anyone be attempting to look through the grimy Victorian windows in the street. It was unlikely, as they were well above head height, but Ant was taking no chances.

The instructions he had received were explicit that the man suffer great pain, but Ant had been left a huge freedom of choice in how to inflict that pain. A veritable torturer's toolkit had been supplied in a large wooden chest in the rear of the building. Some were innocuous in an industrial setting, such as the power tools, saws and vices. Others spoke more clearly of the chest's sinister nature. Acid, barbiturates and cat-o'-nine-tails rounded out the collection. Ant's contact clearly meant business.

Satisfied he had everything he needed, Ant pocketed a couple of pairs of handcuffs. Although the targets would be drugged it was best to restrain them too.

Ant watched them throughout their meal, letting them enjoy a last meal together before he struck. It even gave him time to sample the house delicacies, enjoying a southern fried rack of ribs with a side of slaw.

As they drank the bottle of wine (a gift, on the house, to avoid the chance they wouldn't imbibe alcohol) they fell under the spell of the Rohypnol. Their conversation soon became incoherent, a stream of nonsense no one but they could understand. The waiter signalled it was time to get them into the back of the vehicle waiting out back. It was parked on double yellows, but a disabled badge on the dashboard kept it free of parking attendants.

Ant brushed through the door towards the parked taxi, and unlocked the door. As he left he heard the waiter say to the couple:

'Your taxi has arrived, sir.'

'We ordered a taxi?' Or at least, that's what he tried to say, instead muttering inaudibly.

'Yes, sir. It's waiting outside.'

'I must have had a few to drink!'

'Not to worry, sir, and thank you for the generous tip.'

It was this line that sealed the couple's trust in the waiter. They hadn't paid, of course; Ant had done that for them, but no one would argue to try and pay twice. They allowed the man to lead them through the rear door to the taxi, and staggered in.

'Royal Horseguards Parade please, mate,' the man slurred, the woman already slumped in the back seat.

'Let me help you with your bags,' Ant offered, stepping out towards him. It took the man too long to realise he didn't have a bag with him. His eyes widened in terror as the cuffs clicked about his wrist. Ant could see he was going to scream, and quickly clapped his left hand over the man's mouth, a chloroform-drenched towel in his palm. The man slumped into the seat. He would be out cold for at least an hour, and that would be ample time.

Ant glanced around to make sure no one had witnessed the incident, but his contact had chosen well. There was little foot traffic outside, and the street lamp was broken. Cars could be heard in the distance, but the road was only used for access and no one had tried to pass in the three minutes the whole job had taken. Ant strapped the man in, leaning the woman into him to give the illusion of a cosy scene to any curious onlookers, and then put his foot on the pedal.

Chapter 36: Pain

They awoke in the stark warehouse, but they were unable to see the size of it as the centre had been marked out with dividers, electrical outlets on extension socks visible underneath the boards.

The toolbox was out of sight. Ant didn't want his victims to know what was coming.

A makeshift rack had been put up using old scaffolding, and the man was tied up on it. His arms were bound behind and above him, contorted so that he hung by his shoulders. Too long in the position and they would dislocate.

She had been far more lucky. The chair into which she was tied was not comfortable, but she wasn't in pain, yet. Both of them were bound too tightly to move, and neither could yell out as they had been thoroughly gagged.

Footsteps thundered, echoing through the building. As they grew louder Ant appeared through a gap in the stud walls at the south end, behind the man. Ant knew they were thirsty; the combination of Rohypnol and alcohol would ensure that much. A glass of water was perched on a table in the corner. His instructions had said nothing about deliberately being cruel to the victim. His contact really only wanted to send a message, a warning to anyone considering cheating his contact's client. The body had to remain sufficiently whole that the injuries could be ascertained. An eviscerated body would not serve properly as a disincentive.

He started with a cat-o'-nine-tails, turning the woman to make her watch as he ripped the flesh on her date's back, lacerating it thoroughly. The thongs had been triple knotted to increase the number of points of impact. Not only would it increase the pain caused, but it would make the weapon harder to track. Lead weights on the end of the thongs made light work of the man's skin. In only a handful of lashes welts were beginning to appear, and the man was openly weeping. It was hard to imagine that this was once a legal punishment used in Britain as recently as the Forties in Wandsworth prison. The cat even found modern-day use in Trinidad and Tobago despite international criticism.

Of course, those used judicially hadn't been modified as Ant's had. His arm began to tire, and he lowered the whip. A saline solution was thrown over the man's back, seeping into his open wounds. He yelped, a small sound escaping the rags with which he had been gagged.

The gag was unnecessary. It was to prevent them pleading rather than to prevent anyone hearing. The road was a long way away, and the building's walls were thick and insulated.

He yanked the rag from the man's mouth.

'Stop being a little bitch or I'll make it worse.' Ant's eyes flared and then focussed as if he was staring at something floating in the air. Ant was no longer seeing the businessman In his mind's eye, he was exacting revenge for the treatment he had endured in prison.

'Fuck you,' the man cursed, and spat at Ant. It was a big mistake, and he knew it the moment he spoke. Ant stuffed the gag back in his mouth and grabbed an electric branding iron that was starting to glow with heat.

Once Ant was satisfied it was hot enough he advanced on the man, touching the iron first to his legs, then his arms. Rage coursed through him, but his movements were controlled. He knew what would cause pain. He had suffered worse in prison. The woman watched wide-eyed as Ant methodically scarred the man. His touches were light. Too deep and he would burn out the nerves and the pain would stop.

Alcohol was poured into the trenches he had gouged in the man's flesh. He screamed, or would have if the gag had not been in place.

'Never tell me to fuck off.'

He removed the man's gag, daring him to speak.

'Please, I'll tell you where I put the money.' It was the first thing Ant knew of any money. He didn't want to appear too keen, and ignored him. A pressure washer was applied to the man's flesh. It would sting like crazy but the cold water would take the heat out. Too much and the man would pass out.

'Please!' The man began to beg as Ant moved towards the woman. She tried to shy away, almost toppling the chair over backwards. She had to watch. The order had been explicit.

Her eyes clapped shut, scrunched tightly to avoid watching. It just wouldn't do. Ant didn't want to hurt the woman. She was no threat, and really only a by-product of the deal he had struck, but it was necessary. If she wouldn't open them he would simply remove her eyelids.

He told her as much. Picking up a razor-sharp scalpel he walked towards her.

'We can do this the easy way or the hard way. Open them. Now.'

Her eyes shot open, and Anthony returned his attention to his primary victim.

The next torture Ant had endured in prison had been having his fingernails pulled. It was an easy task requiring only a pair of pliers. Hatred flowing through him, Ant bent the man's index finger back for easy access, keeping it away from the rope bindings.

He pulled one. The man yelled, a guttural sound that resonated around the warehouse. In between anguished moans he tried again.

'I'll give you the goddamn money, just stop!'

'How much is left?' Ant only wanted to ask how much, but added the rest as an afterthought. That way he didn't betray the fact this was new information.

'Just over a million.' The man's head hung lower. It was obvious that there had been much more in the first place.

'Where is it?' Ant demanded.

'Self-storage unit in Kennington. A bank would have been too risky.'

'How do you get in?

'Key code at the gate, key at the locker. Number is 1332 for the door, and the key is in my wallet.'

'You know if you're lying you'll die,' Ant warned him, deciding that the money would buy the man some relief.

The man nodded. Ant decided he'd had enough. The man would die anyway, but he would make it quicker than he had planned. He took a knife, and ran it across the man's neck from behind. Blood spattered out, covering the floor, and the man fell silent.

The woman was next. To keep her from screaming he thrust the knife up through the ribcage, piercing the lung. She would die in a matter of minutes.

He poured kerosene all over the warehouse except for the bodies, set the timer provided that would provide a spark in an hour, and left. The fire would take care of all the evidence he had ever been there.

Chapter 37: Guns

'Thanks, John. We'll be fine, don't worry.' Rosenburg hung up. As much as he protested he wasn't worried, he was. That call was from one of his wife's cousins. Internal affairs were investigating the guns that he'd diverted the previous year, and his disappearing act only compounded the appearance of guilt. His wife's cousin was a junior clerk in their department and he wouldn't be able to affect the investigation, but the heads-up was invaluable.

He hadn't planned to steal the guns originally. His wife Jane ran ARM Disposal UK Ltd. It had been how they had met. It was her father's firm then, and Rosenburg tried to keep work and pleasure strictly separate, but Jane had inherited the firm on the old man's death a few years after they had married. She wasn't great with the paperwork, but she worked hard and kept the business turning over a decent profit.

A lawyer for one of the gang leaders arrested had approached him in the station. They couldn't afford to lose their entire stock, and could he help? The lawyer had traced Jane's maiden name of Friedrich and realised her husband was a detective. He'd taken a gamble approaching him, although simply asking wasn't necessarily criminal without further action.

Rosenburg had fobbed him off initially. He hadn't said no as such, but he certainly hadn't said yes.

He slipped it into conversation with his wife that evening, almost as if it was an inconsequential anecdote. He had waited with bated breath for her response. If she had been shocked and appalled he would have simply agreed with her and dropped it, never to be thought of again.

She hadn't been shocked though. She realised that she was sitting on a gold mine. She couldn't steal every gun. The batch destruction had to be witnessed by law, and her husband wasn't routinely given that duty. She came up with a compromise. In each batch she would remove a few of the weapons, and supply them to the lawyer, who would in turn sell them to his clients.

It was a fairly simple scheme, and it wouldn't make them millionaires by any stretch of the imagination, but it did allow them to live a little beyond their means. With perfect foresight they should have realised that eventually one of the guns would be found by the police and the scheme traced.

The next step would be to ditch the remaining stock quickly, even if it meant actually shredding the weapons. Then they'd choose an office boy to become a patsy, and point the finger at him should the Internal Investigations Unit come knocking. With their mole monitoring the progress reports they'd be informed well in advance if they were going to make a move.

The blaze was enormous. The building caught quickly, with all of the excess junk stored inside helping the fire spread in minutes. Without an alarm or a sprinkler system the fire had a head start before anyone noticed it had started. It was when the fire reached the roof that Joe Public could see there was a problem. A passer-by called 999, and the fire service was on hand less than ten minutes later. It wasn't an unreasonable response time, but the fire had already consumed most of the warehouse and was spreading towards the adjoining buildings. Their efforts were concentrated on preventing damage to those buildings rather than saving the warehouse, as there was little left to save.

By the time the fire had been extinguished it was clear there were lines of extreme heat radiating out from the centre of the blaze. An investigation was started immediately into the cause of the fire, and it was evident that the cause was arson.

The lead investigator, Russell Watts, walked gingerly among the remains.

'Petrol,' he announced, sniffing the charred remains. Chemical analysis would confirm it later, but he was certain.

'What have we here?' he asked no one in particular. A glint of metal had caught his attention. It was sheet metal, and was piled in the centre. It wasn't damaged, although some carbon charring could be seen around the area.

He motioned for his team to come look. With great care they shifted the sheets, only to reveal two bodies underneath. They were cooked thoroughly by the heat, but the injuries Ant had inflicted were still clearly visible.

'Holy Mary, Mother of God!' Russell exclaimed.

'Get away, lads! This is a crime scene.' They retreated from the bodies, and phoned through to the police for back-up.

***

'Something wrong with your food?' Sarah had spent hours preparing his roast dinner. It wasn't easy to find time to prepare something so arduous on a Friday.

'No, dear,' David said glumly.

Sarah looked at him suspiciously. He had spent nearly twenty minutes pushing it around his plate.

He had been listless for a few days, and Sarah suspected that being on desk duty was beginning to wear on him.

'How was work?'

'Good, good.' It was his standard non-response, a hint that he didn't want to talk about it. Sarah wasn't going to let him get away with it that easily.

'Any interesting casework today?' she tried again.

'Not really.'

'For God's sake, David, we've been married for twenty-five years. I know when something is bothering you!' Sarah rarely took the Lord's name in vain, but her patience was frayed.

'I'm not cut out for desk duty,' he said simply. He wasn't good with computers, and typing up incident reports offered no intellectual stimulation. He was being paid an inspector's wage and doing the job of a temp.

'So, take their offer.' It was the first time she had broached the subject of the letter since it had arrived.

'And do what? Sit around and watch the television? Garden?'

'Is that any worse than what you're doing now?' She knew how to manipulate her husband.

'Well, no.'

'Then take the deal.'

'I can't. I'm not ready to be old.' He was in barely into his fifties, but had already started to feel it.

'David, growing old is normal. You've got years ahead of you, but you simply can't be running after criminals all day much longer. Stay home, with me.'

David had begun thinking of a caustic reply as she started that lecture, ready to rant for hours, but his expression softened as he realised that retirement would mean more time for them to spend together. He could fish, cook, read and do all the other things he'd been meaning to do but never found the time for.

'I'll think about it.'

Sarah grinned inwardly. She knew she had him on the ropes, and he'd sign the acceptance note included in the letter in few days. She could afford to wait a week or two; she'd been waiting for almost three decades of marriage.

Chapter 38: Keys to the Castle

A subtle carved sign hung above the entrance to the Internal Investigations Unit: *'Quis custodiet ipsos custodes'*. The unit was the last line of defence in the Met, watching over the guardians that safeguard society to ensure that their work was carried out with due diligence. The Internal Investigations Unit never took chances, preferring caution at every turn. No single person held all the keys to the castle, and so no one could abuse their position within the unit for personal gain.

Every access request on their encrypted computer system was logged, tagged and assigned to an investigation. At one glance an investigator could see who was looking at a jacket, how often, and whether they were involved with the case in any discernible way. The unit had a rigidly enforced policy of Chinese walls. No investigator should ever look at an investigation he was not actively involved in. The system used a flag warning system. If a file was included in a list it shouldn't have been, a small flag was raised. A one-off glance at the index of a jacket would also raise a small flag. Looking at one repeatedly would drop so many flags that the system would raise an alert.

Those alerts then went to the Internal Investigations Unit security officer responsible for enforcing the Chinese wall. When John Friedrich accessed the jacket for Charles Rosenburg the system had flagged it in no time. He was a mere data-entry worker, and had no reason to access active files unless specifically instructed. He wasn't involved in the Rosenburg case, so it came to the attention of the security officer seconds after his first access.

Seeing that he took a break immediately after viewing the illicit data, the security officer had followed him outside, pretending to smoke a cigarette.

He heard the conversation on the phone, and surreptitiously swiped the phone from John's desk when he went back to work. He didn't know who was being called, but he would find out. The boss would threaten John with obstruction of justice, as well as being an accessory to the crimes. There was no way John wouldn't crumble. He was a simple bloke, and wouldn't survive in jail.

***

'No smoke inhalation,' the coroner announced as he walked in.

Charles Rosenburg had never investigated an arson homicide before, and must have looked quizzical because the coroner explained without his even needing to ask.

'It means they were dead before the fire started. The lungs are clean, so they weren't breathing when smoke was in the air.' He spoke slowly, as if explaining something to a child.

'So how did they die?' Rosenburg snapped. He was never patient when he was being patronised.

'Acute blood loss, though the man wasn't in great shape before that. He suffered a pretty thorough beating.' The doc's tone was more conciliatory.

'What happened?'

'Looks like he was whipped, beaten, hung, electrocuted and eventually his throat slit.'

'Fuck. Who'd he piss off?'

'That'd be your job to find out, Inspector.' The coroner grinned. He much preferred the simplicity of the morgue.

'Any hint as to ID?'

'DNA samples have been sent up, but you'll have to get the results yourself.'

'How did she die?'

'Again, blood loss. She took one blow, a knife shoved up through the lungs. It would have collapsed the lungs. A classic stealth takedown. It wasn't needed though; she was wearing a gag, so only the killer could have heard her anyway.'

'So he didn't want to hear her? What about the man?'

'No gag there. Seemed his squeamishness was limited only to the woman.'

'Maybe he knew her, or has woman issues. Time to talk to the head doctor upstairs.'

'My full autopsy report will be on your desk tomorrow morning.'

'Thanks, Doc.'

***

'Dr Jensen?' Rosenburg popped his head around the door to find the doctor dozing in a wing-backed leather chair, a pile of papers scattered across his desk. It looked like Rosenburg wasn't the only one with an excessive caseload.

'What? I was just resting my eyes.' He started to shuffle papers in attempt to feign being organised.

'Relax. Got time for a quick question?'

'Shoot.' Jensen chuckled at his own double entendre.

'Got a double homicide. Killer let the man scream, but prevented the woman from doing so. That strike you as normal?'

'Could be a number of things: difficulty dealing with women, the perception of women as property in need of protection, guilt, rage at the male victim and the need for him to suffer more.'

'What could cause it?'

'Old-fashioned upbringing, elevated hormone levels, post traumatic stress, childhood abuse... Your guess is probably as good as mine without a psych evaluation.'

'So there's a chance he wouldn't be fit to stand trial?' His eyebrows narrowed. The lawyers would jump on it.

'Maybe. Let me have a look at him when you bring him in.'

'Gotta catch the bastard first.'

'Good luck with that.'

The room was cold. John had been asked to join his supervisor in interview suite number one. It was used to conduct interviews for active investigations, and a number of efforts were made to make the subject uncomfortable. Keeping the thermostat down was one of them, and it was working on John. They hadn't told him what they wanted to talk to him about, and he was beginning to stress out.

Despite the frigidity of the room, beads of sweat were beginning to form at his temple. Outside, the security officer was running through what he had witnessed again.

'He dialled from a mobile, but it wasn't a work-issued phone so no tracking that way.'

'Don't worry, it was probably a disposable SIM. You reckon we've let him stew long enough?' The supervisor, Theresa West, jerked a thumb at the one-way mirror between them and John.

'Give him five more minutes. Then he's all yours. I'll be outside if you need me, boss.'

***

'Who'd you call, John?'

'Sorry, what are you talking about?' John feigned ignorance.

'We know you accessed the ARM Disposal jacket.'

'Did I? Must have clicked on the wrong link.' John gulped slightly, the movement of his Adam's apple betraying his nerves.

'Don't think so, John, you spent several minutes on that page. Then you called someone. Who?'

'I must have just left the window open.' This time, it was more of a plea than a defence. He knew they had him.

'John, you're not fooling anyone. Talk now, and all you'll lose is your job. Otherwise I'm arresting you for perverting the course of justice at the least.' The threat was obvious. The charge would be tried on indictment, so John would face anything up to life imprisonment with twelve strangers deciding his fate. The odds were stacked against him.

'I called Rosenburg.'

'Why?'

'His wife is my cousin. She runs the disposal company.'

'How many guns have they faked the destruction of?'

'Hundreds. Not all in one go, but a couple in each consignment. '

'What did they do with them?'

'No idea. Sold them, I assume. Don't know who to.'

'Wait here. I have an idea.' Theresa stood, leaving John where he was. He didn't have much choice but to wait for her to return.

Chapter 39: Honey Trap

The plan was simple. Rosenburg was being watched closely, as was his wife. If he made an early move to the guns they'd simply catch him red-handed and arrest him.

If he didn't then Theresa's plan would come into play. They would use the cousin as a sting by having him offer to help ditch the guns, and then Rosenburg would be arrested in the process.

It didn't take long to set up. John readily agreed to go through with it. They had him bang to rights for perverting the course of justice, and would have added accessory charges to heap on the pressure if needed. It hadn't taken long for him to cave; he was a simple man and not clever enough to even ask for a lawyer. If he had, then the lawyer would almost certainly have put the kibosh on the sting.

He was to be at the ARM Disposal plant at ten that evening. Rosenburg wanted a sentry on the gate as a lookout while he brought the guns back on site from his illicit stash, and once he had he would work the immense shredder the company used to destroy guns. It took a while to fire up, so he would need a large period of time uninterrupted.

The Internal Investigations Unit wanted Rosenburg bang to rights. Anything less and it would probably be swept under the carpet. Rosenburg would simply be fired in light of his service record. Theresa wasn't going to settle for that.

She positioned cameras at the gate to the property. Recording him going in would prevent any argument that the guns were on site, and that the destruction had simply been delayed. Telescopic lenses would catch him as he unloaded them. They would then let him fire up the machine, and wait until he disposed of the first gun. At that point an armed response unit would take him in.

It was a simple plan, and hinged on the guns' not being stored on site already; but Theresa was confident that Rosenburg wouldn't simply leave the guns lying around the property to be found. It wasn't a large building, so it made sense that they would use an external site to hide them. If Theresa had known where it was she might have been tempted to simply stake out the site, but that information wasn't forthcoming.

***

'Surveillance team, in position,' a voice crackled over the radio.

It was ten minutes to ten, and John had been stood at the gates for around ten minutes. Surveillance were in a building a short distance away aiming their lenses through the window. As the lights behind them were out they would be hard to spot even if Rosenburg was looking.

The images they would capture wouldn't be perfect. The distance combined with the low light levels would make for a poor-resolution picture even with high-quality kit. Anything more would be intrusive and obvious though. For the same reason John wasn't wearing a wire, as handy as it would have been.

'Charlie!' John called out as his cousin's wife approached in a pickup. Tarpaulin was stretched taught over the back, secured with nylon cord. Surveillance wouldn't get an image of the guns specifically, but the team waiting to arrest Rosenburg would find the weapons in it later on.

Charles stepped out of the pickup, a bronze key in his left hand. The gates swung open with an almighty creak, and he gestured for John to wait inside while he moved the pickup inside the fence.

Once the pickup was inside, with the rear of the vehicle nearest the door, he stepped out again.

'John. Appreciate the call the other day. I need you to wait with the truck. I'll lock the gates, but if you see so much as a shadow move out there then shout for me.'

'OK. Mind if I wait inside the truck? It's cold out here.' John mock-shivered as he made the request.

Rosenburg shrugged, but tossed him the keys anyway.

He disappeared inside the building with the key to the fence. It didn't matter; the police already had a team inside. They were in the attic, monitoring the building with infrared guns that let them see an outline of a warm body below. Soon, another heat signature appeared as the shredder began to warm up, rows of diamond-tipped teeth whirring at dizzying speed.

It was almost time to make their move. A small camera was aimed at the feeding tube for the shredder, with the feed coming over Bluetooth to their smartphones. Once they saw the first gun go in the shredder there would be an exodus from the attic. It would almost certainly cause a ruckus, but another team would have moved into place outside the building by the time he could react and run.

Rosenburg went back out to the truck, pulled back the tarpaulin and started to unload. With a nod to his lookout, he went back inside with one box. The team watched his heat signature until he reappeared on the camera. When it became evident the box was full of weapons they began to creep towards the attic hatch. It was a pull-down ladder, and as soon as they moved it he would hear them.

Rosenburg had just placed the first few guns in the shredder – only a few at a time to prevent the machine's jamming – when he heard the creak. He knew he wasn't alone, and thanked God he had left a lookout by the truck.

'John! Start the engine!' He paused just long enough to chuck the rest of the box in the shredder. They would take a while for it to churn up into metal dust, but at least it would destroy the evidence.

Seeing the heat signature move, the team sent two men to pursue him out of the building, with the last man dropping behind to stop the shredder and save as much evidence as possible. Rosenburg was quicker than them and jumped into the passenger seat of his getaway vehicle.

'GO!' He screamed. Instead, John hit the driver-side button, locking both doors to the cabin. Charles Rosenburg was going nowhere.

By the time the team inside had caught up with him the team outside was prying Rosenburg off John's limp body. In such cramped confines John took a beating, and was bleeding profusely when the police rescued him.

'Good work, John. Get him to the hospital.'

Teresa turned to the dirty cop in disdain.

'Detective Inspector Rosenburg, you are under arrest. You do not have to say anything, but it may harm your defence if you do not mention when questioned something which you later rely on in court. Anything you do say may be given in evidence.' She had just bagged the biggest collar of her career in the Internal Investigations Unit.

'Spare me.' Rosenburg spat at her feet as a uniform cuffed him. She shoved him roughly into the back of a waiting squad car. Today had been a good day in the fight against police corruption. His wife would be picked up momentarily, and both would be going to jail for a long time.

***

Morton was off duty when his phone beeped. He and Sarah were out having a quiet coffee in Kensington.

It was a text from the duty sergeant: *'Come in to the office. Big news'*.

He showed it to Sarah.

'Go, I've got to get my hair done anyway.' She flicked her hair as she spoke, and David realised she had an ulterior motive in coming out for coffee. It had seemed excessive to spend money on Kensington parking for the sake of a cappuccino. She must have had it booked for weeks.

'Thanks. See you at dinner?'

'Sure, what do you fancy?'

'Steak?' he ventured.

'Again? No. How about Chinese?'

'Yuck. Italian?' It was the old standby.

'Sure thing, Giovanni's at eight.'

He grabbed his coat from the track, drained his coffee cup and left Sarah to finish his lemon slice.

***

'Dave! Wait up!' Alan Sheppard jogged to catch up with Morton as he stepped into the elevator.

'Hey, Al.' Morton's voice was overly chirpy, trying to hide his jealousy that his friend was still actively investigating crimes while he lingered over data-entry work.

'There's something you need to know. I don't know all the details but Charlie Rosenburg has just been nicked. I hear he's been caught flogging seized weapons.'

'Shit. Does the press know yet?' Morton knew better than anyone that there would be a whirlwind of camera vans on site as soon as the press could muster them.

'It's only a matter of time. The whole building seems to know about it already; thought you'd want a heads-up. Anyway, this is my stop.' Alan stepped off the elevator as Morton rode to the sixth-floor briefing room.

As he walked into the briefing room he found out the exact details from WPC Stevenson.

'His wife had inherited an arms company and ran it legitimately for a number of years under her maiden name. A lawyer for the gang he busted with a few hundred weapons approached him seeking their return, having spotted the marital connection. For the six years since, the police have been funnelling the seized guns back to the criminals they were seized from. The lawyer took a cut for organising the sale, but they still cleared thousands.'

'Don't we witness the shredding?' Morton was aghast. He'd confiscated many of those weapons himself.

'Sort of. An officiator sees them start the batch, but they didn't nick the lot. They just keep back a few from each job. I guess it's how they afforded the nice flat with the view of the Thames. I figured they'd just inherited a few bob!'

'Damn. At least we caught it. Bet the press will have a field day. 'Scuse me, I need a word with the Superintendent.'

The Superintendent's office was upstairs, and he had an army of secretaries and support workers guarding the door to his office. Normally it would take at least a week to make an appointment and get past his guardians. Today Morton knew that they'd all be cowering. The Superintendent hated it when the press caught wind of anything negative, and he was liable to yell at anyone who dared enter his lair.

The coast was clear when Morton made it to the top of the stairs. It was six flights up, and he had to pause a moment to catch his breath. A secretary came scuttling past.

'Here to see *him*?' she jerked her head upwards towards the Superindent's office. 'I wouldn't bother today, love.'

Morton rolled his shoulders in a laissez-faire shrug. He wasn't scared of a tongue-lashing. He had nothing to lose by going in there.

'Superintendent?' He rapped smartly on the open door three times in quick succession to announce his presence.

'What?!' he growled. He looked rough, like a man possessed. The arrest had happened late the previous evening, and it didn't look like the Superintendent had slept. His jaw sported a day's growth, giving him a somewhat shady appearance. A press conference was due that afternoon, and he needed to go home and freshen up for the cameras.

'Sir, with Inspector Rosenburg gone the murder investigation team is incredibly shorthanded.'

'You'll have to make do without him, Morton, get back to work.'

'Sir, HR put me on desk duty after I was injured last month.' Morton indicated his leg, where a scar would have been visible had he not been wearing dark trousers.

'Get back to work. I need an experienced hand in charge, and you're it. Tell HR to pull a sergeant if they need someone to work the desks.' With that, the conversation was over. Morton practically skipped as he headed to the Director of Human Resources' office to relay the news. Unsurprisingly he wasn't impressed.

'You aren't fit for duty!' he practically screeched when he heard the order.

'Sorry, sir, but duty calls.' Morton suppressed the grin that wanted to remain plastered across his rugged features.

'Fine, but take WPC Stevenson along with you at all times. No excuses. She sticks on you like a limpet, and if you lose a criminal because you aren't fast enough I'll have your badge, and your pension. Do I make myself clear?' The director's tone suggested the threat was deadly serious.

'Yes, sir!' His hand snapped to his face in a sharp salute. He'd have to sell Sarah on his return to active duty, but then the Superintendent had been most insistent. He was back.

***

His first morning back and his office had already been invaded by the time he had grabbed his morning coffee. A well-dressed gentleman was sat in his chair, his feet up on his desk, well-polished Italian loafers marking the wood. He bolted upright as Morton entered, extending a manicured hand to the Inspector.

'Who are you?' Morton demanded, ignoring the outstretched hand.

'Michael Burrows. Financial Services Authority.'

Morton winced. It explained the suit. The man was probably paid twice as much as him, but still thought of him as a colleague.

'What are you doing abusing my chair?'

'Sorry about that, bad habit. I believe one of your cases may be tied up with one of mine.'

'I doubt it. I'm a murder investigator.'

'I know that. I believe you are investigating the death of a Mr Peter K Sugden. He was found floating in the Thames.'

'That case is closed.' Morton knew that much had changed while he was out of action. He still had a huge number of cases to catch up on, once he had his office back.

'Oh. Well, just to satiate your curiosity I'll tell you anyway. Sugden was under investigation for insider trading.'

'Wasn't curious, and could have guessed as much. You are FSA after all. Now, can I have my office back?' Morton had enough live cases without getting bogged down in the closed ones.

'Don't say I didn't try and be courteous.' The man turned up his nose, grabbed a leather briefcase at his feet that Morton hadn't noticed, and left.

Chapter 40: To Sea

Pierre had seen Barry get on the ferry after him. It was an LD Lines service, and should take a little less than five hours to get to Le Havre. Pierre knew that the kill would take mere minutes, and he wanted to make sure that the execution took place towards the end of the voyage to minimise the chances someone would find the body. He needed to be off the ship by the time that happened.

It was a shame that it was such a small ferry. Barry had not paid the premium for a private cabin, so the possibility of simply killing him there was out of the question. Similarly the cabin Pierre had rented was a no-go as it would lead straight back to him. Instead Barry would need to be ditched somewhere that no one could potentially find him.

Pierre was fortunate that Barry had chosen a place so early to spend the voyage. The Dirty Duck bar had a 24-hour licence, and served alcohol to the many travellers from the moment they disembarked from Portsmouth. Barry had made a beeline straight for the bar, and was quietly sipping a solitary pint washed down with a bag of crisps. It was clear to Pierre that he was trying to keep his outlay down. His clothes were peppered with crumples, and he hadn't shaved for at least a week. The other customers were avoiding sitting too close to him, despite competition for stools at the bar which led Pierre to deduce he probably smelled as bad he looked.

As Barry tucked into his crisps, Pierre took a seat in the back of the mock pub. He was dressed conservatively in chinos and a sweater, and knew he was at home among the middle-class crowds on board that day. Peering over a copy of the *Financial Times*, Pierre surveyed the area. There were cabins nearby, but they were of the shared four-bunk kind. Ditching a body in there would be too risky. He could try and get Barry drunk, and then blame his lack of communication on the alcohol. It would also keep Barry suggestible. The problem was that Barry clearly couldn't afford to get drunk on his own funds, and to buy his drinks would arouse suspicion from the barman.

Pierre would have to resort to his backup plan if he couldn't get him alone. In his pocket was a microscopic vial of taipoxin. Extracted from his personal farm of inland taipan snakes, it was the most easily concealed weapon Pierre owned. It didn't set off alarms, had no odour and was small enough never to be found even during a frisk. It took great personal effort to milk the number of snakes required, and even longer to extract the taipoxin by gel filtering it, and then using a process called electrophoresis to disperse the unnecessary particles in the raw venom. At the dose contained within Pierre's pocket the venom would, within minutes, stop the victim's producing acetylcholine, the neurotransmitter needed to move muscles. In short, the victim's muscles would all cease to function, including his heart.

The plan was pretty simple. As it was a five-hour journey it was likely that Barry would go to use the bathroom. When he did, Pierre would inject him with taipoxin using a needle-free delivery system. A stream of high-pressure liquid would deliver the taipoxin in less than a second, so all Pierre would need to do is brush past him to inject him. He would never see it coming.

It took over an hour before Barry's bladder got the better of him, and when it did it was sudden. He bolted round the corner from the bar for the disabled bathroom, which had been left unlocked.

Pierre didn't follow immediately. Instead he looked in his bag, in which he stored numerous items that might come in handy. One of the items he was carrying was a Radar key that would lock the disabled bathroom door. Pierre slid out of his seat, and stretched languorously before heading towards the corridor. It was empty, and Pierre knew that the moment for him to strike had come.

He waited outside the bathroom, nonchalantly pretending to look out of the porthole at the view. When he heard the door behind him he turned, quickly pulling Barry with his right hand, forcing him back into the bathroom before he could move to go back to the bar. With his left he injected Barry with the taipoxin. Immediately Barry's limbs began to go slack. Even with the best medical care in the world he would never survive now. Pierre cast him to the floor. He wouldn't be able to get up any time soon. He tried to rasp a question.

Pierre leant in to hear him, not fearing a surprise attack as he knew Barry's muscles would not respond to his commands.

'Why?' Barry rasped.

Pierre turned his hands upside down in an 'I don't know' gesture. He had to get away quickly. He applied a line of superglue to the inside of the doorframe, closed the door and locked it with his Radar key. He doubted anyone else on board had one of the keys issued to the disabled, but the line of glue was an extra precaution. Any casual user of the bathroom would simply use another bathroom. By the time Barry was discovered the ship would have pulled into Le Havre.

A few hours later Pierre casually strolled onto the dock, flashed his fake identification and soon found himself once again on familiar French soil.

***

'Damnit!' Morton cursed. He still couldn't sleep. The visit from the berk from the Financial Services Authority had rattled something loose in his brain. He couldn't for the life of him work out what, but his subconscious was on to something, he just knew it. It happened every now and again. His mind stumbled over something, but he couldn't consciously put two and two together, yet.

He had done as he always did when his neurons were on overload, and gently eased out of bed, careful not to disturb Sarah. He'd tiptoed down the hallway to the airing cupboard and dug out an old blanket before trying to get back to sleep on the sofa. Despite his best efforts, his brain wouldn't let him sleep. At half five in the morning he decided that enough was enough. He dressed quickly, grabbed a bagel and headed in to work.

Security was surprised to see him pulling up in his Audi a little after six. It wasn't unheard of for a junior policeman to put in the long hours to try and climb the slippery pole, but Inspector Morton most certainly didn't need to. Sure, he had come in early before when paged, but security got a copy of all page requests to make sure they let them in unhindered.

'Couldn't sleep, Bill. Thought I may as well make myself useful,' Morton said, rolling down his windows as he approached a gate.

'No need to explain yourself to me, boss. You have a good day now.' Bill had a slightly nasal twang, but he was a mild-mannered chap, and had been serving almost as long as Morton.

His Audi A4 parked in the spot marked 'Chief Inspector Morton', he ascended the stairs with a vigour belying his advancing years, and settled himself with a mug of Peruvian coffee and a digestive biscuit.

What he was looking for had to be in the file. It had to be something he'd already read. He read quietly to himself, thinking aloud.

'Mr Peter K Sugden had been found in the Thames, a drowning victim. His body had been tracked back to the point he entered the Thames, where CCTV showed he was thrown in by a man acting in self-defence.'

It was a sparse case summary at best. Morton flicked on his computer monitor, and brought up the electronic case file. The CCTV would be copied there digitally, and he wanted to see how the man had died.

He saw him bumbling down the road towards the camera, before attacking a man who flipped him over the barrier. It was indeed self-defence.

'Holy shit.' Morton spotted the man who he was attacking. It was none other than Barry Fitzgerald. His self-defence death and his person of interest in another death case were linked.

'Shit!' Ant exclaimed. 1332 wasn't the code for the gate. The key looked fine, the logo matched the Kennington branch of the StoreCo building he was outside of, but either he'd been given the wrong code, or the code had been changed since the night of the fire.

He walked away from the gate. It would look odd if he just loitered. He'd have to wait for someone else to come by and simply tailgate them inside. It did mean he'd probably have to come back during a busier period rather than take advantage of the 24/7 access, but it was worth a shot. If the money was worth killing over, it wouldn't be a small sum.

Chapter 41: France

With a scream she let her mop clatter to the floor. Now she knew why the door had been jammed.

'Merde!' the voice of the handyman who had unjammed the door came from behind her. He quickly shooed her away, closed the door and radioed for port security. Then he stood guard by the door to prevent anyone else entering the crime scene. He knew as much from watching crime investigation programs on television. Now all he to do was wait for the gendarmerie.

***

The gendarmerie arrived quickly, and relieved the handyman. A medical examiner was called from the local *institut médico-légal*, the French equivalent of the coroner's office.

'D'origine criminelle?' The gendarmerie demanded to know if it was murder. A shrug was the only response they got. There were no external injuries, but without knowing the dead man's medical history it would be difficult to make a call until laboratory tests had been conducted.

What was obvious was his nationality, as his passport was in his back pocket along with a wallet and a mobile phone. Clearly if it was murder the killer had not deigned to rob him. The British police would be informed of course, and there would undoubtedly be an argument over jurisdiction, but for now the French would begin the investigation into the death of Barry Fitzgerald.

***

The StoreCo had peak traffic at the weekends, with numerous customers coming and going, unloading their wares. It didn't take Ant long to piggyback his way in. All it took was for him to approach another punter, and offer to help them unload their furniture. Job done, he was inside the property and could go in search of locker 146. He had the key, but didn't know how the property was laid out.

After exploring the numbers passed as he helped unload a sofa, Ant noticed that the numbers on the larger storage units he passed were all in single or double digits. Eventually he realised that the smaller units were towards the front of the warehouse. Away from the big yellow-fronted doors of the large units the corridors narrowed. These smaller units were more akin to broom cupboards than the garage-like spaces he had just seen. Instead of a generous loading bay and complimentary forklift truck access, the corridors offered more secure storage. CCTV was obvious throughout the area, and the locker numbers soon ascended above one hundred.

A short way on, locker 146 came into view. It was one of the smallest units, a half-height locker that could fit little in. He leant casually against the wall nearby, fishing in his pocket for the key. The key seemed to fit in, and Ant turned it with bated breath. With a click the lock swung downwards, and Ant was allowed entry to the locker.

'Fuck.'

It was empty.

Chapter 42: Like Old Times

'The body of Barry Fitzgerald, a British man wanted by the Metropolitan Police in conjunction with an active murder investigation, was found today aboard the Nordic Giant, *a ferry on the popular Portsmouth to Le Havre route. The French authorities are stymied as to the method of his death, as the body is in pristine condition and he had no known previous health problems. Our reporter was refused access to the morgue...'*

Edwin felt the weight of the world lift from his shoulders as his eyes traversed the article on page five of *The Impartial*. The last living link to him was gone. It had taken a professional to remove him, but it had been done. The loop of kills wasn't closed yet, but it didn't matter. Edwin was home free.

Edwin was curious as to how Barry had died, but then anyone who read the *Impartial* article would be. No visible signs of trauma, and an otherwise healthy man found dead in a sealed toilet on an international ferry. The press would be running articles speculating for months. They might never know how or why he died.

He would now be able to put in an insurance claim without worrying that the police or the insurance company might flag it up. He was the rightful beneficiary, and the proceeds would clear the mortgage on the house as well as providing a valuable lump sum. Edwin chuckled. It was astonishing to think that Eleanor's prudence in life had essentially provided a bounty on her head. By insuring herself she incentivised him to kill her. The policy would pay out fairly easily. Edwin had already been formally cleared by the police and had a solid alibi, and the policy was mature rather than a recently taken-out policy. It would be a prudent killer who waited over a decade to collect on the life insurance payment. Besides, in Edwin's mind he wasn't claiming money he wasn't entitled to, he was simply expediting the process.

***

The cases just didn't add up. The work Rosenburg had done was by the book, if not particularly imaginative. Barry Fitzgerald was murdered by persons unknown on a ferry leaving the country mere days after a rich banker from the suburbs tried to kill him and fell to his death. The same suspect was wanted in connection with an earlier death of a barmaid from North London.

It just seemed so random. The only clue was the warning from the Financial Services Authority. It had to be about money. No other motive could connect such disparate persons together. If Sugden was involved in insider trading then Fitzgerald had to know about it in order for Sugden to try and kill him. It was logical to assume therefore that the eventual murderer of Mr Barry Fitzgerald was in some way linked to Sugden – perhaps another financier linked to the active FSA investigation – but how did Barry link to Vanhi Deepak? It could be pure coincidence. The evidence against him was purely circumstantial. Then again, he had attempted to flee when Morton had attempted to question him.

Morton shook his head; it was enough to give him a headache. He reached inside his desk and withdrew a packet of morphine tablets. They were supposed to be for his leg, but his head was killing him. It could simply be that Barry assumed the police wanted him in connection not with Miss Deepak, but with the financial crime, in which case his presence in the alley of the One Eyed Dog could be the result of his regular patronage of the establishment. That begged the question of why he thought fleeing the country would assist in evading the Financial Services Authority. The French had confirmed that the body on the ferry was him, so he had to be heading to France to meet someone. What was the connection?

Without more to go on, Morton could only guess. Hopefully the Fitzgerald body would yield some sort of a clue. As the most recent case it was the hottest, the most likely to be solved quickly. The killer's identity wasn't a complete mystery. They were one of the finite number of passengers and crew on board the *Nordic Giant*. There couldn't be that many on board with a link to Peter Sugden or his associates. Perhaps Morton had been rash in dismissing the dandy from the FSA. It might be fruitful to cross reference the passenger manifest with those involved in their investigation.

***

It was a Thursday when the third gold-embossed envelope landed on the doormat of Mrs Sugden.

It was a similar invitation to the first one, but much less formal and far more heartfelt.

'Dear Mrs Sugden,

His Excellency Qadi Qumas and his exalted wife will be holding a dinner party for the village residents the coming Saturday. They would be delighted if you would honour them by agreeing to attend as the guest of honour. They appreciate if you wish to decline, but sincerely hope to see you.

Warmest regards,

Qadi Qumas.'

It wasn't long before his wife turned up to chase the invitation in person. She was deeply concerned at Mrs Sugden's growing isolation. It was, in her opinion, too easy to turn inwards upon the death of a loved one, and by reaching out and offering her support she might be able to help Mrs Sugden at a difficult time. It was hard for Mrs Sugden to decline. The family had been there to support her when her own had not. She had scarcely seen anyone other than her sister, and even then the visits were becoming more fleeting.

Chapter 43: Schengen

Mere moments after stepping foot on French soil Pierre was leaving again. He had left the UK on a French passport identifying him as a 'Guillaume Racine'. The name existed only on that passport, the passenger manifest for the journey, and a prepaid Visa with which he had paid. Both the card and the passport would be shredded shortly.

Pierre was once again within the Schengen Zone, a collection of countries that didn't believe in internal border controls. He would travel freely onwards, through France then Switzerland, Germany, the Netherlands and Denmark. From there his next job awaited in Finland. Not once would he be requested to supply any sort of documentation, although he was in fact carrying yet another set of fake documents just in case. He was now an Italian, Giuseppe Berlingieri.

His appearance would be changed dramatically, his hair shortened and darkened. A few licks of grey would be added around the temples to age him, and his clothes would transform his attire from casual businessman to stylised Italian. Square designer specs and a woollen neck scarf rendered him unrecognisable. The police would look for Guillaume Racine for a while, but when they found no trace of him the case would join the growing mountain of unsolved murders in the European Union. With 490 million people in the EU, hiding in the crowd would be child's play for an experienced professional.

***

The gendarmerie were feeling the heat. The death was, as far as they were concerned, their responsibility to investigate. The ship was flying a French flag, and the body was found in a French port. The problem was they had nothing to go on other than a name. The British were being uncooperative, claiming that jurisdiction should be passed over to them as the deceased was a British citizen and might be related to crimes in the UK that were under active investigation.

Jacques Nazaire didn't care about nautical jurisdiction rules. The gendarmerie only took orders from within the military. If the powers that be wanted to fight it out over jurisdiction he would happily leave them to it. Until then, the case was his and he would treat it like any other case.

The problem was it wasn't just any other case. It was exceptionally rare for a death case to fall to the gendarmerie. If the body had been found outside the port the case would be in the hands of the French police, and they had far more experienced investigators than Jacques.

Jacques had seen more contraband cases than most, but this was a different kettle of fish and he was beginning to feel out of his comfort zone. The visual inspection of the body in the morgue had revealed precisely nothing. Other than being dead the man was in excellent health. It was as if his heart had simply stopped of its own accord. Jacques knew this supposition to be false. Dead men do not seal themselves inside rooms. There was a killer out there, and he intended to catch him.

***

Tempers were riding high. The lawyer from the British Crown Prosecution Service, Kiaran O'Connor, arrived unannounced that morning, demanding to talk to the gendarmerie. Those in charged deemed it prudent not to be rude to him, as much as they wanted the lawyer to leave.

As a compromise, they let him into the port but holed him up in the one building without air conditioning. A sweltering thirty-degree day, it had tempers fraying before an official meeting had even begun.

The argument was, in Jacques' opinion, completely unnecessary. He had been called in by those up the food chain to give evidence why the gendarmerie felt the death was on their turf. The French claim was obvious enough to Jacques. The man died on a ship sailing a French flag, and the body was discovered within French national waters. The ship's CCTV showed he had stayed alive long enough to make it to the bar. The barman corroborated this and estimated he didn't disappear from the bar until at least a couple of hours into the journey, by far long enough to leave British territorial waters.

For Jacques, the question wasn't in which jurisdiction the man died but how best to find his killer. It was more likely the killer was in France than in Britain, given he had to disembark in Le Havre. That meant if the British wanted to arrest him they would have to go through the kerfuffle of obtaining a European Arrest Warrant. Domestic police had no such jurisdictional issues to contend with. The problem was that the French knew little about the man, and it would be difficult to track his killer when there was no forensic evidence, no cause of death and no apparent motive. He hadn't been robbed, he had no known acquaintances on board the ship, and so Jacques was at a loss as to how to begin to investigate.

The British had the fact that he was a British national, and that he had departed from the UK. Kiaran O'Connor was already yelling about their supposed trump card, a domestic provision known as section nine of the Offences Against the Person Act that supposedly gave the UK extra-territorial jurisdiction when a British subject was involved in a murder. Jacques didn't know who would win the legal case. He was happy for both to investigate. It was a shame the British simply wouldn't accept that. They wanted the body shipped back to be dealt with by their own coroner.

Interpol had sent a representative to mediate. Her presence should have diffused the tension in the room somewhat, but it was ultimately only a supervisory role, and the tension could be cut with a knife.

Jacques resolved to say whatever he needed, and get out. It wasn't his job to wrangle over cases. He just investigated them.

***

The blood work came back negative. No foreign bodies, no poison, no drugs. Every drug that the French tested for had been marked 'négatif', except for alcohol, which showed a minimal concentration. He certainly hadn't drunk enough for it to kill him. The medical examiner was stumped.

'Can we not do a more detailed screening?' Jacques asked.

'Yes, but the tests don't just look for everything. We have to know what we're looking for. It's not a common poison, virus, or other such pathogen. That means we're in the territory of neurotransmitters. I don't have the kit to test for that.'

'Who does?'

'Université de Bordeaux.' The medical examiner named one of the most prestigious universities in France for natural sciences.

'Merde.' Jacques knew it would take time to get an external consultation. Maybe the British could help.

Chapter 44: Dishonourable

Yosef's heart pounded as he opened the latest darknet message. It had all seemed so easy when he had agreed to the plan. His son deserved not to have to suffer any more, and if this was how Yosef could alleviate his suffering, then so be it.

That didn't stop his nerves as he read the name and biographical details of the man he was supposed to kill. His hands shook as he copy-pasted the name Jake Randall into Facebook, and brought up a photo. It seemed so personal now that he was looking at the smiling face of his victim. Jake was a lecturer, a bona fide Doctor of Philosophy in International Relations, and an avid member of his local council. Yosef wondered what he had done to deserve death.

He wrenched his eyes away from the screen. He knew he had to memorise that face, lest he kill the wrong person, but to gaze at the bright spectacled green eyes of the man on the screen was to shake Yosef to the core. He believed adamantly in the sanctity of life. As an orthodox Jew there was nothing more precious in his religion. It took his only son's suffering every day with Tay-Sachs to convince him that the rule against killing was not absolute. It was dishonourable to let him live.

The problem for Yosef was that Jake did not have Tay-Sachs. He was an apparently healthy young man, one of God's children whether he knew it or not. Yosef steeled himself, forcing himself to look at the Facebook profile in front of him. If this man had to die to prevent his son's suffering any further, then so be it. He would be Yosef's sacrificial lamb.

***

It took three days for the French to capitulate. They would agree to let the British take a lead role in the investigation into the death of Barry Fitzgerald, including repatriating the body to be examined in London. The gendarmerie would continue to investigate locally, including the hunt for the eventual suspect, but the bulk of the investigative process would fall on the Metropolitan police. Jacques was off the hook, and Detective Chief Inspector David Morton once again had a full caseload to investigate. Blood work samples were already winging their way to the coroner's office, a full battery of exotic tests waiting to be carried out once the samples were in London.

Interpol would supervise, including enforcing open information sharing. Anything the British knew would be passed to the French, and vice versa. If the suspect left France, Interpol would be on hand to rope in any necessary police departments as well as assisting with the procurement, and enforcement, of a European Arrest Warrant should one prove necessary.

Yosef had never travelled south before. He had been a Londoner for a long time, and liked to spend his vacations somewhere hot or exotic. Visiting the southern counties was low on his list of priorities, but this time he had no choice.

The kill had to take place out of London because the intended victim resided in Portsmouth. Yosef wasn't too happy about this, but at a little over sixty miles away from the capital it was about the same in terms of travelling time as crossing the breadth of London by underground. It was certainly quicker than the bus network.

To avoid being too obvious Yosef had taken a National Rail coach to get to his destination. It was cramped, stuffy and uncomfortable, and Yosef's legs did not appreciate being confined in a space that was a few inches smaller than their length. Rather than being direct, the route was most circuitous, visiting a huge number of towns and hamlets before finally setting Yosef down at the hard interchange in Portsmouth.

The target's veneer of respectability would never lead Yosef to suspect it, but the man he was to kill that evening was a drug dealer who had caused a young Anthony Duvall to spend the prime of his life in prison.

He was greeted by a sea of bus stops in front of him, stretching out to every possible destination in the area. Behind him the train station sat, squat and squalid, graffiti tagging evident on almost every surface at hand height. It was clearly a hub for transportation in the region. With train, road and sea links it was an easy place to stage a getaway, as the police would be forced to spread their resources thinly to cover all the bases.

The water churned nearby, a murky brown that lapped against the hull of HMS *Victory*. Above him, the Spinnaker tower loomed, a concrete sail guarding the harbour. It was an unusual sight, and there was something different in every direction that Yosef looked.

His destination was the university at which his target taught. Yosef wanted to get a visual handle on the man, and he knew which building he taught classes in. Unfortunately for Jake his schedule was publicly viewable on the university website, and so Yosef knew exactly where Jake would be at any given time.

It was only a short walk away. Directly down College Road, and to the right, the Mildam building was easy to find. A former navy office, it had become part of the university portfolio long before Jake became first a student, and then a tutor at the institution. It was easy enough to find him, clearly visible through the windowed door at the side of the lecture theatre his next class was being taught in. He was the spitting image of his Facebook persona.

Yosef still didn't have an exact plan as to how to kill the man. He knew the when was certain. It would go down tonight, and he would be back in London before midnight. That gave him a window of a little less than eight hours before he would need to leave the city. The rest of the plan lacked finality.

He could attempt to take him out in the university, but with the foot traffic around the area it would be almost impossible not to be seen. That left accosting him after he finished, which was likely to be around six judging by his rather regular schedule. Traffic would be heavy around then, with commuters leaving the city after work. With the city being on an island it was especially dense in terms of population, and several naval ships were in the harbour. While that was great for covering up Yosef's presence, as he could easily be lost among the crowds, he knew that he couldn't afford to be seen either in person or by CCTV. The population was transient due to the student and naval nature of the city, but they weren't blind. If he attempted anything in broad daylight it would be seen.

It was a dangerous city to attempt anything in. There were few quiet areas, and even fewer areas not covered by the ever-watchful cameras, but Yosef was not just anybody. Before moving to Britain Yosef had been in Shin Bet, the Israeli national body for internal security. While not as famous as its brother agency dealing with intelligence, Mossad, it was just as effectively trained. Yosef had been accepted to both agencies, but it was his preference for avoiding violence that stayed him from joining Mossad. Instead he had taken a role that saw him liaising with foreign security agencies. It was just as demanding, but primarily paper-based rather than field-based. He had still gone through the basic combat training required of all employees, and was therefore more than capable of defending himself, but he was not as bloodthirsty as some of his fellow candidates.

As a disciple of Krav Maga, Yosef was well placed to carry out the hit itself. He had always focussed on training to defend himself, but the techniques he had learned were easily adaptable. Krav Maga taught him to strike hard and fast, targeting exposed areas such as eyes, throat, groin and knee. Yosef would disarm the target by taking out his knees from behind, and end his life with a swift kick to the temple.

Yosef knew that he had to wait until the target went to a less populous area to make his move. He knew from a search of the electoral roll that the target lived in Southsea. Taswell Road was in the residential section, ending in a cul-de-sac. Before that the streets were well lit, and it would be reckless to proceed.

Yosef knew he also couldn't afford to wait too long. The house had a number of occupants according to the electoral roll. Witnesses could easily get him caught, and if they were to actively become involved then he might well be caught quickly. He would therefore have to strike while his target was heading indoors.

A pub less than two minutes' walk away proved the ideal waiting place for Yosef. There were hundreds all over the city, ideal locations to simply bide time. He knew from his instructions the target would take twenty-five minutes or so to walk back after finishing his five-to-six lecture. At 6:20 p.m. his target came into view ambling down Clarendon Road. His demeanour was relaxed, with his hands in his pockets and a slight strut to his step. It was clear he wasn't expecting to be ambushed at any moment.

Yosef waited a little distance away until his target turned off the main road. He then quickly began to close the distance, power-walking rather than running. His target continued to saunter, fishing in his pocket for a key as he turned into his road.

Yosef's step quickened. The gap closed to mere metres, and Yosef made his move.

He kicked out, slamming his foot into the man's right knee. The target's legs gave way underneath him and he fell to the uneven pavement. Yosef's shoes were steel-toe capped, and Jake would not be able to get up quickly.

Struggling to pull himself up he flopped forward, exposing his temple to a blow from the right. Yosef twisted in position, and pulled back his muscled leg, ready to deliver the fatal blow. As Yosef prepared to take a life, his thoughts drifted. Life was too precious. This man wasn't threatening him. Yosef was the aggressor, and the Talmud places a high value on life. It came down to a simple choice: his son, or his faith. Yosef found himself paralysed. He simply couldn't do it. He could not take a man's life, even if it would end his son's suffering.

Snapping out of it, he fled, leaving a dazed and confused Jake sprawled on the pavement more than a little worse for the wear.

Chapter 45: Repatriation

The body arrived back in a plywood coffin. Someone had thoughtfully draped the union flag over it before it had been flown back to London. On arrival the Metropolitan police's in-house chaplain saw fit to give the deceased his last rites. He didn't know whether the dead man had been a practising Christian, so he veered towards the non-denominational. That duty fulfilled, he witnessed the transfer of the corpse to the morgue, ensuring that the chain of custody was rock solid.

The gendarmerie had done most of the work for the coroner's office. A 'T' shaped incision had been made in the body rather than the British 'Y' incision, and the organs had been removed *en lutelle*, where the organs were removed together rather than in groups. It wasn't how the coroner would have done it himself, but the work was certainly proficient, and it had been thoroughly documented on tape.

It did not take long to confirm the initial French finding. The man was, but for being dead, perfectly healthy. The testing that would take place on various samples would be extensive. Blood work would be done of course, with a much-extended battery of tests run to check for foreign particulates. Samples of skin and hair would also be examined. Sometimes trace could be found in the hair long after it had been cleansed from the blood.

The brain had been removed by the French authorities. Their notes suggested that they had observed the brain in situ, but did not spot anything out of the ordinary. The medical examiner did endorse his report to note that brain functions were not his specialism, and if he had retained the case he would have called in a neurologist to inspect the brain. To facilitate that, the brain had been removed and put in a buffered water solution containing 15% formalin that would preserve the brain as well as helping it to retain its original shape, allowing it to be handled for inspection.

No expense would be spared in determining cause of death. The eyes of the international media were now firmly fixed on London, and the heat would continue to build until the manner of death was established.

***

Nothing. Ant had been looking out for a newspaper article to confirm that his hit had taken place as planned for three days. He realised that a run-of-the-mill murder rarely made the national press anymore, but the local press should have picked it up. Nothing had appeared on the Internet news sites, and Ant was beginning to wonder if he had been conned.

He hoped it was simply that the body had yet to be found, but something in his gut told him it wasn't true. He would give it a few days before trying to confirm himself whether Jake was still alive. Hopefully it was simply taking a while for the police to release details to the press.

If he hadn't heard anything inside a week then he would have to take matters into his own hands, and pose as a student on the telephone to determine whether or not Jake was alive.

***

'If I have to take many more samples then we'll run out of blood,' Larry joked. The coroner was a jovial sort. Morton supposed he needed to be to work with the dead all day.

'How many samples have you taken?'

'Dozens. One came back with a result.'

'What was that?' Morton inquired.

The doc spread the reports on his desk, wetting his finger to help him unstick two pages before finding the results he was looking for.

'We found taipoxin.' The doc's face had become ashen as he had read the results. It was a startling transformation. A cherub-like glee had turned sunken in a nanosecond.

'What the hell is that?' Morton's brow creased. He had never heard of taipoxin.

'It's an incredibly rare neurotoxin. I hadn't seen it before but I did some research.' The doc spun around to the desktop computer on one of the few exposed work surfaces in the room, and begun to hit hyperlinks in quick succession.

The screen glowed with reams of information, little of which made much sense to Morton.

'Taipoxin is an acetylcholine inhibitor.'

'Hey, Doc, in English?'

'Acetylcholine is the neurotransmitter the brain uses to tell muscles to move. Without it, muscles don't move. That includes the heart.'

'That'd explain why he appeared to literally just stop breathing then.'

'Yes, as well as why no other symptoms were present. Whoever killed him knew what they were doing.'

'Where would one get taipoxin?'

'You don't get it, you make it. It's made from snake venom, from a particularly rare snake.'

'Which snake?'

'Oxyuranus microlepidotus.'

Morton just looked at him.

'An Australian inland taipan.' The doc looked a tad flustered at having to translate himself.

'I'm guessing those aren't found in pet stores.'

'No. Mostly zoos and the like here in Britain. The snake is the easy part though. Even once you have the snake you still need to milk huge quantities of venom, and then process the venom. You'd then need to filter it using gel filtration. That bit isn't too hard, as long as you have access to a laboratory.'

'Could it be done here?'

'Yes. We'd simply use Sephadex 75.'

'What does that do?'

'It removes certain molecules by weight. In this case, all the bits we wouldn't want in the venom would be taken out and chucked away.'

'Is that it?'

'No. The next and final part is what makes it almost impossible. You'd then need to use column zone electrophoresis.'

'You what?' Morton couldn't even pronounce it.

'You use electricity to sort by ion in an electric field.'

'Try me again.'

'You purify the toxin.'

'So who could do it then, Doc? Am I looking for a mad scientist?' Morton tried to lighten the mood.

'Can't help you there. Good luck.'

It looked like the source of the taipoxin would be the key to nailing the killer.

***

He had waited long enough. Picking up his pay-as-you-go mobile, Ant dialled the switchboard, and made his request to be put through. Moments later Jake answered the phone. He was alive.

Ant rang off. The darknet contact had broken their deal, and failed to deliver. He thrust his fist into the coffee table in anger. He had been duped.

In a fit of rage he almost threw his laptop. Before he did a small voice told him to contact the other party. A simple delay he could live with.

'You haven't carried out your end of the bargain. Why the delay? Let me know new date for delivery.'

He reread his message. It certainly made it plain he wasn't happy, but it fell short of a threat. If the situation wasn't remedied soon, the threats would follow.

Chapter 46: Loose Links

Edwin should have known it wouldn't be that easy.

An invisible hand had Edwin's heart in a vice grip when he saw the darknet message light appear. He had thought it was over. Eleanor was dead, and so were those who knew anything about him.

The problem was one of his contacts had baulked. He had passed on the details of the last kill personally, acting as the connection between the two without either side realising it. Now one of them had failed to carry out their end of the deal, and Ant was demanding the deal be fulfilled.

Edwin debated ignoring it. He could just play ignorant, never check the darknet messages ever again, but there was the most meagre of all chances that Ant would use his darknet details to try and track him. Edwin was perfectly willing to risk that. Indeed, the whole plan had hinged on Edwin's having confidence in his own ability to conceal both his identity and his whereabouts on the network. There was, however, a cleaner solution.

He could simply reply to the message telling him the deal was off, and slip Yosef's details into the equation somewhere. He had enough to identify him, and that way the inevitable backlash would solve a problem rather than creating a new one. It was ruthless, but Edwin had abandoned any semblance of a conscience long ago.

First, though, he would check that it wasn't simply a delay. If so, then he could urge Yosef to advance his plans and fulfil his obligations.

***

Yosef knew that his contact would realise he had not killed Jake eventually. He should never have agreed to take part in any such swap. As much as he wanted to help his son, he believed in the sanctity of life. He could at least be satisfied that, because he was going first in the deal, nobody had lost out. They could both simply walk away, having never committed a crime. All they had done was plan the murders, and as far as Yosef was concerned that was a moral crime for which he could receive redemption.

His reply was simple, and to the point.

'The deal is off. We both walk away, and pretend this exchange of messages never happened.'

It was non-negotiable, but that much was implied. His contact couldn't force him to kill somebody, and as they had lost nothing it was likely they would simply move on to find another prospect. He doubted he was the only one in London who knew how to work a computer and be willing to accept such a deal. All Yosef could do was pray for their souls.

***

London Zoo had two inland taipans. They were the only known examples of the species in the capital. As a potentially lethal animal anyone who wanted to keep them was required by law to obtain a licence to do so under the Dangerous Wild Animals Act 1976. These were granted by the local council to prospective owners after they had proved that they could care for the animal safely and securely. Morton thanked his lucky stars for such bureaucracy. Normally, such rules and layers of red tape were the bane of his existence, but in the Fitzgerald case the snake venom was the only real lead he had to go on. The need for a licence showed how finite a pool of suspects there were for the murder. They had to get the venom from somewhere, after all, and fewer people still would be able to process it properly.

He called out to the WPC who was now acting as his personal assistant.

'Stevenson! Five minutes, we're going to the zoo!'

It was one of the oddest commands that WPC Stevenson had heard in her time at the Met, and she couldn't help but be a wiseass, even though she knew Morton might chew her up for it later.

'OK, Daddy, will you buy me an ice cream?' She smirked, but grabbed the car keys all the same.

It was clear Yosef had no intention of carrying out the hit he had agreed to. Edwin could engage in verbal sparring with him over the darknet, but it would be of no use. It would be far better to let Yosef think he had accepted the withdrawal, and simply pass his details on to Ant. If there was one thing Edwin had learnt as a newspaper editor it was that, when possible, you let someone else deal with your mess. Edwin had never been a fantastic writer, but his ability to delegate was extraordinary.

He knew he would have to slip the information in casually. Not:

'Sorry, couldn't fulfil on time. My kid was in hospital due to his Tay-Sachs. When next? Yosef'

That one message would probably be enough to identify him, but Edwin wanted to string Ant out a bit further. There wasn't much benefit to it, other than gaining him credibility for slipping info in, but Edwin had begun to enjoy the feeling of power that surged through him when he successfully manipulated people.

Chapter 47: Snakes

WPC Stevenson wouldn't stop talking. She had a tendency to babble when excited, and it been non-stop since they got in the car.

'Did you know the reptile house is almost a century old, and it was used to film Harry Potter in?'

Thankfully, it was a short car journey. The keeper in the snake house had readily agreed to talk to them when they had phoned ahead. When they got there, the snakes were waiting, as was the keeper.

'Hi, are you the keeper we spoke to on the phone?' Stevenson opened her mouth before Morton could raise a hand to stay her.

'I'm not a keeper, but yes, we did speak on the phone.' A wry smile appeared on Dr Philippa Aldridge's face.

'If you're not a keeper, what are you then?' It was Morton's turn to seize the lead in the conversation.

'I'm a herpetologist. I study amphibians,' she explained.

'We're investigating a death involving taipoxin. Who could have access to your inland taipans?'

'Anyone with a key to that door.' She pointed at the keeper's entrance allowing access to the rear of the tanks.

'Got a list?'

'Nope, but I can tell you no one's been near these babies but me.' Her voice was strong and confident.

'How's that?'

'Look there.' She was pointing at the corner of the snake habitat. It took a moment for Morton to spot what she was gesturing at. London Zoo had installed web cameras in the cages to help monitor all the animals, as well as provide marketing footage. Anyone who had been in contact with the snakes would have been on the video.

'We're going to have to see the footage,' Morton said calmly. She had just made herself the only viable suspect, and Morton doubted this woman was a deadly killer. He'd check her alibi anyway, but his gut was rarely wrong.

'Sure thing, just talk to our IT department. They keep it for about six months before it gets trashed.'

'Thank you for your time, Dr Aldridge.' Morton nodded respectfully as they made their departure.

***

It was obvious that the contact was a time-waster. Ant had exchanged dozens of messages with him, and he was still no closer to getting the deal upheld. They had agreed that it would be carried out the previous evening, but once again the darknet contact was full of apologies and excuses when Ant confirmed that Jake was still breathing. It simply wouldn't suffice. Ant would have to do it himself. He already had blood on his hands, so the risk of a second life sentence was not much of a deterrent. He'd been in jail already, and he knew that being known as a mass murderer would actually get him respect in the joint. With a reputation for multiple kills the rumours would spread, and no one would dare touch him. He might be back inside, but it wasn't as bad as the general public thought. He could even do a degree for free, when on the outside he'd be charged nearly nine large per year. Ant chuckled; so much for its being a punishment.

A decent lawyer and he might even get away with it. He could act crazy if it would see him walk away scot-free. It was time for Ant to take matters into his own hands.

***

Morton's hunch was on the money. The herpetologist was clean. No one else had been near the snakes, and she hadn't been on the ferry. It was possible she'd milked the snakes and sold the venom, but her lifestyle was modest and nothing in her financials suggested such impropriety.

The IT techs said the video file was clean too, so Morton could rule out tampering there to cover up illicit access. That left three categories for possible access to the snakes: other licensed dealers outside London but in the UK such as other zoos, unlicensed owners, or foreign import. The research said that the venom remained viable for a considerable period after it was milked, and with proper storage it was perfectly possible that access had happened months ago, or that the venom was shipped in. It was the only angle that the police had to pursue on the forensic front, but it was beginning to look like a dead end.

Morton sighed. It looked like the investigation would need to delve more deeply into the victim's past, which he knew was tied up with the previous attack by the late Peter K Sugden. He suspected that the whole thing might be a tangled web of insider trading, but he just couldn't find the right thread to pull to start unravelling the mystery. It pained Morton, but it was time to swallow his pride, and go talk to the dandy from the FSA.

***

To get the job done properly, Ant knew he would have to do it himself, and he firmly believed that there was no point putting off until tomorrow that which could be done today. His plan was already coming together. This time, it would be fatal. The kill would take place in another city, and he hadn't had contact with the victim in a long time.

He had been careful to avoid the obvious trap of exacting revenge within a short period after his release from prison. He would have liked nothing more, but it would have been extremely obvious, and almost certainly have required him to break the conditions of his parole.

Ant knew he had a significant height advantage over his intended victim, but he would be recognised if Jake spotted him, so he would have to move with considerable stealth. He would hire a car on Saturday, and drive it to Southampton airport ostensibly for a holiday. There, it would be returned to the vehicle hire company. The last leg of the journey would be done by train. It wasn't quite a direct route, but he intended to stay in Southampton in the evening to provide something of an alibi.

Tickets for a gig he had no intention of going to were primed and ready in his wallet. A copy of the band's latest album was on his MP3 player, so if he was questioned he could answer general questions without any cause for concern. The venue he had chosen was an old-fashioned one. The newer gig venues used electronic tickets, and would flag the fact he never went.

In reality he intended to place a small explosive inside Jake's car. The device would be simple in the extreme. A radio switch would be placed inside his petrol tank that would create a spark, exploding the car from the inside out. The range of the switch would be limited to around a metre, and the activation key would be receiving a mobile phone text. Given that he parked on the driveway at his home, the odds that someone other than him would be that close at the time of receiving a text would be minimal. Assuming that the tank was full it would create an explosion encompassing around fifteen feet, with the car chassis acting as shrapnel.

Chapter 48: The Colonnade

The office was among the highest in the building. With views out over Canary Wharf, 25 The Colonnade was a building that any bank would be proud to inhabit. Instead it was home to a government regulator, the Financial Services Authority.

Morton, with WPC Stevenson in tow, had easily cleared security and they were now faced with a heavy oak door leading to a corner office on the eleventh floor. Morton rapped loudly on the door, and proceeded to open it.

'Mr Burrows?'

'My my, Detective Chief Inspector Morton. How the mighty have fallen, eh?' Michael Burrows was as obnoxious as Morton remembered him being the first time they had met, when he had found Burrows sat in his office, feet on his desk. It was unlikely the two men would ever be more than cordial to each other after such an aggressive first meeting.

'Mr Burrows, I need to ask you a few questions.' Morton tried to avoid a churlish response.

'Fine, what do you want?' He snapped his laptop lid down, and turned his attention to the two police officers now occupying his office.

'Your investigation into Mr Sugden. What evidence did you have that he was involved in insider trading?'

Burrows sighed, buzzed his secretary to bring in three coffees, and settled in for the long haul.

'All stock trades are now electronic. One trader posts an offer to buy, another to sell, and the system matches the offers. Most professionals make a reasonable sum of money, but Sugden, among others, was consistently buying bull stock right before big news was announced, as well as going bear on stocks before losses came to light.'

'Bull and bear?'

'Bull stocks are those on the up, so you want to buy them. Bear are those that are about to crash, so you want to sell, or even short them.'

'OK, and Sugden was right too often?'

'A certain amount of it can be attributed to market rumours. Most traders live by how much confidence they think the market has in a stock. It's often more about the perception of a stock's value than how much it is really worth. The problem is that Sugden wasn't going by the rumour mill. Several times in the last year stocks have been rumoured about to crash, and instead of selling like everyone else Sugden would buy the stocks everyone was offloading on the cheap. The news would then turn out to be false, and Sugden would double his money in a single morning. As a one-off, it might be lauded, but his group consistently made huge amounts.'

'How did he find out about the stocks?' Stevenson chipped in.

'We can only speculate.'

'What's your best guess?' Morton asked as the coffee arrived. He declined sugar as Burrows stirred three into his coffee, black.

'Come with me.' Burrows rose, striding quickly for the door. Slightly perplexed, the investigators tailed him, curious expressions splashed across their faces.

He led them into a larger room, with a conference table in the middle and a number of charts, documents and photos on displays down the length of the wall. It was eerily reminiscent of the police squad room when everyone was roped into a particularly intriguing case.

Burrows gestured at a collection of photographs near one end.

'These gentlemen have all appeared on our radar after making gains that would be hard to explain by mere luck. They all make losses, but those losses are without exception far smaller than the gargantuan gains they make. All the men are connected personally, even if only remotely. Several of them are linked by alma mater, professional training, place of birth and past employment. The connections are slim at best and don't appear to point to a cohesive group. Their market positions, however, almost always coincide, even when the general market opinion is against them.'

'So you think they are working together?'

'Yes. Between them they seem to have developed an extensive collective network, one that would explain how they are getting their information.'

'I'm sensing a "but" in there?' Morton smiled mirthlessly.

'Yes. The "but" in the equation is: I can't for the life of me work out how they are communicating. No letters, texts, calls, emails, couriered messages or in-person meetings have taken place. I have extensive surveillance on all of them, and my agents have seen nothing.'

'Doesn't sound like you've got much to go on. I guess we're on our own.'

***

The journey took Ant longer than he expected. It was nearing nightfall when he made it into Portsmouth. His jury-rigged device was safe inside a backpack. Without the petrol inside the car, it posed no threat. A jiggler key rounded out the required kit, and was tucked safely inside a pocket, hidden from prying eyes. Jake's car was an older-style Fiat, and getting into the fuel cap would be fairly trivial. By bumping the inside of a tumbler lock Ant could force the pins up above the lock for a fraction of a second. If done while nudging the jiggler forward and turning, it would allow the cap to be opened without the proper key. It was an old lag's trick, and Ant had heard about it many times while in prison. It wasn't something he had much experience in doing, but he had practised on his own car, and was confident that he could open the cap inside thirty seconds flat.

The plan was to wait for dark before making his move. He would need a full two minutes to get to the car, open the cap and get out without being seen. Daylight would put him in plain view, and while the house was at the end of a cul-de-sac, there was the possibility that there would be neighbours around that could spot the movement.

Google Street View had shown Ant that a solitary street lamp lit the road in the evening, and Ant guessed it would kick in around six. On a Wednesday night Ant was fairly certain that footfall would drop to zero after around ten o'clock. There would likely be a few students in the various pubs in the area, but Taswell Road wasn't on any of the major routes, and few lived there. The houses were largely recessed from the road, fences and hedges obscuring the driveways from view.

At eleven o'clock, Ant made his way to the street. A few drunks could be seen near the Taswell Arms pub. The road was laid out as an inverted T section, with one side running north-south, and the bottom of the T containing the target house. The north of the cul-de-sac was a school, and the CCTV on the gates would cover part of the pavement on that side of the road.

Ant was careful to stick to the south side of the road, avoiding the ever-watchful cameras. No one was in sight, and he passed into the driveway of Jake's home without being challenged. A crackle rang out in the darkness, somewhere nearby, and Ant drew closer to the wall for cover, holding his breath to ensure silence. Thirty seconds passed, and he heard nothing. By the one-minute mark his blood was pumping, beginning to pound in his ears, and a sharp intake of breath ensued as his lungs screamed out for air. He didn't know how long passed before he allowed himself to move again, his muscles a little stiffer for the experience.

He slowly inched towards the fuel cap. It was at the back right of the car, close to the house. If anyone inside went past the bay window that guarded the lounge he would be caught. Moving quickly he jiggled the lock. A forensic examination would show that the lock had been bumped, but Ant was confident that the explosion would destroy all the evidence.

With a wrench the fuel cap came off in his hand. He delved inside the bag at his feet, and pulled out the device. He had balled up the device his Irish cellmate had taught him to build. He had tied one end to a short length of string. He held the string, then lowered it in carefully, listening out for the splash that would indicate he had gone too far. The device needed to be near the petrol, but not in it as only the fumes could be lit from the spark. If the device were to become submerged, it would fail. He taped it off inside the fuel cap, and replaced the cap to conceal his treachery.

He rose slowly to avoid making any further noise and lifted his bag gently onto his back. It was now redundant, and he would dump it somewhere before returning to London in case the police traced him by CCTV – a man with a bag would be seen far more easily than one without. He moved on the balls of his feet, scarpering out of the driveway and doubling back along the road away from the house.

He debated finding a 24-hour bar to wait out the night, but a lone drinker arriving near the witching hour would be remembered, and the explosion was bound to make the national media sit up and take notice. Instead he would sleep on the seafront. It was quiet, and he knew that the many benches would be a magnet for the homeless. He could easily kill time there before catching a cab in the morning.

***

As the sun rose over the ocean, Ant realised that he was exposed. He had not expected to fall asleep on the hard bench, and to regain consciousness as early morning runners jogged by was disconcerting. He had to get out of Portsmouth before he was seen. He made his way to the train station. He could have simply taken a train, but the police would be bound to look at the CCTV covering those leaving the city in the wake of an explosion.

Instead, his destination was the nearby taxi rank. With the air of someone in a hurry he demanded to be taken to Petersfield. It was a regional trading hub, and he knew it would be easy to get onwards passage there via train back to London. As his taxi pulled into the market town, Ant sent a text to Jake's phone which set off the receiver in his car. The resulting explosion engulfed the car in a ball of flames that blew out the windows of his house, scattering metal and glass over a fifteen yard radius.

Chapter 49: Panic

Half the city had been cordoned off by the police. They had no idea whether or not it was an isolated incident, and they were taking no chances. The road was photographed from every angle, with every shard, fragment and remnant being bagged and tagged. The forensic evidence would be so extensive that the regional processing centre used by the Hampshire Constabulary would be backed up for weeks. The point of origin was discovered in little time. All the damage radiated out from the car parked in front of 2 Taswell Street.

'It was a miracle that there was only one casualty,' Detective Inspector Brown said to the group assembled as they broke for a quick coffee, and a chance to survey the scene.

'Yes, sir. Plenty of property damage though. Must be a few million quid in damage,' one of Brown's junior officers chipped in.

'True enough, but the insurance companies will put that right.' Brown was unconcerned with the smashed windows and scratched cars.

'You think it was Al Qaeda?' a crime scene tech ventured.

'If I hear any of you say that near the press, you'll be fired. No one here is to use the term terrorist. Do I make myself clear?' Brown glared at them.

They nodded quickly, knowing they'd simply wait until he was gone before they finished their conversation.

'Right, back to work.'

There was one victim, the driver of the car. His body was better preserved than Brown had expected. Rather than the complete immolation he had expected from an explosion, the body was remarkably well preserved. The fireball had not been hot enough or long enough to incinerate the remains. Forensics had explained that the concussive force was minimal for an explosion, and that it was safe to rule out any controlled substance being used to fuel the explosion. It was simply the petrol tank exploding.

Brown knelt near the car. There wasn't much left of whatever trigger had been used to set off the explosion. The shrapnel fragments would have to be sorted by hand for any evidence of the requisite electronics, but it would take a while to collect all visible evidence. Until that had been done the search for the trigger couldn't begin.

CCTV was being analysed by the audio-visual department, but coverage on the Portsea peninsula was spotty at best, with most of the coverage focussing on the tourist areas such as Gunwharf and the Historic Dockyards. Most of the other shops carried their own cameras, but in the residential areas the blanket ceased and a few cameras were dotted around the major throughways.

The work was being hindered by the media. Minutes after the emergency services were called they began to converge on the scene. Roads that would normally flow freely were being clogged with journalists, and camera crews. Combined with the road closures the police instituted near possible targets for attack such as the Guildhall, the city was at a standstill. Even the Navy had the good sense to remain on base with tightened security checks on the entrance.

Every officer on the force was under strict order to only reply with 'no comment', yet the journalists were getting some of the information anyway.

Inspector Brown knew he would have to call a press conference sooner rather than later to address the public's concern. They deserved to know the truth, but at the same time the last thing he needed was to incite public panic. Before that happened he had been asked to meet with an Executive Liaison Group from MI5. It probably wasn't a terrorist organisation. None had claimed responsibility yet. Nonetheless, they couldn't afford to risk it, and it would be actively pursued as a possibility.

For now, the police would have to follow up on the bomb, and hope that something could be seen on the CCTV.

***

Grim satisfaction resonated through Ant as he saw the aftermath of his handiwork on television. The road had been devastated, bits of car and masonry scattered over the street. He was glad no one else had been hurt. His anger was great, but it was directed only at the man who had caused him to wind up in prison. He had extracted his revenge. The talking heads on television were haring off in the wrong direction. More than one had been quick to attribute the blame to Al Qaeda, despite a denial being issued by their spokesperson through Al-Jazeera. Ant didn't mind; the speculation was fuelled by ignorance, and the more he heard about terrorist groups the further away from the truth the police had become. The device might give them some hints, but even it was a design he had stolen from a former cellmate who had attempted to use it during the Troubles.

He knew that there was a danger he would become overconfident. He had killed two people, and so far the police were none the wiser. There was one more death that he had to bring about, the man who set him up to carry out the first kill but reneged on the deal. He had enough information to piece together who he was. Now all he needed to do was find out where he went and when. With that information he could begin to form his plan, and then revenge would be his.

Chapter 50: Implications

Edwin felt smug. He knew he'd layered just enough information into the darknet exchange to implicate Yosef. Neither of them had any idea he was involved as they both believed they were dealing directly with the other. Yosef didn't deserve to die. He wasn't the one who had benefited from the kill Ant carried out, but Ant didn't know that. By giving Ant the chance to take it out on Yosef he removed the chance that someone with knowledge of the darknet would try and hunt him down. Eleanor was long since dead and buried, and the police were still nowhere near finding out what had happened.

He knew that the pile of carcasses on his conscience had grown steadily since then, but he had no personal connection with any of them. He hadn't so much as seen them, so it was easy for him to rationalise them as just numbers. It was the same way he felt when he first read of the tsunami that had killed 1.7 million people back in 2004. He knew that it was a devastating loss of life, and that every victim would be mourned by someone, but without a face to put to each number it was easy to disassociate the deaths from his actions.

Knocking back a whisky, Edwin toasted his freedom.

***

Ant didn't bother planning his last kill. He knew the man couldn't carry out a hit, so he certainly couldn't pose a threat to a hardened lag like Ant. He knew the man had a child with a rare illness, which meant he probably spent a lot of time at Guy's Hospital in Southwark, as it was the only hospital in the capital to deal with Tay-Sachs children. He knew he was looking for a Jewish gentleman, and he knew his first name.

Finding out who his son was had required him to be bold, but had worked like a dream. He walked into the hospital, and asked the nurse which room Yosef's son was in, holding an armful of toys. The nurse immediately showed him to the private room that Zachariah occupied. Surreptitiously glancing at his charts gave him a surname, Gershwin. He thanked the nurse for her help, and made a hasty retreat. He now had all the information he needed.

***

Inspector Brown was being stonewalled. The 'liaison' group had seized a great deal of evidence in the name of national security, and the police were in the dark. CCTV had shown nothing. With over 200,000 people milling around an island city it was impossible to keep track of just one individual. Per square mile Inspector Brown had responsibility for more people than London, and when cases like this came along his department was overstretched.

A backlog of forensics was being examined, and in the three days since the explosion the debris had been sorted according to source. This was mainly done by visual inspection. Glass was separated from metal from plastic, and placed into mountains of evidence. Each piece over an inch long was individually logged and numbered, with the position at the scene noted carefully. 360-degree imagery allowed Brown to explore the crime scene as it was on arrival, but the resolution left something to be desired.

The team were still looking for traces of electronic debris in a bid to find something that could identify the bomber. The problem was that it was at the epicentre of the blast, and was likely to have been melted by the heat. Brown also feared that the electronics from the car itself would contaminate anything found, and render it worthless as a means to trace the bomber.

Instead of focussing on the slim chance of finding something forensically significant he had been homing in on the life of the victim. Four people shared the house which was bombed, and the car was used by just one of them. Brown had assigned deputies to investigate all four, but his personal hunch was that the bomb had hit its mark when Jake Randall had died in the blast.

Mr Randall was a lecturer in international relations at the university, and outside his housemates and students he appeared to have a fairly closed social group. It would be somewhere to start, even if unlikely to be fruitful. Even if the university proved a dead end it would beat sitting around waiting for forensics to come up trumps.

Ant lay in wait on a dark street near Guy's. He knew Yosef drove to the hospital after watching him leave his son's bedside the previous evening. Finding the car again took some time, as there were no car parks in the area, and with London congestion it was impossible to park in the same place twice. Yosef was clearly affluent though, as the car was a new-model BMW. It wasn't brand new, but at barely eighteen months old it would still cost a pretty penny.

He found the vehicle parked near Vinegar Yard, a short walk east of the hospital, and far enough away from London Bridge Station to have lower footfall. On foot, the quickest way to it was to take Melior Street straight from Guy's and cut down an alleyway.

He debated breaking into the car and hiding inside, but it would increase the odds of his being seen. It seemed like he was loitering for an age when Yosef appeared. When he walked past, Ant waited a moment before following. He reached his BMW around thirty seconds before Ant got there and there were simply too many watching for Ant to be able to make his move. Mr Gershwin would survive that evening, but it was only a temporary reprieve.

***

Morton could see what the FSA meant. He'd done his own research on the individuals Burrows had pointed the finger at. It was a loose collection, and he wondered if Burrows was clutching at straws trying to find a connection. Thirty individuals could be found who had made vastly more than their peers. Much of the work in the investigation had already been done by journalists astounded at the profits. Morton doubted he and WPC Stevenson would be able to dig anything more up, at least not without alerting them to the investigation, and he knew Burrows wanted to keep it hush-hush to avoid ruling out a sting.

The links the media had highlighted were spurious at best. Two had gone to the same school. Another pair shared the same golf club. Three more graduated from Oxford together. All of the links were of the same ilk, connecting together small subgroups, but nothing suggested that they were all linked. Burrows' own case file that he had sent over unabridged ran to hundreds of pages including detailed surveillance work, and not once had all of the suspects met, or communicated in any way known to the FSA.

Feeling a migraine come over him as he pored over dozens of financial statements, Morton shouted for WPC Debra Stevenson.

'Debs, be a doll and get me two aspirin, would you?' He grinned, knowing she hated to be called doll.

'Get it yourself!' She turned to go.

'C'mon, doll, my leg.' He gestured at the scar left by his previous encounter with Barry Fitzgerald, and suppressed a wry grin. He knew he had her over a barrel.

'Fine, but I'm telling Sarah.' She pulled out the ultimate threat, telling his wife. Morton knew it had been a mistake to let them meet at a police function the previous Christmas. He was normally savvy enough to skip work socials, or at least leave Sarah at home. She didn't do much for his macho image, as she loved to tell embarrassing stories, even from decades ago. She took after her mother that way.

Morton mimed having been shot in the head as Debra went to fetch his coffee.

Chapter 51: Marylebone

The failed attempt had forced Ant back to the drawing board. Now that he had followed Josef once, there was a chance that he would recognise Ant the next time, and be on guard. Ant hadn't planned for that, and knew that he needed to follow through the second time because there might not be a third opportunity.

Extensive web searches helped pinpoint Gershwin's workplace. He was an architect based at Greagor, Gershwin and Hopkins LLP in Palgrave Gardens. A Marylebone firm, their offices overlooked the railway leading out of the station of Monopoly board fame. It was a noisy area, particularly during peak commuting times, and Ant knew that he could simply shift his plan's location but leave it otherwise unchanged. The obvious place to attempt to extract revenge would be the firm's car park, which appeared to be in the basement. If he could get in there then the odds of a witness would be greatly diminished, as it was fairly private.

The danger this time would be coworkers using the same car park. If one saw him he'd be rumbled. He'd also have to avoid any internal CCTV, and manage to sneak into the car park without being seen. It was a tall order, but not impossible. The car park had one entrance for cars that came up on the road, and was just about wide enough to allow one car in and one out at the same time. Barriers were used to prevent unauthorised entry, but a pedestrian could easily duck under, or climb over those.

The issue was the CCTV. The entrance was bound to be covered, and it would be even harder to obtain access through the building's internal lift as he would certainly be seen trying to go through reception.

A disguise would be the only way to go in unnoticed. In London maintenance men were virtually invisible. Jeans, a blue shirt and a tool kit would open more doors than trying to pretend to work there. A suit that wasn't a regular would be greeted, asked questions of, and remembered even if the individual encountered didn't call security. A man repainting a few lines on the floor had an excellent excuse to loiter for hours, slowly repainting the demarcation lines of the parking spaces. If he was challenged he'd simply say the landlord sent him. With several floors, and different leaseholders on each, they would all assume that one of the other tenants had hired him, and leave him be with minimal questioning.

It also gave him a great excuse to carry a makeshift weapon. A wrench would be an easy way to clobber Yosef Gershwin, and he could always pop the wrench back in the tool kit to carry it out of there unnoticed. By the time anyone realised malfeasance had taken place, he would be long gone.

***

His attire was almost that of the archetypal handyman. A waterproof beanie obscured his brow to help prevent identification, and a bulky toolset around the waist made him appear far more rotund than he was in reality. This was reinforced by baggy jeans, and a dark blue work shirt that was so fungible it could have been worn by anyone. He wore a ratty grey jacket over the top to add pocket space to his attire. A large blue toolbox rounded off the look, bought that morning from a charity shop in Wimbledon. Even the boots were as mass-market as they could be, and the newness would mean that the soles had not had time to wear, so any footprint impressions would be rendered virtually useless.

He had a tin of paint in the opposing hand to the toolbox, and was carrying a small brush to repaint the four-inch lines in the car park. He aimed to get to the car park at half four. Much later than that and he would be cutting it too fine, not to mention it would be odd seeing a handyman start so late in the day. He knew his target would want to get to Guy's Hospital after work, and the visiting hours in his son's ward began at six and ended at eight. It was likely therefore that he would make an appearance between half past five, and quarter to six.

By the time 5.30 p.m. rolled around Ant had repainted almost sixty of the hundred or so spaces in the car park. His work had been surprisingly neat. He knew that diligence would let him work without being accosted, whereas sloppy lines would garner attention.

He didn't have to wait much longer, as his target emerged from the lift at 5.34 p.m. The problem was that he was not alone. He stopped to talk to the other man beside his car, and Ant began to tense, knowing what he had to do. He kept his head down, watching the pair out of the corner of his eye. They were over fifty feet away, and so far Yosef had not recognised Ant from their brief encounter near the hospital.

The pair broke apart with a handshake, with the stranger getting into his car. Ant knew the timing would be tight. He needed the potential witness to leave, but Yosef to remain behind. He was a few feet from Yosef's car, and began to redo the line adjacent to it. As Yosef strolled over he realised that the car would have to be reversed carefully to avoid getting paint on his tyres.

'What are you doing? Get that paint away from my alloys!' Yosef's tone was haggard, as if he had had a particularly arduous day.

'Jus' paintin'.' Ant replied, his voice thick and nasal. He played up the idiotic handyman stereotype. He needed to buy time.

'Well, stop.'

'No can do, suh. I got me deadlines.' Each syllable was slow and deliberate. As he finished talking the first man's car left the parking lot. It was now or never.

'Hurry up and get out of my bloody way.' Yosef tone turned aggressive, the weariness from before melting in an instant.

Ant seized his toolbox with his left hand, putting the paint brush in as if to comply. He stood slowly, with his back to Yosef. The wrench fit snugly in the pit of an elbow as he held his arm to his chest to conceal it. He placed the right hand on one end, and turned quickly, lunging at Yosef.

Yosef reacted far quicker than he expected, seizing his wrist, and bringing a knee up to his groin. He doubled over, briefly wracked with pain as a throbbing sensation emanated from the hit. With a howl of pain he charged forward, knocking Yosef to the floor. His wrench lay abandoned on the floor a few feet behind him, dropped during the struggle. Yosef went for his eyes, attempting a quick jab that Ant narrowly dodged before rolling to his side and straightening up.

Yosef tensed, one foot in front of the other in a stance Ant didn't recognise. In full bloodlust, he charged, right fisted cocked behind him. As the blow landed Yosef turned his cheek, diffusing the force of the throw. Ant yelped. He had broken one of the cardinal rules of hitting someone. Jaws break fingers, not the other way around.

Blood oozed from his fingers as he considered his next move. Realising that he couldn't win hand-to-hand he dove for the wrench. Picking it up he spun on his right heel, swinging the tool violently. He caught Yosef's arm, sending him crumpling to the floor. Yosef tried to kick out as Ant advanced, but this time he was ready and deftly sidestepped. Seconds later he crushed Yosef's skull with one powerful blow, the weight of his body behind the blow. Yosef's body went into spasm then fell still.

He was dead.

Ant turned to flee, his bloodied hand tucked up inside his jacket pocket. The paint can lay abandoned. With one good hand he had to make a choice between it and the toolbox. He gave the paint can a quick wipe with his shirt to remove any fingerprints, and fled.

Chapter 52: Devastation

Forensics had finally sorted all the debris collected on site, and were slowly processing it all. Plastics, glass and organics had been ignored temporarily to focus on the metal shrapnel, as it would be the only source of clues as to what kind of trigger had been used, and whom by.

Several fused chunks of electronics were found, but a great deal of heat had been applied to them during the explosion. Where the victim had been shielded by the metal bodywork of the car, the electronics inside the petrol tank had not been so fortunate. While that did make it easy to distinguish between the electronics used in the bomb, which were worst hit, and the electronics in the car itself such as the CD player, which were shielded by the other components, it did mean the evidence had been irreversibly damaged.

At the most basic level the device appeared to be a circuit board for receiving radio signals, connected to an even smaller device that generated the killer spark. It was likely the receiver had been salvaged from a cheap mobile. A basic GSM 900 mobile would have been perfect for the job as it would only receive signals in one radio frequency band, and not be set off accidentally by a television or radio signal, which operates at lower frequencies than the mobile phone network.

'Could the bomber have simply set it off by text?' Brown asked the tech showing him the remains.

'Yes, sir, perfectly possible.'

'But then he'd need line of sight in order to target the timing of the explosion.'

'If he had a specific target in mind, then yes, sir.'

'You think it wasn't deliberate? That the bomber just picked a random house and rigged their car to explode?'

'Possibly but not necessarily sir. It could have been a signal, a warning shot, not intended to kill. Or it could have been an attempt to kill any one of those living with Mr Jake Randall.'

'Hmm. I can't rule it out, but my gut says if you just wanted to send a signal then you would simply use a timer. It's much quicker and easier. Salvaging the circuits for a remote activation takes a fair amount of effort, even if it isn't all that complicated.'

'You're the Inspector, sir.'

Inspector Brown glowered at him. He hated the passive-aggressive types that he often dealt with in the lab.

'If you've got something to say, say it. No? I thought not.' With that, he left the tech to sort through the rubble, and went back to his office to collect his thoughts.

***

Nurse Jayne Milligan was desperate to get through.

'Come on, come on. Pick up!' She urged the phone. It was no use; the number kept ringing off to voicemail after eight rings. She shook her head in dismay. At this rate she'd simply have to leave a voicemail. The mobile number wasn't getting through either, and come to think of it she hadn't seen Mr Gershwin for a while. It wasn't unusual for her to miss a patient's visitors though. Guy's worked on a rota basis, so she was often working at different times each week.

She sighed, resigning herself to conveying bad news by voicemail. Dialling through one more time, she waited for the obnoxious voice mail message begging her to leave a message. The tone beeped, and Jayne began to speak. She knew she had to keep the message short and professional.

'Mr Gershwin, Jayne Milligan here from Guy's Hospital. Your son's condition has deteriorated. Please come in, or call me back at your earliest convenience.'

She wanted to say more. Yosef wasn't just the father of one of her patients; she had begun to get to know him over a number of cups of tea while he sat at Zachariah's bedside over the past four years. Hospital policy, however, had other ideas. It was against departmental rules to give out details on the phone, both because of data protection concerns and to prevent the parent becoming panicked. Thus Jayne was constrained to using catch-all terms like 'deteriorated' when in reality the situation was much more dire.

Zachariah had suffered with recurrent infections since birth, a complication of being a Tay-Sachs child. For the most part these had been treated with simple antibiotics, albeit at a dose much greater than that usually wielded by general practitioners. The problem with long-term use was that the body built up a tolerance to the antibiotics, necessitating ever-greater concentrations be used.

The most recent infection was mastoiditis. Jayne read from the chart, trying to work out when his next dose was due.

'Looks like you had one dose after your headache this morning.' The boy couldn't hear her. The Tay-Sachs had already rendered him almost deaf, and it was because of this that they missed the first major warning sign of mastoiditis, hearing loss. Without the warning signs the infection had advanced unchecked. Complications had arisen before treatment had even begun, with an epidural abscess arising first.

They needed consent to insert a catheter into the epidural space to drain the pus, but without contacting Yosef they would be unable to proceed unless the procedure became necessary to prevent loss of life. Jayne's hands were tied. She could only act once it was established the treatment was vital, and it would be unsafe to wait for consent, but at the moment Zachariah was stable. He wouldn't remain that way for long.

Detective Chief Inspector Morton rubbed his hands with glee. The crime scene was spattered with blood. The last few scenes he had attended were pristine, almost clinical in their presentation, and the lack of forensics had made it nearly impossible to hunt down those responsible.

'The question is, whose blood is it?' Morton's WPC, Debra Stevenson, was quick to jump in with the obvious as always.

'I doubt one man got beaten this badly without the other getting nicked at all. Look.' Morton gestured at the spatters leading away from the body towards the car. The scene was peppered with droplets of blood.

Mitch, the crime scene tech, was pretending not to listen to the detectives' conversation but couldn't prevent himself from chiming in.

'Look at the spatter closely. We've got several clear concentrations of droplets on the scene. Near the body we've got low-velocity spatter.'

'What's that?' WPC Stevenson chirped up again. Morton's face fell to his hands. Didn't they teach the basics anymore?

'Blood drips from an injury. These show us where the bleeder went after being injured. It's mostly gravity moving the drops, but with a little bit of directionality as the person moved. See, there is a thicker concentration near the point of origin.'

'What about this?' She pointed at a thinner line pointing away from the body towards one of the columns supporting the building above.

'Medium-velocity spatter. Probably the victim's. The heart pumps fast-spewing blood out of the fresh wound. It's likely what killed him, although the coroner will say for sure. It wasn't done with a gun, otherwise the spray would be much finer. I'd hazard a guess at blunt force trauma. Again, don't quote me on that.'

'Thanks, Mitch.' Morton had everything he needed. If the blood didn't match the victim, he'd be able to nail his killer.

Forensics would finish up without any further input from Morton. By noon a manila folder full of scene photos would be on his desk, neatly printed on ten-by-eight-inch photographic paper. At the same time the body would make its way to the morgue for examination. Morton had a few hours before he would be needed at the conclusion of the autopsy.

'C'mon, doll, let's go see if we can get ourselves some CCTV footage.' He gestured at the entrance, where a camera hung over the 'in' lane to the underground car park.

***

Jayne had taken the decision to proceed without Yosef's consent. She had honestly tried to respect his wishes, but she had not been able to reach him after a full day of trying. Her voicemail messages went unanswered, and she had to assume responsibility for making the decisions regarding Zach's care. Pus had built up between the dura, or outer membrane covering the spinal cord, and the skull. Pressure built rapidly, increasing intracranial pressure. His brain was being crushed inside his skull. The boy was being surprisingly stiff-upper-lipped about the whole thing. Jayne had barely heard a peep out of him in hours, and it worried her. The pain should have been immense, and the lack of fanfare made her wonder if he had begun to lose brain function.

In some ways it was a blessing. Zach had suffered immensely during his four short years on the planet. It was immeasurably cruel that someone so young and innocent should suffer so. Now he was preparing once again for surgery. The pressure needed to be relieved, and the pus drawn off to prevent the pressure building once again. He was not an ideal candidate for surgery. His tolerance for anaesthesia was low, after being subjected to it innumerable times to help deal with the symptoms of his condition. He was not a healthy boy, but they had no choice but to operate. To fail to act would be a death sentence.

***

'I need the feeds from the camera at the car park entrance,' Morton demanded.

He was in a small office in the building above the car park, surrounded by computer equipment. The ventilation was sadly lacking. Beads of perspiration began to roll down Morton's brow as he felt the heat coming off the mainframes.

'Sure, but it ain't gonna do ya much good.' The reply came from a fat, toad-like man splayed out in a leather office chair, crumbs from his mid-morning snack scattered over his clothing. He clearly didn't get many visitors to his realm.

'Just give me the tapes.'

'There ain't none.'

'They're dummy cameras?' Morton shook his head in disbelief. Only in London would a multi-million-pound building cheap out on basic security.

'Naw. LPR, mate.'

'Damn.' LPR, or licence plate recognition, was a relatively new technology. Rather than storing huge amounts of data recording on analogue video feed, the cameras just focussed on the licence plates of the vehicles entering.

'I can give you the logs.' The man wheezed slightly as he rose to print them off.

'What do you record?'

'A number of data points. The number plate of course, but also which space they park in, as each space has a sensor above them indicating occupancy. We needed that as some of the companies were moaning that the others were using their spaces. They're all pre-allocated, see, goes with the lease. Then we got time logged for both entry and exit.'

'Why use it?'

'Central London, innit? Loads of people looking for a free place to park, 'specially this close to the station.'

'So you've got nothing useful for me.'

'Didn't say that, did I? The system also logs when it fails to read a plate. It's got an entry for yesterday at 4.31 p.m. and an unauthorised exit at 5.58 p.m.'

'A car?'

'Naw, not unless they use high-gloss paint to reflect the lights and obscure the plate. My bet would be someone on foot. They ain't got a number plate, so the system logs it as an anomaly, see.'

'Thanks, you've been useful.'

***

Even modern medicine didn't work every time. Zachariah hadn't reacted well to the surgery, and the swelling had increased too quickly for anything to be done. A tear rolled down Jayne's cheek, and then another before it built to a steady stream. The entire team had spent four years fighting for that little boy. They had genuinely begun to believe he might defy the odds. No Tay-Sachs baby had ever survived much beyond their fourth birthday, and at Guy's the average was close to two. Zach had been almost halfway to his fifth birthday, a record for a Tay-Sachs child. He was deaf, almost blind, had a respirator to breath and a feeding tube to keep him nourished, but he was alive. Jayne knew it would be devastating for his father to know Zachariah had passed away while he wasn't there. He had been present virtually every day for the boy's entire life, and had even managed to take him home for brief spells in the first few years of treatment.

The body would be taken to the morgue, and as per Yosef's wishes a rabbi would be summoned from the multi-faith chapel located in an outbuilding at Guy's.

Jayne picked up the phone one last time. This time, she hoped she would get through.

***

'What have you got for me?' Morton was in the forensics lab.

'We've got two sets of blood on the floor at the Gershwin crime scene.'

Morton almost did a little dance. Now all he had to do was find his suspect and DNA would do the rest. He settled for a little yip of glee that escaped him before he could contain his excitement.

'Please tell me we've got fingerprints too.'

'Sorry, got zip for you there.'

'Damn.' Fingerprints would have been the icing on the cake. Few criminals jump from zero to cold -blooded killer, so there were good odds the perpetrator would be in the system.

'You got anything else for me?'

'Working on the processing still; I'll page you if anything comes up.'

'Fine.' His tone was flat. He knew that 'I'll page you if anything comes up' was techspeak for 'get out of my lab'. He lifted himself out of the seat he'd assumed possession of for the session, and headed down to the morgue.

***

'Afternoon, David.'

'Hi, Doc. Please tell me you've got something for me.'

'Yes and no. Cause of death was easy. Blunt force trauma to the rear of the skull. He literally had his head smashed in. That means a huge amount of force. I'd guess you are looking for a beefy guy in the six-foot plus range. Definitely not a woman in my opinion.'

'What about these other injuries?' The body had suffered badly before the final blow was delivered.

'He gave as good as he got. This injury here.' The doc pointed at the jawline, which was peppered with abrasions. 'This would have done some serious injury to the hand that did it.'

'Bad enough he would have sought medical treatment?'

'He'd be pretty dumb to, but it's worth checking with accident and emergency departments. We've got a few.'

'I'll do it.' WPC Stevenson spoke up for the first time since entering the morgue. She hated seeing the recently deceased, and had loitered near the doorway as far from the men as she could have been without physically leaving. Before waiting for affirmation from her boss she dashed off to make the inquiries with A&E.

'Got anything else?'

'Nope, that's your lot. Audio-visual might have better news. That end of London is crawling with cameras, and our guy will have busted up his hand pretty hard. It might well be visible.'

'Great; thanks, Doc.'

Chapter 53: Getting Ready

'No bloody way.' Eleanor's father, Oliver, had been particularly blunt. Usually slothful and willing to sit and listen, he had leapt to his feet when Edwin had announced his plans.

'You didn't have a problem with Eleanor taking her to New York for work!' Edwin knew arguing was pointless, and he was going to do what he wanted anyway, but he needed to vent at the unfairness of their position.

'That was different.' Eleanor's mother, Victoria, chipped in.

'How?!'

'Well, she's our daughter.'

'Look. I'm taking the Vancouver job whether you like it or not, and Chelsea is coming with me.'

'Please,' Victoria beseeched him, her eyes welling up at the thought of not seeing her. Chelsea clung to her grandmother's leg, trying to reassure her with a silent hug.

'It's my choice.' Edwin put his foot down firmly.

'Don't make me call our solicitor,' Oliver practically barked. His voice was beginning to become hoarse as emotions welled up inside his wrinkled facade. Calling a solicitor had become almost an in-joke in the family ever since Eleanor had qualified, but this time Oliver was deadly serious.

'Chelsea, why don't you run and get yourself a slice of cake in the kitchen, dear?' Victoria silenced the men momentarily with a hand gesture. Chelsea didn't need to hear this.

'Go for it. It'll cost you a fortune, and won't gain you a thing. Grandparents don't have rights.' It wasn't strictly true, but Edwin didn't care. English law wasn't concerned with rights of family members so much as it was the best interests of the child.

Oliver leapt to his feet, pain shooting down his aging legs as he straightened up. He was on the cusp of turning violent.

'Please.' Victoria tried again, beginning to beg. Chelsea was her only granddaughter, and her son was unlikely to be providing her further progeny anytime soon as he was still in rehab.

'I'm not trying to be deliberately hurtful here. I've got to go with the work, and the Canadians are offering me an amazing job opportunity.' Edwin tried to be conciliatory. He hadn't come here to be aggravating.

'Will you let us visit?' she asked.

Edwin nodded. He wouldn't deny Chelsea access to either set of grandparents. His own parents weren't too happy either, but had grudgingly agreed to support their only son. Oliver's clenched fist began to unfold as he realised that Chelsea would still be in his life.

'How about I make sure to ring you when we come back to visit my parents, and you can see Chelsea then?' Edwin offered the only olive branch he was willing to concede.

Victoria's face flooded with a smile, and even Oliver relaxed as they realised that Edwin was willing to be reasonable.

'Deal.'

With that it was settled; the Murphy family was going to Vancouver.

***

The boys in AV were excited. Their work was often under-appreciated, but David Morton was well known for giving credit when due, and what they had would break the case.

'You paged me. It better be good.' Inspector Morton had to duck to fit inside the booth used for audio-visual analysis. Monitors were crammed along every inch of the wall, and its operator was sitting cross-legged in his chair, waiting proudly to show off what he had found.

'It is, sir. Marylebone comes under the City of Westminster council, so we retrieved all the CCTV for the day in question, and began to look for who was in the general area.'

'You find someone?'

'Hundreds of people. It's a busy area. We know from the canvassing deputies did in the area that a workman was in the garage. We started trying to find him, as we thought he could potentially be our star witness.'

'But he's not a witness. He's the perp.' A light bulb clicked on in Morton's head.

'Exactly. No one else went in or out, and it explains why no one noticed him.'

'So, you tracked him on the CCTV?'

'Yep. He disappears after a while, but not before leaning against a bus stop while flagging down a taxi.'

'Where?' If they were quick, they might still be able to pull prints, and run them through the national database.

'Park road. Opposite the Royal College of Obstetricians and Gynaecologists.'

'I'm on my way.'

***

Morton pulled the prints from the bus stop himself. It wasn't a job he was required to do, but he hated sitting around waiting for someone else to carry out the grunt work, especially when he was fully certified to do something so basic. The job took much longer than he expected as there were hundreds of prints.

By the time he was finished it looked like someone had dusted the whole bus stop, as if a bag of cocaine had been exploded nearby. Each print was lifted by hand, and the techs back at the lab would scan the lot to digitise them, and then compare them all with the national database.

By the time he had logged all the prints, it was nearing dark. He dropped the lot off for the graveyard shift to begin processing, and headed home. Sarah would be annoyed if he didn't make it back by the time dinner was on the table.

Edwin had begun packing moments after sending his acceptance email.

He wanted to leave the bulk of the furniture in the house, as he knew that would aid an eventual sale, and he didn't fancy the cost of transatlantic shipping anyway. The rest would be put in storage until he needed it. The paper had agreed to a relocation allowance for him, so his new pad would be furnished exactly how he liked it, rather than to Eleanor's more refined taste. A huge flat-screen television was top of his to-buy list.

The plan was to rent at first. The move wasn't irrevocable if he found that he missed the big smoke. His townhouse in Belgrave Square would rent out for an obscene amount that might well eclipse his new salary, and a similar property in Vancouver, while pricey, would certainly not run to quite as much. He was ready for a smaller place, less showy and not so central. A decent garden would go a long way to keeping him in Canada.

Chelsea wasn't so enthusiastic. As he boxed up, she was kicking and screaming in that infuriatingly high-pitched way that only little girls can do.

'I don't *want to*!' she screamed, her pigtails bouncing up and down as she jumped.

'Why not, baby?'

'My friends are *here*!'

'You'll make new friends, princess.'

It didn't matter how reasoned Edwin's reply was, the conversation always looped back to the beginning.

'Don't want to!' was the order of the day, and nothing he could say was going to change that.

***

The prints at the bus stop belonged to almost fifty individuals. Thirty-six were in the system for one reason or another. Morton immediately discounted all the women, the non-whites and the sole disabled person on the list. The photos clearly showed a tall white male. That still left ten possibilities among the known prints, and a further fourteen in the unknown pile.

Morton fervently hoped that the perpetrator was among those on file, as otherwise it was almost back to square one again. He was actively pursuing the victim angle as well, and had sent deputies to canvass work colleagues, friends and family, but nothing useful had surfaced yet. If the forensics team didn't find him a potential suspect he would have to concentrate his personal efforts on getting inside the life of the victim.

He gave WPC Stevenson the job of sorting the suspects into a list. She'd have to prioritise the order in which he approached them to try and maximise his efficiency. He could get used to having a personal WPC following him around like a puppy. It wouldn't last of course. Sooner or later HR would pronounce him fully fit to return to work, and then he'd have to do his own grunt work.

Chapter 54: Shotgun Reflexes

'Police! Open up!' Morton called out.

They heard someone scrabbling around inside.

'He's going for the fire escape! Open it!' He gestured for the man with the ram to step in.

The door splintered in one hit, the metal ram making short work of the plywood. WPC Stevenson thrust a hand in front of Morton, gesturing for him to stay back.

'Remember what happened last time?' she whispered with a wink.

'Snarky bitch,' he muttered, under his breath. He stepped back all the same.

She raced in, followed by three more deputies. They pressed forwards, advancing on different rooms.

'Clear!'

'Clear!'

'Got visual!'

WPC Debra Stevenson made it first. A shot rang out, and she crumpled to the floor, clutching at her abdomen to try and stem the bleeding.

'Shit!' Morton pulled his weapon, and charged in. The target, Antonio Milano, was shaking violently. He had never fired a gun before. Morton nudged the gun gently out of his hands, passing it backwards to the waiting hands of a constable.

'Antonio Milano, you are under arrest...' Morton began, clicking the handcuffs onto the suspect. Another officer radioed for medical attention. She was bleeding out fast, a rosy stain spreading across her blouse.

***

WPC Stevenson was rushed to hospital faster than Morton thought humanly possible. But first he kept pressure on the wound until the paramedics arrived, and only reluctantly let go even then.

The bleeding was profuse. Gushing spurts of blood erupted between the paramedic's fingers. By the time she was taken to the ambulance the group looked like a horror film. With the level of bleeding she was experiencing it quickly became apparent she would need a blood transfusion on arrival at the hospital.

'What's her blood type?' The paramedic demanded.

'Oh god.' Morton's usually-perfect memory turned up a blank.

'Think, damn it!' The paramedic actually yelled at him.

'O Positive,' he replied as the ambulance screeched to a stop.

'Good man. Let's get her inside.'

***

WPC Debra Stevenson was pronounced dead less than fifteen minutes after she arrived. The blood loss had been too dramatic. Morton howled as he was given the news. Her foibles had annoyed him, but in the two short weeks they had been working together he had become quite fond of her.

He'd have to inform the family personally. She was his responsibility, and died as a direct result of a live investigation. Then he'd get revenge on the bastard that did this. Five minutes alone with Antonio Milano would be all he'd need. Beyond that he didn't care what happened. The serial-killing bastard would suffer.

***

'Give me a few minutes.' Morton gestured for the custody sergeant to leave the interview suite.

Without a word to the suspect, Morton kicked his chair over backwards, toppling him to the floor.

'She's dead.' He spat at Antonio Milano, narrowly missing his face.

'I didn't mean-a to do it,' he said with a thick accent that added an 'a' to the end of every word.

'You shot her in cold blood.' He shook Antonio as rage coursed through him, avoiding the urge to punch him, so there wouldn't be any marks.

'You burst in on me, with guns!' He had a point.

'We came to talk to you, and you shot at us.'

'Whaddya wanna talk about?'

'Yosef Gershwin.'

339

'Who's-a that?' His accent was grating on Morton, who was by now convinced it was being put on just to piss him off.

'Don't play games with me,' Morton growled; his voice was gravelly, barely containing his anger.

'I don't-a know him!'

As Morton was about to berate him further someone knocked on the door.

'Come in,' Morton said, edging away from the floored man.

A uniformed officer walked in, his eyebrow cocked at the scene in front of him.

'He fell over.' Morton knew he was convincing no one.

'OK. Got some results back for you, boss.' He handed him an envelope.

Morton tore open the strip at the top and decanted the contents into his hands.

Antonio Milano's DNA didn't match. He didn't kill Yosef Gershwin.

***

The list was getting shorter by the hour. A number had been interviewed by deputies, and all had alibis for the time of the killing. None had any connection to Yosef Gershwin.

There were three possible suspects left when Morton struck gold. Anthony Duvall was a low-level drugs dealer who had spent time at Her Majesty's pleasure, and his previous line-up photos, while out of date, did conform to the CCTV upon a visual inspection.

Morton pulled up his address in the system; it was still listed, as his parole was fairly recent and the system hadn't been purged since. It was local.

He shouted for a few deputies to join him. This time they were taking no chances. They would surround the property with enough deputies to guarantee they nailed their man.

Thirty minutes later, and they were outside in unmarked vehicles. They couldn't afford to spook their man lest someone else end up getting hurt. Morton hung back. He was under strict instructions from HR not to take any risks. One more bullet or blade, and that would be the end of his career.

It was with great trepidation that he kept back, waiting near the entrance to the apartment building. There were two doors into the building, and each was manned by two officers. No one would go in or out without their say-so, and Morton was fully prepared to go door-to-door to find their man. This time, they had found him. Morton knew it in his gut.

The first two deputies, McShane and Dockerty, were given the go-ahead to advance. Six flights up they paused on the landing to make sure neither had built up an oxygen debt.

'Ready?'

Dockerty nodded. Flat 617 was just down the hall.

'Police! Open up!'

A chain rattled, and the door inched open.

'Got some ID?' Anthony Duvall was cool as a cucumber.

Dockerty flashed his badge, and the door slammed shut. He expected to hear the chain rattle again, and the door open. Instead he heard the toilet flush.

'Open her up!' McShane slammed the battering ram into the door. It stayed in one piece, but swung open. Anthony Duvall could be seen flushing packages down the toilet.

'Drugs? He thought we were here for drugs?' Dockerty was quizzical.

'Aye. Well, we arrest the laddie for possession, process him and let Morton deal with 'im after that.'

Dockerty nodded and stepped towards Duvall.

'Anthony Duvall, you are under arrest for possession of a controlled substance. You do not have to say anything but it may harm your defence if you do not mention when questioned something which you later rely on in Court. Anything you do say may be given in evidence. Do you understand?'

He nodded.

'Cart him away.'

Chapter 55: Taped

'We've got the bastard.' This time, CCTV analysis confirmed the match. They could hold initially him thanks to the drugs charge. Morton had tried to start the interrogation as soon as he was in-station, but the greasy bastard had clammed up and demanded a lawyer within seconds of their opening fresh tapes.

'Get the Crown Prosecution Service on the phone. I may need them to extend the time period for detention.' The police could detain without charge for 36 hours before they needed to go to court. They would charge him with the drugs, but there was the possibility he'd make bail on that charge at the first hearing, and they might need to keep him off the streets a bit longer. With a magistrate agreeing they could keep him for 72 hours.

'Is his lawyer here yet? Good. Let's go.' He wanted another officer watching from the one-way mirror to see if their opinions matched.

'Afternoon, Mr Duvall.' The politeness was for the lawyer, not the suspect.

'I'm Theodore Leigh, and I represent Mr Duvall.' The portly lawyer rose, extending a pudgy hand to Morton. Morton waved it away. Leigh did not look like a typical defence solicitor. He was too well-dressed, even wearing a waistcoat. All that was missing was a pocket watch, and then Morton would have sworn on record that he had been transported back in time.

'Detective Chief Inspector David Morton. For the benefit of the tape, have you had time to counsel your client?'

'I have.' Leigh had been given thirty minutes' grace before both lawyer and client were hauled into the interview suite.

'Mr Duvall. Where were you on Tuesday afternoon?'

Duvall's face dropped. He thought he was in on simple drug possession charges, and had suddenly realised the extent of the trouble he was in.

'Can't remember.'

'That's unfortunate. Mr Leigh, have you explained to your client that the courts can draw an adverse inference from Mr Duvall's non-cooperation?' The question was intended to stick the needles in Duvall, but he sat there looking smug, the panic of the previous moment shuttered down behind glassy eyes as if someone had flipped a switch.

When he got no response, Morton continued.

'Were you at the car park of Greagor, Gershwin and Hopkins LLP on Tuesday afternoon?'

Duvall didn't dare lie directly. He simply shrugged, a slight glare thrown in the inspector's direction.

'Silence won't help you, Mr Duvall. We have blood evidence that links you to the scene.' The tests hadn't come back yet, but the police were allowed to lie to a suspect. He was pushing the limits of his ethical obligations, but he squared the white lie with his conscience with ease. It wasn't even a fallacy anyway, as the results were bound to come back positive.

Duvall's face paled, and he turned to whisper to his lawyer. It was the lawyer who spoke next.

'He wants to cut a deal.' The lawyer confirmed Morton's suspicions, forcing him to conceal a thin smile.

'Deal? He killed someone in cold blood.'

'That may be true, but there's more to it than that.'

'In what way?'

'He was put up to it. You want the big boss, not the little guy.'

'Interview terminated. 16:32. I need to speak to the prosecutor. If he agrees to a deal, I'll listen to what you've got to say. If it's no good, your client is going down for murder.'

'Fine with us,' Duvall said in a confident voice.

Morton left, wondering what the hell he had just stumbled into.

***

'The lab report came back in a rush. DNA confirmed that Anthony Duvall was involved in the altercation with Yosef Gershwin.'

'Then why are you asking me to cut a deal?'
Kiaran O'Connor looked perplexed. He had known
David Morton for years. Not once had he
suggested a deal.

'I don't want to. I want this guy bang to rights.'

'Best I can do for him is manslaughter anyway,
conditional on a guilty plea. The judge can still send
him down for life.'

'I don't like this.' Morton switched sides,
knowing that he could let the lawyer back himself
into a corner. It was a technique he had perfected
on suspects.

'Let's offer the deal, and see what he has to say.'

'Fine.'

Kiaran went into the interview suite first. It was
no longer solely a police interrogation.

'Mr Duvall, I am willing to drop the charge to
constructive-act manslaughter if and only if the
information you provide is sufficiently valuable. I
will decide that in my sole discretion.'

'That don't seem fair. You deciding, that is.'

'It's what I'm offering.' The lawyer entrenched
his position.

'Naw. He decides.' Duvall gestured at Morton.

No one looked more surprised than Duvall's
lawyer. Leigh almost sputtered as he took a sip of
his water.

Morton shrugged.

'Let's hear it then.'

'That Gershwin guy stiffed me. He agreed to kill
someone for me, and in return I was going to kill
for him. Only he didn't do it, kept making excuses.'

'You move in different social circles. How'd you find him?' Morton 's tone was sceptical. It was only curiosity driving him; he didn't think there was any deal in this, yet.

'On the Internet.'

'We searched his computer, and didn't find anything.'

Duvall should have looked crestfallen, but instead he became even more smug.

'That's cause we used a darknet, didn't we?'

'You what?'

'A private network. Heard about 'em in prison. It's not on Google or anything, you just connect port-to-port.'

Morton was in over his head. The terms meant nothing. Thankfully Kiaran was more up-to-date. 'So you used an anonymous group to find each other?'

'Yeah, it's like a newsgroup, man. I use it for dealing weed.' That explained what he was flushing. With a class C substance, it was hardly worth bringing him in for just the drugs.

'Onion routing?'

'Yeah, man. All peer-to-peer stuff. We connected through Tor.' He named a common program for concealing his Internet presence.

'How'd you modify it?'

'Some white dude over the Silicon roundabout fixed us up. Said something about adding more latency to the darknet. Meant we couldn't be monitored, anyway. I don't know exactly how it works.'

'Can you show us?'

'Does this mean I've got a deal?'

'If we bust this network wide open, then yes, you've got your deal.'

Chapter 56: Darknet

The dark web wasn't something Morton readily understood. The idea of swapping murders on the Internet was anathema to traditional policing, and was unlike anything he had come across in his three decades with the Met.

Still, he logged on quickly enough, and found Yosef's message in Ant's inbox. It occurred to Morton that while it wasn't the perfect crime, it might well be the perfect defence. Without prosecution knowledge of the murder swap plan it easily gave rise to reasonable doubt. A half-decent defence lawyer would have a field day pointing the finger at everyone else in sight.

Morton wondered how Yosef knew about the darknet, and what else he might have used it for. Ant's messages were less than subtle. Punks scoring weed online was nothing new, but Gershwin was a respected architect, not a petty thief.

'You.' He collared the nearest constable as one ambled by his open office door.

'Yes, sir?'

'Get me Gershwin's laptop, and send someone up from IT when it gets here.'

The man nodded briskly, and set about his task.

It didn't take long to arrive. The unlucky constable was sent straight out to fetch the laptop from among the late Mr Gershwin's possessions. Morton felt a certain chill as he rifled through it, but it was no longer simply a dead man's property; it was evidence in a murder investigation, and one that might lead him to a larger network of criminality.

'We have a suspect in custody who claims to have used a darknet to secure a deal whereby he would kill someone in return for someone's killing for him. I need to get into this laptop.'

'Yes sir. May I?' He gestured at the spare seat next to the desk.

Before long his fingers were typing at lightning speed, prising open the dead man's system to expose it for Morton to see. As he worked, Morton lazily read his name badge, Conway Lee.

Morton's coffee had cooled to room temperature when the laptop bleeped acceptance of its new master.

'We're in.' Conway announced, pride tingeing his speech.

'Good. I need to know who he talked to, and when.'

'Looks like just one darknet contact, sir, but this laptop is only a few months old.'

'I assume that the contact is Mr Anthony Duvall?'

'Doesn't have a name, sir. Got the messages Duvall sent? I can see if they match.'

Morton passed him the printout Duvall's lawyer had faxed over.

'Nope, he's not the one, sir.'

'What? That can't be right.'

'I'm afraid so, sir. The exchange in your printout doesn't match. Duvall demands performance in his messages, but Mr Gershwin didn't receive those messages.'

'There's a third person involved.' Morton surmised, absentmindedly drinking his cold coffee.

'I'd agree with that.'

'It's not just one murder swap, but a whole web. The question is, who's the puppet master?'

'Perhaps, sir, but I think it's more of a chain than a web. It had to start somewhere, right?'

***

Morton laid out all the unsolved death cases from the last three months on the conference table. He went back to the date on the first message Gershwin and Duvall had responded to.

The case files relating to the deaths of Eleanor Murphy, Janet Morgan, Vanhi Deepak and Barry Fitzgerald joined Yosef Gershwin on the table.

As their faces stared vacantly up at him, Morton realised he only wanted the cases where the suspect had no apparent connection to the victim. That removed Janet Morgan from contention. Her husband had almost certainly killed her; they just couldn't prove it. She clearly wasn't linked to the other deaths. Murphy was the earliest death that there was no other suspect for.

All of the others had died at the hands of someone who appeared to be a complete stranger. Gershwin had died by Duvall's hand, and Fitzgerald was killed in a spectacularly anonymous fashion on the ferry to Le Havre.

'Wasn't Fitzgerald involved in that other odd case, sir?' asked the man assisting him for the afternoon, Rob Dean.

'Oh yes, the death by self-defence case. Peter Sugden.'

Something clicked as he said the name. Sugden had been involved in an FSA investigation. Were the two connected? Morton made a mental note to contact Michael Burrows at the FSA.

'Five deaths? Nothing to link them. Get me their laptops.'

'On it, sir.'

'You do that; I'll phone the FSA.'

***

'Does the term darknet mean anything to you?'

'No, enlighten me.' Burrows' tone was too polite, as if he was humouring the detective.

'It's a private network using an Internet technology that lets users communicate anonymously, without anyone being able to discern the identity of those using it.'

'Great Scott! You think that Sugden was using this to share insider information?!'

'Yes, and more. He tried to kill a man. I think he's involved in something far darker than artificially manipulating share prices. '

'I don't know. He didn't come off that way when we interviewed him. A polite, courteous fellow. I could see him as a white collar criminal, but nothing more sinister.'

'We've got him on tape.'

'Well, I'll be damned. Thought I had the measure of the man.'

'Looks like you need to re-examine your case. I've requested his laptop, should be here any moment. You want it after we're done with our investigation? Shouldn't take long; he's dead after all, and can't be prosecuted, but it might help to bring down your insider trading ring.'

'Thank you, Chief Inspector. I appreciate the call.'

***

The laptops all went through the same treatment, and it took almost a day to crack them all.

'Every victim except Murphy had been involved in darknet use,' Dean announced to the room. He needn't have bothered; they all knew why they were there. After the laptops had arrived Chief Inspector Morton had called in every able body to help dig through the electronic paper trail.

'So Murphy wasn't involved. Does that mean our web was limited to the others plus Duvall?' Morton asked.

'No, sir, at least one other person was involved, as there were messages sent from all these laptops that weren't received by the others.'

'This person got messages from all of them?'

'Yes, sir.'

'So we've got our ringleader. Can we work out who agreed what?'

'Sort of, sir. We know Deepak was killed by another member of the group, Barry Fitzgerald. We don't know if she carried out a kill but if she did, it was one before her death.'

'Did she agree to one?'

'Yes, sir, she wanted someone who abused her killed, according to the messages. I think it was the Brixton kill. Her name was in his case file. It was redacted for her privacy, but the CPS got the original jackets when you asked for this taskforce.'

'Good to see the lawyers can do something right. Who killed Barry?'

'Well, Sugden tried to. Then someone else succeeded.'

'Who? Gershwin?'

'No. From his messages he didn't carry out the kill. That's why Duvall killed him.'

'So who did Duvall want dead?'

'He won't say, sir, something about the right against self-incrimination.'

'We don't have one. Lean on his lawyer.'

'Yes, sir. We know he killed someone else. He felt stiffed by the deal agreed."

Morton nodded. "So who did he kill?'

'We don't know, sir. We've got a few John Does that could fit. Does it really matter? He's going down for life anyway.'

'Of course it bloody matters! The victim's family deserve closure, and justice,' Morton thundered. Dean paled, and didn't respond.

'Anyone have an idea who our puppet master is?'

No one raised a hand to volunteer their thoughts. It was getting late.

'We'll reconvene at half past eight. Don't be late.'

With that, the Operation Darknet staff were dismissed for the evening.

***

'Morning, ladies and gentleman. I've been reviewing all the cases we dealt with yesterday. It looks like this isn't just limited to London. One of Mr Duvall's requests was for an out-of-London hit. We believe that Yosef Gershwin agreed to kill for him a man in Portsmouth. We don't know if that hit ever took place, but if it did, it wasn't Gershwin that did it, as Duvall exacted revenge for his non-performance.

'Someone also had to kill Barry Fitzgerald, and none of the messages indicate who. We also have our ringleader. That leaves up to three unknown persons, or we have multiple serial killers among our group.'

'I think I can help,' piped up a small voice from the back. It was a newer tech, Cindy Jacobs, who had stayed up all night with Morton as they worked through the evidence.

'We know from her messages Vanhi Deepak planned to carry out a kill. She then got killed, and her killer was killed. That makes me think those later kills were a facade for the earlier ones.'

'Good work, Jacobs.' Morton rarely praised those under his command, but if someone truly deserved it he would go to hell to get them a commendation.

'We also know she killed someone,' Jacobs ventured tentatively.

'No, we don't. We can only speculate.'

'With all due respect, sir, it's well-founded if it's speculation. She was killed to cover up another murder. If she hadn't gone through with it then persons unknown would not have needed to kill her to cover it up. They could simply have ignored her.'

A few nods bobbed in the room, and a few deputies murmured their assent. It was a reasonable assumption. Morton had other ideas.

'I like your thinking, but if she was the first then she knew the original target. That would be enough to get her killed, whether she performed or not.'

'Yes, sir.' Jacobs blushed.

'You got Deepak's messages? Put them up on the projector.'

Jacobs did so, and a collective gasp went round the room. The information on her target was enough to isolate her victim.

It was Eleanor Murphy. She was the first victim, and only one person stood to gain from her death.

'Issue an arrest warrant for the husband. Now.' Morton knew something about him hadn't been quite right.

'And for God's sake get his laptop. It might be the only evidence we've got.'

The team dispersed. A manhunt was on.

***

Edwin had already stored or shipped most of his stuff. He'd auctioned some of the knickknacks too, as his new flat was much smaller than the townhouse he and Chelsea were used to. With the new apartment awaiting their imminent arrival, and the old townhouse tenanted out, the London era was drawing to a close.

He and Chelsea had moved into the Hilton a few days ago, as the new tenants at Belgrave Square wanted immediate possession. It was a bit of a rush job, but Edwin didn't mind. With all the memories of Eleanor, the house had a bad vibe and he was glad to see the back of it.

He was now technically home-schooling Chelsea, having withdrawn her from the private school at the end of the last week. That in reality had meant letting her play tourist in her own city for a few days. They'd visited all of the free museums in Kensington, been up in the Millennium Eye and even posed with a Beefeater. Chelsea had smiled more in those few days than she had in the weeks since her mother's death.

Edwin picked his shirt up off the floor. He only had a couple of items left to pack, and they should all fit into the set of matching luggage he and Chelsea would share for their morning flight out to Vancouver.

Chapter 57: Right Place, Wrong Time

'Police! Open up!'

Footsteps came down the stairs to the door of 51 Belgrave Square, and the door swung open to reveal a middle-aged man dressed in silk pyjamas. He was not Edwin Murphy.

'We're looking for Mr Edwin Murphy,' Morton announced.

'Afraid I can't help you, officers.' The voice had a lisp to it that matched the pyjamas.

'Who are you?'

'Freddy Maynard.'

'What are you doing here?' Morton frowned.

'We live here, silly. Me and my partner.'

'I'll rephrase that. How long have you lived here?'

'Oo, a week tomorrow,' Freddy replied.

'Did you buy it from Mr Murphy?'

'No, we've jus' leased it. Through Prestige Homes in Chelsea.'

'Damn it. Thank you for your time, Mr Maynard.'

'Any time, officers.'

The door closed behind him, and Morton retreated, dejected. The warrant in his pocket was for the home of Edwin Murphy, and if he didn't live there it couldn't be searched. Where the hell was Edwin Murphy?

***

The town car was late. Edwin had specifically asked for it to arrive at seven-thirty sharp. The flight was at eleven o'clock, and he knew that the airports liked to have people checked in early. Besides, he still had Diamond Club membership, and he intended to abuse it for all the free drinks he could get. He hated flying, even though intellectually he knew it was safe. The alcohol helped to take the edge off.

Chelsea was being an angel. She had a teddy backpack, and had stuffed enough toys inside it to amuse her for a week, let alone a direct flight. They were going first class anyway, so she'd be able to sit back and watch a few movies in comfort, or recline her chair back and get some shut-eye.

A limousine pulled up outside the hotel, the engine gently purring. It was for them.

'Got your passport?' Edwin asked her. He had her real one of course – he couldn't trust a four year old with it – but he'd had a mock one printed for both her and Teddy to make the journey feel more normal. It seemed to have worked.

'Come on then.'

The porter carried out their luggage, and Edwin tipped him generously. He certainly didn't want to lug cases that heavy around early in the morning. As the door clicked shut, Edwin began to relax. He was off to begin a fabulous new life in a vibrant city. He wasn't rich, but he was comfortable, and more importantly he had his little girl.

✳✳✳

Morton was stupefied. It was as if Edwin Murphy had been wiped off the face of the planet.

His daughter had been withdrawn from school, and his house was in someone else's name.

'Sir, we've just got the bank records through,' Dean announced, entering Morton's office without knocking.

Morton glared at him for a moment, and grudgingly took the photocopies. He hated rudeness, but now was not the time to call young Dean on his lack of manners. He scanned down the latest Visa charges on Edwin Murphy's credit card.

'The Hilton Park Avenue! Let's go.' Seeing a hotel on the charges list, Morton was spurred into action. He was going to nail this bastard. As he jumped in the car, the charges list lay abandoned on his desk. If he had taken a little longer to look, he might have spotted the charge from Canadian Air.

Lights on, they sped across town at faster than the legal speed limit.

'Another red!' Dean exclaimed. The morning's commuter traffic hadn't hit the late morning lull yet, and they seemed to be getting caught at every turn.

'Jump it.'

'But, sir...' Dean began to protest.

'Do it!' Seeing the stern look on his superior officer's face, he pushed the metal pedal down, and lurched forward, narrowly avoiding oncoming traffic.

Minutes later they burst into the lobby of the Hilton Park Avenue.

'Edwin Murphy. What room?' Morton demanded of the girl on the desk.

For what seemed like an eternity, she went through the computer system looking for Mr Murphy's reservation.

'Sorry, sir, no one by that name is staying here.'

'Then where the hell is he?' Morton lost his cool, drawing the attention of the manager in the back office.

'Sir, could you stop yelling in...' The manager's voice trailed off as he realised it was the police.

'Can I help you, officers?'

'We're looking for Edwin Murphy. He has a charge from this hotel on his Visa.'

'You've just missed him. He checked out this morning.'

'Fuck.'

'I believe we called transportation for him. I might be able to look up where he was going in our notes.'

'Do it!' Morton's impatience grew. Twice they had missed him.

'It seems we called a limousine firm for him, sir, Sierra Limousines Ltd. I don't have a destination on record.'

'Call them, and find out where they took him. Now.'

'Very well, sir.' His tone was huffy. The manager was not used to being bullied, even if they were the police.

'It's going to voicemail, sir.'

'Give me the number, now.'

He passed over a business card with the company's registered office and contact details on.

'Dean, keep trying to get through, and stick that postcode in the satnav. We're paying them a visit, and I'm driving.' Morton was already halfway out the door.

'Yes, sir!'

***

The limousine company picked up when they were halfway to their head office.

'Sierra Limousines, how may I help you?'

'Good afternoon. This is Detective Robert Dean, Metropolitan Police. You picked up a suspect of ours this morning from the Hilton, a Mr Edwin Murphy. We need to know where he was going.'

The operator paused, unsure if this was a hoax.

'I need to speak to my supervisor about that.'

'Do it.'

By the time she came back on the line, they were parking up.

Still talking, Dean walked in and flashed his badge at the receptionist. He gestured for her to put down the phone.

'Where did you take Mr Murphy?'

'Gatwick Airport. North Terminal.'

'Thank you.' His tone was exasperated. He didn't mean it. Those ten minutes might have cost them the chance to catch their man.

They dove back into the car. Morton hoped they weren't too late.

Chapter 58: Flight or Fight

Edwin and his daughter cleared airport security in no time at all. Priority check-in had taken care of their bags, and Edwin decided to browse the airport bookshop for something to read on the plane. Chelsea had other ideas.

'Daddy, I'm hungry,' she pouted.

'We'll be in the lounge in a few minutes, honey. We'll eat then.'

'Don't want 'dult food!' She began to stomp her feet, and passers-by began to stare.

'Well, what do you want?'

'McDonalds!'

Edwin cursed airport food. Several hours confined inside a terminal, and it was child's play to sell burgers to children. With Happy Meal toys it was even easier, and Edwin was beginning to succumb to pester power.

'Let me get a book first.' He turned his back on her, knowing that she wouldn't give up that easily.

'No, Daddy, *now*!'

Edwin sighed; she could be a proper princess when she wanted to be. She took after her mother that way.

'Fine, but we're coming back here afterwards.' He reluctantly put down the thriller he was half-way through reading the blurb on, and led his daughter by the hand to the dreaded golden arches.

***

The squad car screeched to a halt in front of Gatwick North, the road tearing up rubber as Dean slammed on the breaks. Morton sprinted, wincing every time he put weight on his injured leg. The huge glass frontage drew closer.

They'd left the car in the valet parking bay outside. The Met would almost certainly get a call from an irate valet company when they realised their bay had been blocked, but Morton didn't care.

'That way!' he huffed to Dean, who was a little ahead of him, but unsure which way to run.

The hallway was huge. Three conjoined halls lay side by side, with businessmen and holidaymakers flitting all over. It was impossible to run. Security was on the north side, and Edwin Murphy was bound to be in departures on the other side.

'Police!' Morton flashed his badge at the woman on the gate.

The female security guard reappeared, and shouted at them: "Hold it!"

'Great, a jobsworth. Just what we need.' Dean's voice was barely audible.

'We're in pursuit of a murder suspect.'

'Who?' she demanded.

'Mr Edwin Murphy.'

'Got an arrest warrant?'

'I don't need one! He's about to abscond with all our evidence!' It was a common misconception. Arrest warrants were normal, but there hadn't been time, and Morton was relying on his right to arrest without warrant where he had reasonable cause to suspect that Murphy was about to commit an offence, in this case perversion of the course of justice by leaving the jurisdiction with the offending laptop.

'I'll escort you.' She wasn't taking no for an answer.

'Fine. Go!'

She picked up a radio. 'Dispatch, I need the whereabouts of an Edwin Murphy. I have a Detective Chief Inspector Morton on site to arrest him.'

The radio crackled.

'One second,' came a flustered voice.

They jumped into the security vehicle as they waited for a reply. It wouldn't go fast, but it would clear the foot traffic out of their way, and ten miles per hour beat walking in a crowd.

The voice came back.

'We've got him somewhere between final security and check-in. His flight leaves in twenty minutes. Gate 22. Over.'

'Roger that, thanks, dispatch. Over and out.'

She clicked off the radio, and swung the cart violently around.

'Where are we going?'

'Gate 22. We'll catch him there. If he tries to go back through security, my boys will pick him up.'

'Gotcha.'

With a honk, she parted the crowds, and raced towards the gate.

'This is far as this baby will go.' She patted her cart appreciatively.

Morton stepped off the cart, glad to have firm ground back under his feet. The woman drove like a devil. Ahead, two moving conveyer belts moved in opposite directions, spanning a huge corridor.

Gate numbers ascended on the left, and descended on the right. The even numbers were on the left-hand side, going up from 14. Seven gates down on the left, the suspect waited.

Bypassing the moving floors, they ran down the centre. Too many pedestrians occupied the conveyer belts, and once they were on them it would be hard to get off. The last thing they wanted was their man spotting them and having time to ditch.

They sped into the lounge. The crowd was huge, over a hundred travellers milling around. More were having their bags searched on the way in.

'Has Edwin Murphy checked in?'

The stewardess on the desk scanned down her list. She had his boarding card tear-off. He was there.

She nodded.

'Him and his daughter.'

'How old is she?'

'Four, sir.'

'Shit. Dean, call Social Services, we're going to need a foster carer for the kid.'

Morton struggled up on tiptoes, straining his calf muscles to get a small height advantage.

'Can you see him?' Dean asked.

'No. Can't see much over the crowd.'

Only Morton had seen him in person. Dean was working off a description, and he wasn't too confident in his ability to spot Murphy.

'Fuck it.' Morton jumped on the table being used to search bags, clambering among the hand luggage at his feet. Now he had a vantage point from which he could see the whole room.

'I can't see him!' Morton frowned.

'Sir?'

'Damn it, what is it, Dean?'

'Don't first class get their own lounge to wait in?'

'Fuck!'

Glancing at the sign, Morton sped towards the rear of the lounge, where a cordoned door was attended by a suited young man.

'Ticket please, sir.' the young man requested as Morton barged past, knocking the velvet cordon to the floor.

'There!' By the window, with his back to the door, was Edwin Murphy. He was lazing in a winged armchair, a broadsheet spread out in front of him, and a little girl playing by his side.

'Edwin Murphy?'

He looked up, expecting to be told it was his turn to board. He saw the Inspector's face, and bolted for the door, upturning his chair into Morton's path as he leapt to his feet.

'Dean! The door!' Morton barked.

Dean leapt into action, sprinting back towards the door, weaving his way through the crowd. Rolling over the table, he leapt at Murphy as he tried to make good on his escape. With a thud the rugby tackle landed, and Murphy was felled. The pair tumbled through the air, rolling violently as they hit the ground.

'Edwin Murphy, you are under arrest for the murder of Eleanor Murphy. You do not have to say anything but it may harm your defence if you do not mention when questioned something which you later rely on in Court. Anything you do say may be given in evidence. Do you understand?'

Edwin remained defiantly silent. He wasn't giving up that easily.

Chapter 59: Lawyering Up

They had barely stowed the suspect in the rear of the squad car before he demanded a lawyer. He didn't want just any lawyer either, but one of the slick young hotshots that Morton had only ever seen on television, ranting and raving in front of the Old Bailey. He probably cost more per hour than Morton earned in a week, but then how can you put a price on getting away with murder?

Kirby turned up in short order, demanding a private audience with his client. Far from the conservative cut Morton was expecting, the lawyer was positively flamboyant. A silk-lined jacket matched a pocket square on his left breast, the suit exquisitely tailored around the man's slender frame. As for the shoes, they were so shiny that Morton could have shaved using his reflection in them.

Once the formalities of introductions, and starting the tape recorder, had been finished, Morton began the initial interview.

'Mr. Murphy. Where is your laptop?'

'What laptop?' Edwin had been smart enough to ditch it. It was among the items he had sold online as part of his preparation for the Vancouver move.

'Your personal laptop, Mr Murphy.'

'Don't have one, officer.'

'When did you last have one?' Morton tried another tactic.

'Not long ago.'

'Where is it now?'

'Don't know.' Murphy knew how useful evasive and vague answers could be. His lawyer had prepared him well, advising him to avoid giving any information up.

'Where was it last time you saw it?'

'In a box.'

'Where was that box?'

'In my hands.'

'What did you do with it?'

'Posted it.'

'To whom?'

'The new owner.'

'Who is that?'

'Can't remember. Check my eBay feedback?' Murphy was treating it like a game.

He knew the laptop wouldn't help to incriminate him. Before sale he'd degaussed the hard drive to remove the data. It was the most secure way to wipe out the evidence, as degaussing reversed the magnetic charge that was used to store the data. No charge, no data.

'We will.' Morton set aside the whereabouts of the laptop for the moment. Someone would have to track it down after the interviews.

'Did you kill your wife?'

'No.'

'Did you cause someone else to do so?'

'I loved my wife.' Murphy smiled inwardly. The past tense didn't give a clue as to when he had last loved her, and he knew it.

'Did you know what a darknet is?' Morton knew he could lead with the inquisition here, as Edwin had publicly written articles on the subject as an undergraduate. It was public knowledge, and a denial would be invaluable in catching him out in the lie.

'Yes, of course.' Edwin wasn't taking the bait.

'Have you used one?'

'Yes.'

'When?'

'When I was an undergraduate.' Edwin tried to be evasive again. He didn't claim it was the only time he had used one. It was almost a lie by omission, but his lawyer had approved it.

'Anytime since then?'

'Yes.'

'When?'

'I don't recall every time I have connected to a darknet. Could you list every time you logged onto the Internet?'

'I'll ask the questions. Did you contact a Vanhi Deepak on a darknet?'

'I'm afraid I don't know that name, officer.' It was a half-truth. He did know the name, but the police couldn't prove it. It could have been a pseudonym anyway.

'We believe she killed your wife.'

'Then you should arrest her, not me.'

'Did you put her up to it?'

'How could I put someone I've never met up to anything?' Murphy had a sarcastic response for everything. Morton needed something concrete.

'Did you post a message on a London darknet seeking a killer?'

'No.' It was the first lie he had been forced to make. Morton could have tried to push this advantage, but he changed tack, seeking to unnerve Edwin.

'How much was the life insurance policy on your wife worth?'

'£350,000.' It was too easy to verify to bother lying.

'That's a lot of money.'

'I suppose, for some people.'

'You also got the house, didn't you, Mr Murphy?'

'It was always my house.'

'But now it's just yours.'

'Yes.'

'She was divorcing you, wasn't she, Mr Murphy?'

Edwin's jaw dropped. He'd forgotten they had seen her copies of the divorce papers.

'You can't use that! It's legally privileged!'

'Not so, Mr Murphy, ask your lawyer.'

Edwin looked deploringly at his new lawyer, who refused to meet his gaze. They'd just proven motive beyond a shadow of a doubt. It was a classic, the jilted ex angle.

'But you know I didn't kill her! I wasn't even in the country.'

'No, but you did put Vanhi Deepak up to it.'

'I didn't!'

'Our analysis says otherwise. We used the messages sent by the other parties involved, and compared the grammatical structure, syntax and language used with your editorial column at *The Impartial*. It was a perfect match.' Such analysis was not yet admissible in court, but Morton knew his suspect wouldn't know that. Even if he did, the CPS would fight for its admissibility, and Dr Jensen was raring to get on the stand and defend his theory.

'Shit.' Murphy swore before he realised the implications of his reaction.

'Mr Murphy. I advise you to remain silent,' Kirby chirped up for the first time since the interview had started.

'You engaged the services of someone online to carry out a murder swap, didn't you?'

'No comment.'

'You then had another person kill Vanhi Deepak to cover up the first kill, didn't you?'

'No comment.'

'That person was Barry Fitzgerald, wasn't it?'

'No comment.'

'Mr Fitzgerald killed Vanhi Deepak, and then went on the run. Isn't that true?'

'No comment.'

'He was a loose end. You tried to have him killed by Peter Sugden, didn't you?'

'No comment.'

'When he failed you needed someone else, but they wouldn't do it for free, would they?'

'No comment.'

'You had Barry killed on board the *Nordic Giant*.'

'No comment.'

'Who killed Barry?'

'No comment.'

'We know it wasn't anyone we've traced. How were the others involved? Anthony Duvall and Yosef Gershwin?'

'No comment.'

'The courts can infer guilt from your lack of comment, Mr Murphy.'

'I think it's plain you'll be getting no further comment from Mr Murphy.' Kirby spoke up again, a slow and authoritative voice. The interview was over.

***

'Charge him.' Kiaran O'Connor, the Crown Prosecution Service lawyer, smelled blood.

'It's a bit circumstantial, Kiaran,' Morton, ever the voice of reason, pointed out.

'You want this scum to get away with multiple murders?'

'No. Of course not, but he can only be tried once. We don't want to miss our shot.'

'Where are we with the laptop?' Kiaran needed something physical to tie up his theory of the case.

'We've got it, but it's clean. Professionally wiped.'

'That's pretty incriminating.'

'His position is he cleaned it for sale, to protect his personal data.'

'Bullshit.'

'We've got Duvall as a witness.'

'Great, a crook who's also going down for killing someone, out to save his own bacon, is our star witness. Still, he is compelling but he only gives us the darknet contact.'

'We can leverage his reaction to the darknet accusation as our proof.'

'It's shaky.'

'It's all we've got.'

'Do it, but we'll only put a few specimen counts down. Then we can recharge on the other murders he procured later if we lose. We've got multiple bites at the cherry here.'

Chapter 60: First Blood

'Bail denied.' As the gavel came down Kiaran almost whooped. The presumption in favour of bail was a strong one, but the flight risk argument was indefensible. He had already tried to flee the jurisdiction, and simply surrendering his passport wouldn't necessarily stop him.

He also made headway with the darknet evidence. While he couldn't show a physical item such as the newly wiped laptop, he could ask Murphy for an alibi for each of the times that the messages were sent. The timestamps were contained within the recipient's computers. Without anything else to corroborate, simply not having an alibi for any one time would not have been sufficient to convince a jury of Edwin's guilt, but the case was a house of cards. By layering each denial it became implausible that Edwin was simply unavailable every single time the messages were sent. In a way he had damaged his own defence by having such strong alibis at all other times.

The question would be whether or not twelve men and women would find him guilty. The Crown Court was a notoriously unreliable place for a prosecutor. The jury didn't have to explain their verdict, so all sorts of whacky decisions had been reached even in just the cases that Kiaran had dealt with.

Pictures of the victims would be laid before them. The dead were butchered in horrendous ways, and the carnage would leave a strong impression on the jury.

His opening speech was what truly laid the foundations for the prosecution case.

'Ladies and gentlemen.

'Mr Murphy has been charged with multiple counts of procuring murder. It is my job to prove this case to you beyond reasonable doubt. That does not mean you cannot have any doubts, but you must be sure that he has acted criminally in order to convict him.

'Over the course of this trial, we will show how he methodically manipulated vulnerable persons over the Internet to convince them to act out his heinous plan. The defence has no alibi for any of the times the messages were sent, although he was in a conveniently public place at the time of each death, as if he knew they were going to die.

'We'll adduce testimony from one of those manipulated to show that Mr Murphy attempted to solicit "murder swaps" multiple times. The first time he did so, he used Vanhi Deepak to kill his wife while she was on her morning run. He did this to benefit financially, and gain custody of their child. One week his wife serves him with divorce papers, and mere weeks later she is found face down in Battersea Park, dead.

'Then the person guilty for that murder, the only direct witness who could identify Edwin Murphy, is killed outside the pub where she worked. This might seem like a case of karma, justice even, but ladies and gentlemen, make no mistake – Edwin Murphy is a sociopath who used this death to cover up his own liability.

'Then Barry Sullivan, her killer, had to die. Not to cover up the Deepak death, but so that Murphy wouldn't have to deliver on his promise. He had Peter Sugden try and kill him. He died in the attempt, and doesn't appear on the indictment, but video footage of this will be adduced showing Mr Sugden attempting to kill Barry Fitzgerald.

'When Sugden failed, Mr Murphy simply tried again. He used persons unknown to kill Barry, using a rare neurotoxin to do so, in a sealed disabled toilet on an international ferry. Presumably he then owed this person for the kill, and roped in another to take part.

'Enter Anthony Duvall, now a prosecution witness, who killed multiple times. His first kill was of an unknown person whom he refuses to disclose, but the details are shown in the exchange of messages which will be adduced as a prosecution exhibit.

'Yosef Gershwin was supposed to kill another unknown person for Duvall, but had an attack of conscience. Duvall killed him, as a direct result of manipulation by Edwin Murphy, who was in fact the dealmaker in the transaction. Murphy let slip Gershwin's details in order to get him killed.

'By this time, Mr Murphy thought he was free and clear. No witnesses or physical evidence tied him to the crimes, and he made a plan to emigrate to Canada, fleeing the devastation he had unleashed on London.

'We caught him, at the airport, after detectives realised that all the persons manipulated by the darknet spoke to one single puppet master. That puppet master was Edwin Murphy. His reaction when accused during an interview under caution says it all, ladies and gentleman. Murphy is guilty as sin. He is a charlatan who will to try and convince you otherwise. Don't let him get away with it. Edwin Murphy is guilty of murder, ladies and gentlemen, and the sooner he is off our streets the better.'

Kiaran sat, noting a slight murmur of assent spread among the jury. The trial wouldn't last long. Without physical evidence the circumstances could be dealt with in mere days as opposed to the weeks Kiaran was used to.

In a few short days, he would get back their verdict.

***

The jury took a long time. At the end of forty-eight hours of deliberation, His Honour Judge Milligan, QC, called them back into the courtroom.

'Have you reached a verdict upon which you are all agreed? Please answer, yes or no.'

'No.'

'Do you believe you could reach a unanimous verdict?'

'No, Your Honour.' The foreman shot a nasty look at juror number twelve.

'I am going to ask you to retire one more time to try and reach a unanimous verdict. If you are unable to do so, I will accept a majority verdict.'

The bailiff led them back out of the courtroom.

Kiaran's hands began to shake. It was a close call. That meant he wasn't way out of the ballpark with his arguments. He hoped the holdouts were of the not guilty kind, and would agree this time around to vote guilty.

He knew that the second time, juries were often much quicker. Both lawyers waited in open court, watching the clock on the wall tick in an infuriating manner. Two hours later, the bailiff was back.

'They are ready, Your Honour.'

'Bring them in.'

The jury came in, single file, and took their seats. They looked weary, but triumphant. Kiaran hoped it wasn't just the triumph of being home for the weekend.

'Have you reached a verdict upon which at least ten of you agree?'

'We have.'

'What is your verdict?'

'We find the defendant, Edwin Murphy, guilty.'

Kiaran exhaled in relief. He could breathe again. At the defence table both lawyer and client looked deflated.

'Is that the verdict of you all, or a majority?'

'Majority, Your Honour.'

'How many of you agreed to the verdict and how many dissented?'

'Ten and two respectively Your Honour.'

'Thank you for your service, you are dismissed.'

The bailiff led them from the courtroom while Judge Milligan waited.

'Mr Murphy, you have been found guilty of three counts of murder. You are hereby sentenced to life in prison.'

His lawyer leapt up.

'Permission to appeal, Your Honour?'

'Denied.'

The defence lawyer sank back into his seat. He had lost. He could still apply directly to the appellate court for permission to appeal, and he would, but he wasn't confident. There was nothing procedurally wrong with the verdict.

***

Edwin stared at the floor in his cell, trying to avoid making eye contact with his new cellmate. As he focussed on a spot of the cell floor between his feet his mind began to wander.

It had been lunchtime in Finnigan'sWake when Eleanor's brother Mark had joined him. He couldn't remember what the bar looked like, but the taste of the grease on the burger was fresh in his memory, making bile rise in his throat as he fought to keep the contents of his stomach down.

He'd had more than his share of the booze when Mark arrived, and his arrival didn't stop the flow of beer. It simply substituted it with whisky, Mark's poison of choice. He and Mark had known each other for a long time. It was through him Edwin had met Eleanor.

'So, my bitch sister wants a divorce then?'

Edwin nodded.

'What you gonna do?'

'What can I do?' Edwin slurred.

'Stop her.'

'She's entitled to half.'

'Mate, you earned that money. She doesn't need it anyway, she's a bloody lawyer. You know how much they get paid.'

'I can't do anything.'

'Hold that thought.' Mark stood.

Mark fetched another few rounds, returning to the table laden with an overloaded tray of assorted spirits.

'Cheers!'

'Cheers? I'm gonna be broke, and she'll get Chelsea.'

'So, you're a creative man. Find a solution.'

'Like what? Kill her?'

'That would do it,' he laughed.

Edwin nodded. If only she'd get hit by a bus tomorrow, his life would be perfect.

'Sometimes you have to make bad things happen to get what you want.'

'I can't!' Edwin protested.

'What was it you worked on during your undergrad?'

'Darknet research on private networks. How the fuck's that gonna help?' Edwin frowned.

' It's anonymous, right?'

'If you do it right, yeah.'

'So, there are criminals on the Internet, aren't there?'

'But they'll know who I wanted killed.'

'So, you could hire someone else to kill them. Then no one would you are involved.'

Edwin's lopsided smile returned.

'That might just work.'

'Yeah, it might, now let's go get pissed.'

Mark grabbed him by the armpit and lifted him up, before half carrying him to the street to hail a cab to the next bar. If the idiot went through with it, Mark's parents would have no choice but to put him back in their will. Without Eleanor, he was their only child, and would inherit the whole estate. Problem son or not, they'd love him again when his sister wasn't there to steal the limelight.

All he needed to do now was convince Edwin that the plan was all his idea. Enough alcohol should do the trick.